ORACLE OF ILLARIA

BOOK TWO OF THE ILLARIA SERIES

DYAN CHICK

ILLARIA PUBLISHING LLC

This book is a work of fiction. The names, characters and events in this book are the products of the author's imagination or are used fictitiously. Any similarity to real persons living or dead is coincidental and not intended by the author.

Cover Artwork by Clarissa Yeo
Editing by Laura Kingsley

For my mom

1

MAX

Max's footsteps echoed through the cavernous entrance to the Dragon's Keep. He ignited a fireball in his hand, sending shadows dancing across the dark, stone walls. The sorcerers behind him followed his lead. The group walked with purpose, focused on the next step in their plan. They may have failed to eliminate the princess and keep Max as the leader of the Ravens, but they were determined to get him on the throne.

The castle at the Dragon's Keep had not been used as a permanent home in generations. The Order of the Dragon used it as their meeting place. Occasionally, a member would stay for an extended time if they needed a place to go. Aside from the two housekeepers, the castle was often empty.

Max closed his fist around the fireball in his hand as he crossed the threshold from the cave into the castle proper. The ground changed from stone to shiny marble. The housekeepers kept the place spotless since there wasn't much for them to do besides clean.

Without breaking his step, Max turned the corner and walked into a formal sitting room. The other sorcerers followed every step, not daring to ask any questions of their leader.

Max stopped when he reached the center of the room and ran his hands through his hair. Dropping his arms to his side, he let out a frustrated scream. Sparks flew from his palms and he had to squeeze his hands into fists to keep from igniting into larger flames.

Closing his eyes, he took a deep breath before turning to face his followers. Working hard to force his face into a calm expression, he turned to address them.

"Things didn't go according to plan tonight. It's time to initiate our backup plan." Max took a moment to look each of the sorcerers in the eye. They returned his gaze with equal fierceness. His Dragons, ten fire sorcerers who didn't question his authority, were ready. They would fight for him. They would help him reclaim his throne. What else did he need?

A young woman with bright red hair walked silently into the room. Her long black dress slid across the floor as she entered. She stopped near the doorway, green eyes locked on Max.

Max's mood shifted as he returned her gaze. He felt lighter, empowered. The king's daughter had been a fixture in Max's life now for a few months. She wanted her father removed from the throne even more than Max did and their relationship deepened with every conspiracy they conceived. Of all the people he'd ever met, she alone understood his ambition. His need to be king. Max smiled and walked over to her. "Nora."

One edge of her mouth tilted up as she watched him approach.

Max lifted her chin with his fingertips. "I'm going to need you to talk to your father. Can you do that for me?"

"Of course," she said. "I already arranged to have dinner with him tomorrow."

Max lowered his head and whispered to her, "We're going to get everything we deserve." He pressed his mouth against hers, then pulled away. He turned to address the group. "Get some rest tonight, tomorrow, we reclaim our kingdom."

The black-clad sorcerers bowed to Max and left the sitting room. They'd be staying in the castle until their plan was complete and Max was on the throne.

Max and Nora were the only ones left in the room.

"I saw your sister come to the castle. Father wouldn't let me stay. He told her about your mother?" Nora's brows creased, a rare sign of sympathy.

"Yes, he did." Max tightened his jaw, not wanting his emotions to show on his face. He wasn't used to not getting his way. Ever since the day the Ravens asked him to take the role of the future king, he'd felt like all of his past disgraces had been atoned for. Having it ripped from him by the same child who had taken it from him when she was born was not part of the plan. If only Etta had never been born.

Nora lifted an eyebrow. "And he didn't try to have her killed."

The king hadn't done as Max expected. While Max hadn't sought his sister's death, it was clear she needed to be removed from the equation. The king could have killed her when he found out where the trials were being held. Instead, he'd sent his sorcerers to test her power and see what she was truly capable of. Now everyone knew how powerful she was and the whole thing had backfired. She was more loved than ever and the king no longer wanted her dead.

Max sat down on a couch. "I think he wants her to join him."

Nora sat next to him. "She'll never agree to it."

Max sat quietly for a moment, thinking about what he knew of his sister. They had spent very little time together and he didn't yet know all of her strengths. She'd hidden her magic from him. She was smart, but he knew her weakness. A smile crept across his face.

"I know that look," Nora said. "You've got an idea."

"If we want to try to get my sister to join us, we can't go through her. She's too noble. But we can go through those who are close to her. She's in love with Ashton."

"Your apprentice?" Nora's eyebrows pressed together. "Was that the one she brought with her to the castle?"

Max nodded.

"So that's why he's not here," Nora said. "He's in love with the little princess. It'd be sweet if it wasn't so inconvenient for us."

"It's still possible that we'll be able to get Ashton to join us. We could use him on our side. All we have to do is get them away from each other," Max said. "We have to break their little hearts."

"Sounds fun," Nora said. "Have you been practicing your shadows?"

Max waved his fingers through the air and a pair of slithering, dark forms floated away from him. They circled the room like silent ghosts. He snapped his fingers and the shadows vanished.

"Well done," Nora said. "If you infiltrate their heads with those, you'll have no problem breaking them up."

Max smiled at his companion. "You are more devious than I ever was."

"I learned from the best," she said.

"Can't argue that," Max said. "It's really too bad we can't control your father. It's a waste of a good sorcerer."

She leaned in toward Max, her mouth almost touching his. "But once he's gone. You'll be king."

Max could feel the heat rising from her. His temperature rose to match hers as he ran his hands up her arms, leaning in for another kiss.

She pulled away and lifted her mouth to his ear. "I missed you while you were off playing the hero."

He wrapped his arms around her, pulling her on to his lap. "You know I'm not the hero type."

"That's what I love about you." She reached down to his waist and slid her hands under his tunic up to his chest.

He raised his arms in the air, allowing her to lift the shirt over his head. His nimble fingers reached behind her, working her buttons open one at a time.

She pulled her upper body out of her loosened bodice, wrapping her bare arms around Max's neck.

With a growl, Max hoisted her up and threw her on the couch, lowering his mouth to hers as his hands explored her body. His lips found her neck and traced a line of kisses down to her waist.

"Don't go easy on me," she said.

Max looked up at her, eyes wild. "I'd never dream of it."

NORA'S naked body was draped across Max when he woke the next morning. They'd managed to make it to the bedroom at some point. He lifted her arm off of his chest and slid out from under the leg resting on his. He didn't want to wake her. She was not a morning person.

Max sat on the edge of the bed for a moment. He never thought he'd end up here, in bed with the king's daughter. It had all been so innocent when they first met. Nora, like her father, was aligned with fire. She'd come to the Order of the Dragon seeking training because it had been denied to her. She didn't realize who Max was when they met. He'd hesitated to take her on as an apprentice, but with her connection to the king, Max figured she'd be useful. After weeks of sneaking away to train her, their relationship took a turn he didn't expect.

It wasn't love, it was something different. Something born of heat and ambition. It was the same thing that drove them both and when they were together, it was unlike anything he'd ever experienced. The first few times had left him so guilt-ridden, he'd broken things off with Saffron.

Glancing behind him, he looked at Nora's sleeping form. She was so young. So different from Saffron. Despite ending things, Max had never been able to stay completely away from Saffron. When he sent her to watch Etta at the camp outside the village, he thought he'd be on the throne before Saffron returned. Instead, she'd returned with his half-sister and all of the old feelings came rushing back to him. She was a part of him but he couldn't stay with her if he wanted to be king. Nora was the key to finding the king's weakness and gaining the throne.

Standing, he walked over to a wardrobe in the corner where he kept a change of clothes. This wasn't the time to dwell on what could have been. He'd made his choice.

The black robes of the Order of the Dragon felt like his second skin. The world of sorcery made sense. There were rules, traditions, and expectations that didn't get broken. Sorcerers were less complicated than kings.

Max pulled a blanket over Nora. Nora rolled over, letting out a sigh. Max turned away from her and left the room.

The early morning light filtered through the stained-glass windows in the long hallway, giving off a warm red glow. While the castle hadn't been built with the Order of the Dragon in mind, it was filled with symbols and elements that evoked images of fire. The original owners had been obsessed with Dragons, thus, building the castle on top of an old dragon keep.

It was as good a place as any to wait. Certainly better than the tent he'd been living in. He shook his head, still finding it hard to believe how badly his plan had failed. He'd underestimated the power his sister held. He'd underestimated the fact people would be willing to follow a woman. If only he could have married her off right away, everything would have worked out.

It didn't matter. His mother taught him to have a back up plan at all times. Joining with the king wasn't ideal, but at least he wouldn't have to sneak out of the Raven camp to meet up with Nora anymore. He could stop living a double life, at least as far as the Ravens were concerned. Instead, he'd work with the king long enough to learn his weaknesses so he could destroy him. He didn't need the Ravens.

Max followed the hallway to a wide, twisting staircase that led to the grand entrance of the castle. Traveling past the dragon sculpture that greeted visitors who used the main entry, he headed for the renovated library.

The library was a large room with rich, dark wood paneling. One whole wall was lined with bookshelves. Most of the books had been sold long ago when the Order first took over this estate. A small collection of books on magic had been built in the last decade. Mostly at Max's request. He walked to the shelf and dragged his fingers over the bound leather copies. Eyes fixed on the titles, he searched for the one he wanted. Stopping about halfway down, he paused, finger resting on a burgundy book with gold lettering on the spine. He pulled it out and walked to the long, rectangular table that filled most of the room.

His fingers traced over the letters on the front cover, *History of the Illarian Kings*. Printed shortly after his father's coronation, this book was full of his ancestors. He should be in this book. Illaria had never been ruled by a woman. Why break hundreds of years of tradition just because he had been born of the wrong womb? He still had his father's blood running through his veins. That should be enough.

Flipping through the pages, he skimmed through, looking at each of the king's names, the important dates, and the element they aligned with. He slumped back in his chair. Not a single man in this book aligned with fire. With the exception of a few air sorcerers, they all aligned with water. It was almost as if they were mocking him. Telling him that he didn't belong. Things would have been so much easier if he'd just inherited his father's water alignment.

Max's mother had told him that his fire made him special. Now, in contrast to his sister's water alignment, it felt like a weakness. He closed the book and slammed his fist against the cover. *I will be king of Illaria.*

Max looked up to see Nora framed by the doorway. Her usual black dress flowed behind her as she glided across the room to where Max sat. She moved like the shadows, like the Reapers. Max had to remind himself that she was his apprentice, she didn't have the same power he had.

He closed the book, resting his hands over the title. Nora slid his hands away, leaning over the book. "Why do you do this to yourself?" She picked the book up and returned it to the shelf. She stood behind Max, arms draped over his shoulders. "You'll be king soon enough."

Max sighed. He knew that was the truth, his ambition wouldn't allow him to quit until he was King of Illaria.

Nora rested her chin on Max's shoulder. "I know you wanted to have that moment." She kissed his cheek. "The crowds of people cheering as you walked through the streets. Their support behind you as you claimed the throne. But you don't need to have the love of the people to be king. Look at my father, nobody loves him."

"I want to be a good king, Nora." Max didn't think he'd ever told her that before. For Nora, it was about eliminating her father and becoming queen. Without Max, she'd never live to see her father's reign end. The dark magic coursing through his veins had already prolonged his life. Once he channeled all of the Darkness entering Illaria, he'd be unstoppable, immortal.

"My father probably started out the same way." Nora stroked Max's shoulder the way a mother would soothe an upset child.

Max caught her arm in his hand, squeezing harder than he should have.

Nora gasped.

"I'm nothing like your father," Max said.

Nora leaned in toward Max, her mouth inches from his. "Of course you are. Look how easily you gave up the love of your life for me. You think I don't know how you feel about me? You think this is easy for me? Being in love with somebody who loves another?"

Max let go of her and turned his face away. Even if he wanted to leave Nora for her, it was too late. He'd chosen Nora over Saffron. Ambition over Saffron. Nothing would change that. "Don't be a child. You know I'm not in love with anybody else."

Nora twisted a strand of her red hair around a finger. "So when I kill Saffron, you won't be upset?"

Max's jaw clenched. He could feel the heat rising inside. He could picture Saffron's smile. The way the long, blonde curls cascaded down her bare back when they were alone. He slammed his fist on the table. "I ended things with her for you. I sent her away. She spent months in the woods, watching Etta. That should be enough."

"According to my sources, there were still stolen kisses between the two of you after you sent her away to watch your sister."

Max pushed his chair back from the table and stood. The chair tumbled to the ground with a crash. "You are the student, here. Remember that."

He walked toward the door, ignoring Nora's smile. He had too much to do to worry about a jealous eighteen year old. He knew his relationship with her was built on their common desire to overthrow the king. But somewhere along the way, she'd started to get attached to him. He could learn something from the king, he didn't remarry after his wife died. Women were too much work to keep around.

"Max," Nora called down the hallway.

Max stopped walking and clenched his fists. He wasn't in the mood for another fight with her. He turned slowly to face her. Her footsteps were silent as she approached him.

"Don't be cross with me, Max." Her smile was too sweet. She set a hand on her stomach. "We may have a new prince joining us, soon."

Max's stomach tightened and his mind reeled. Was this possible? They'd talked about it. They'd certainly done what was required to create a child but it never felt real. If it was true, if she was with child, the king would have to accept Max's offer.

Max's hand shook as he reached out, resting his palm on top of the hand that was covering her stomach. "Are you sure?"

"The ladies at the castle say you can't be sure until two months has passed with no bleeding, but we've passed the first month. We'll know for sure in a few weeks."

A wave of affection for Nora flowed through Max. He brushed his fingers over her cheek and traced her lips with his thumb. "I never thought it would happen so quickly."

"I suppose even the gods agree with our plan," Nora said.

Max pulled her into a hug, his anger toward her melting away. She was going to give him a son. A king with no heir was at greater risk of being overthrown. Nora would be showing by the time Max claimed the throne, heir already established.

Nora backed away, keeping her hands on Max's sides. "We have to go to my father, together. There's no way he can say no. Once you're given his blessing, you'll have access to everything. You'll know all of his weaknesses. Come to dinner tomorrow."

Max nodded. His throat felt dry. In front of Nora, in front of the Ravens, he always tried to show a brave face. He didn't want anybody to think he was afraid of the king, but he knew it was foolish to underestimate him. Max didn't want to end up as an undead puppet, forced to live out the king's wishes for eternity. He swallowed back his fear. "I'll be there."

Nora stood on her toes and kissed Max's cheek. "I better get back to my father's castle before he notices me missing. I'll meet you at the back entrance tomorrow."

Max watched the gray smoke rise in a cloud around her as she teleported away.

2

"**E**tta." Saffron shook me gently. A lantern glowed on the ground next to her. It was still dark outside.

I rolled on to my back and looked up at her. "I actually fell asleep."

"Yes, you did." She held a dress out to me. "The scouts are back."

I sat up with a start. *It's too soon.* They had only been gone for a week. My heart raced in my chest. "What's wrong?"

"They brought news, but I told them to wait for you before sharing it." Saffron pressed her mouth into a line. She looked like she wanted to say more.

Tossing aside the blanket, I jumped off of my bedroll. "What are you not telling me?" My stomach twisted into knots. *Ashton.* He was part of the group of scouts we sent to see what was going on in the kingdom. In the weeks since Max left, we'd found a new camp and began recruiting to replace our depleted numbers. Many of the members of the Ravens had left. Some went to follow Max, others didn't trust me yet. Part of me didn't blame them. I hadn't done anything to prove myself. Max had been with the Ravens for fifteen years, earning their trust. Who was I to step in to this role?

I pulled the dress over my head and looked at Saffron. Her expression wasn't giving anything away. I was afraid to ask, but I didn't want to walk into something I wasn't prepared for. There was already enough talk about me being too young and too emotional. I had to appear strong in front of the members of the Ravens. "Ashton?"

Saffron nodded. "He's waiting for you. I didn't think it proper for him to come to your tent."

My stomach filled with butterflies. We'd only had two weeks together from the time Max left and when Ashton left with the other scouts. In that short time, we'd been busy with moving camp, setting up a council, and organizing what was left of the Ravens. Our moments together were few and were carefully planned to hide them from the others. Saffron and Celeste knew we were meeting each other. There wasn't any way I could hide anything from them. While she didn't say anything about it, I knew Saffron still didn't approve. I wondered if it reminded her too much of her relationship with Max.

I didn't know much about her past with him and I didn't have the courage to ask her about it. All I knew was that she'd been distant since he left. She tried to hide it, but it was as if she wasn't quite the same. She seemed broken since he left. Max had betrayed all of us, but what he did to her was a betrayal far worse than what he did to me. One day soon, I hoped she'd open up to me. With the scouts unexpected return, I knew today wasn't the day.

We walked from my tent toward the crumbling barn we used as our meeting place. Saffron held the lantern out in front of her. There wasn't a moon tonight and the early fall air was crisp in the darkness. I shivered, wrapping my arms around my chest.

"No clues as to what is wrong?" I glanced at Saffron, trying to read her expression. The scouts were scheduled to report back next week. If they were here early, they'd found something or had an emergency that required them to return.

"I told you, I didn't ask yet. I came to wake you so you could be there to hear the report before the whole camp finds out." She slid open the barn door just wide enough for us to pass through.

The inside of the barn was well lit. Glancing up, I noticed several fireballs floating above the large table that filled the center of the room. The people who were seated at the table rose when I walked in.

I lifted my hand. "Please sit." The formality insisted upon by my council was not something I was fond of. Despite the number of times I've asked them not to treat me differently, there were certain things I couldn't get them to give up. Standing when I entered was one of them.

My eyes searched the table, looking for the familiar head of honey-blonde hair that I'd missed so much this last week. When I found him, my breath caught it my chest and my mouth dropped open. I stood frozen in place, unable to continue to the table.

Ashton's hair was almost black from dirt and soot. His face was smeared with a mixture of dirt and blood. One side of his face had a long cut that began near his eye and ended by his jaw. His clothes were torn and singed.

This wasn't supposed to happen. The scouts had been sent out to evaluate different parts of the Kingdom of Illaria. To see how the people were faring and find out where the king had more power. They weren't supposed to get involved with anything. They were supposed to hide and stay out of trouble.

Ashton's green eyes stared into my blue ones. He mouthed the words *I'm fine*.

How could he be fine? My forehead creased in concern. All I wanted to do was to run to him.

Saffron cleared her throat. "Your highness?"

I tore my gaze away from Ashton and looked at Saffron. She pulled out a chair for me. Forcing a smile on my face, I nodded at her and took the seat. When I risked a quick glance at Ashton, I saw Celeste next to him. Her fingers were on his cheek. A flicker of jealousy rose inside me, but it was brief. Celeste and I had become friends over the last several weeks. I knew she was there to check on him for my benefit as much as for his. She knew I'd be concerned and couldn't act on my worries. Plus, she'd been friends with Ashton for a long time. She was likely just as worried as I was about him.

I looked away, knowing that he was in good hands. Celeste was a natural healer. She'd been taking lessons with Master Flanders in the afternoons to improve her skills. The two of them had even been working on the full size orb together since she'd obtained a dragon egg from her uncle.

The people sitting around the table were silent. Blank faces watched me. I counted the heads at the table, there were five of the eight scouts we'd sent out. "Where are the others?"

"Josiah and Greg haven't returned yet," Saffron said.

I looked around, trying to place who else we were missing. "Ashton, where's Nathan?"

We'd sent the scouts out in groups of two. Each group had one sorcerer to make sure they could teleport in case of an emergency. Ashton's non-sorcerer partner, Nathan, wasn't sitting at the table with us.

Celeste was cleaning Ashton's face with a handkerchief. Ashton pushed her hand away and looked around the table before his eyes settled on mine. "We ran into trouble at the Temple of Seven." He took a deep breath. "The king and the Reapers teleported in while we were there. We didn't stand a chance. I did everything I could to save Nathan." He shook his head.

I shuddered at the thought of the king and his Reapers. I could almost smell their rotted flesh as memories of their ethereal floating black cloaks haunted me. They were monsters controlled by a monster who looked like a man. The king was no better than them, but his appearance was deceptive. He didn't look the part of a monster the way the Reapers did but I knew he was worse than all of them put together.

Ashton was lucky to be alive after being surprised by them. I looked over at him and met his eyes. My heart felt full as relief washed through me. What would I have done if he hadn't made it back to me? "I'm so sorry, Ashton."

"How did you escape?" Celeste asked.

"I teleported out with Nathan, hoping I could make it to a healer." He lowered his eyes and shook his head.

The table went silent as the loss of Nathan sunk in. We hadn't planned for any conflict with these scouting trips. I could feel the weight of the news around the table and wished I had something encouraging to add.

Ann, a small sorcerer from Gallia who had stayed to help us, broke the silence. "The Temple of Seven is a sacred place, even to those outside of Illaria. The gods will carry his essence through the Astral Realm."

Nods and quiet affirmations surrounded me. The Temple of Seven was the most sacred of the ancient sites. For anybody who practiced the old religion, it was an honorable place to meet your end.

My brow creased in confusion. The ruins were not a likely place to come across the king. They weren't near his castle or any major city. It wasn't somewhere we'd expect to see him. "What was the king doing at the Temple of Seven?"

"What were you doing at the Temple of Seven?" Saffron asked.

Ashton looked from me to Saffron. "We'd heard there was a small resistance group using the ruins as their base. We went to look for them."

Saffron fidgeted in her seat next to me. "Was the king there to destroy the resistance group?"

She seemed uncomfortable with the idea that the king was personally hunting down resistance groups. I didn't blame her. If that was his intention, he was likely looking for us.

"That's the strange part. There wasn't any sign of people at the ruins. I don't know why we were sent there. I thought the source was reliable."

"Do you think you were set-up?" I asked.

"It's possible. But the king seemed surprised to find us there so I don't know. It's hard to know who to trust anymore. Things have changed in Illaria." Ashton shook his head.

Herman, a member of he Ravens who had gone out to scout for us spoke. "He's right. Things are changing. It's hard to explain. There were reports of the king and his Reapers in Marina. The people told us they had been looking for something. Nobody knew what it was."

Ann stood. "Your highness."

I turned to look at her. She wore a grim expression. Whatever she had to say wasn't something she wanted to share.

"What is it?" I asked.

She took a deep breath. "I didn't want to be the one to share this." She glanced from me to Saffron, then back again. "It's about your brother."

My whole body tensed. Where was this going? In the last few weeks, I had imagined seeing Max again. I'd hoped he would come to camp, tell me he wanted to join me and that we could do this together. Though he'd have to apologize to Saffron, he wouldn't have to apologize to me. I'd forgive him without a second thought. I had a feeling that whatever she was about to say was going to ruin that hope.

"Your highness, we saw Max." She nodded to Herman, the man who had gone with her. "He was with the king." She bit down on her lip.

I'd imagined a hundred different things Max could be doing with his time since he left the camp. Working with the king never once crossed my mind. He hated the king as much as I did. "No, no, that's not possible. It must have been somebody else."

"Your highness, it was Max. And we watched him raise the dead."

I stared at Ann, not believing her words. "You must be mistaken. There's no way Max would join the king." I looked around the room at the blank faces staring at me. Why wasn't anyone speaking up to defend him? How could they all accept this so quickly? It had to be a lie.

"It had to have been the king raising the dead. Max would never do that." I turned to look at Saffron, expecting her to support me. "Would he?"

Saffron's face was drained of color. She didn't speak. I looked at Ashton. Somebody had to speak up. I wasn't ready to accept that Max would do this to us. "Tell me he wouldn't do that."

"I don't know. I thought I knew Max, but maybe I don't. Ann, are you sure?"

Ann nodded. "I didn't want to be the one to tell you. But it looks like Max has joined the king. It looked like he was getting lessons."

"Where were you? Maybe it was a misunderstanding. Maybe you were too far away. It could be somebody who looked like Max." I scrambled to come up with a reason why Max would even be in the same place as the king, let alone performing spells with him.

"We were outside of Campari. We set up camp at the ruins of Lenihan and heard some noise from the old necropolis. Thankfully, we weren't noticed but we watched for a while. It really looked like he was getting lessons." Ann played with a pendant around her neck. She looked uncomfortable.

I leaned back in my chair and ran a hand through my hair. If Max was learning dark magic from the king, we had bigger problems than just worrying about how to defeat the king.

"You're sure it was Max who completed the spell?" Saffron finally spoke.

"It was," Ann said. "I'm sorry, Saffron."

Saffron stood. "Excuse me, your highness." She walked away from the table and slid through the still open door. I stared after her, wondering if I should follow her. Like me, she had probably spent the last few weeks hoping Max would return. His alliance with the king solidified his betrayal, making him our enemy instead of just someone we had a falling out with.

"Lenihan?" Ashton's voice brought my attention back to the table. He straightened in his chair. "Nobody lives in Lenihan anymore."

"It was empty, aside from the two of them and us," Ann said. "We thought it would be a quiet place to camp. Never thought we'd see anybody there, let alone the king."

"Lenihan is the site of the old sun dais, right?" Ashton looked around the table.

"The dais isn't there anymore, but yes, it was." Ann said.

"Why the ancient sites?" Ashton asked. "Why an old solar calendar? Why the necropolis? Or the Temple of Seven?"

I rubbed my forehead and tried to think of a connection between the places they'd seen the king. For some reason he was visiting places that were sacred to the ancient Illarians. All seven of the ancient sacred sites were said to be nothing but ruins, all of the buildings and temples had long been destroyed. I'd learned about the gods from my grandmother, but I couldn't think of why they would be connected. "Maybe it was coincidence? If they needed a necropolis that was abandoned, Lenihan may have been the best place to go."

Ashton covered a yawn. I looked at the weary faces looking back at me around the table. The scouts needed to rest. They had all been through a lot. Of the five scouts who had returned, one group hadn't talked at all. "Patrick, Ralph, can you give us a report?"

Patrick shifted in his chair before pushing his chair back and standing. Ralph stood next to him. "We have to show you something, your highness."

My heartbeat quickened as they walked toward me. "What is it?" Before I could react, Ralph had his arms around my neck, pulling me free from my chair. Patrick's arms closed around my waist, keeping me from breaking away from them. A cloud of gray smoke rose around my feet.

"Etta!" I heard Ashton screaming my name but couldn't find him in the chaos. I pushed away from my captors, fighting to escape their grip. Every time I moved, the arm on my neck tightened and less air found its way into my lungs. My head started to spin and I had to fight for the few breaths of air I could get.

Arms tightened around my waist, pressing into me. I cried out in pain as the smoke swallowed me whole.

3

S moke clouded my vision for a moment as I dug my nails into the arm around my waist. As we landed, the arm let go of me and a hand made contact with my cheek, sending me stumbling backward.

I covered my stinging cheek and took a few steps away from the men who had taken me from the Raven camp. In the clearing smoke, I noticed there were three figures. Maybe the slap had jarred my vision. Blinking, I looked again. Flames erupted before my eyes and I let out a gasp. The third figure was Ashton.

In the gray light of early dawn, I was able to see some details around us. We were standing in a familiar field. My whole body tensed as the king's castle came into view through the clearing smoke. *They're taking me to the king.*

Patrick threw his arm around my neck again, pulling me against him. I closed my eyes and took a deep breath, calling to my magic. Even just a little arctic fire should be enough to get him to let go of me.

The feel of cold steel against my throat made my eyes snap open. Time seemed to stop as I glanced down to see Patrick's hand gripping a dagger. I held my breath for a moment, trying not to move. The blade was pressed against my skin and I was afraid Patrick's hand might slip.

"Put the fire away," Patrick said.

Ashton lowered his hands. "Think this through. You don't want to hurt her. Let her go."

The grip around me tightened as Patrick spoke. "Why are you even following her? The only thing I can figure is that the rumors about you two are true."

Ashton's hands closed into fists and he stepped closer to us.

"Stop right there, Ashton. I don't want you to move." Patrick pressed the blade into my skin. Pain bit into my neck and I gasped. He adjusted the blade again, pulling it back and the pain eased. It was as if he didn't want to hurt me.

Ashton stopped and put his hands up in surrender. "Just let her go. I'll take her back to camp, you go wherever you want to go."

"You don't get it, do you?" Patrick said. "We've lost. There is no way we can fight back against the king, especially with Max on his side."

My stomach knotted. Did all the Ravens feel this way? I knew taking a stand against the king wouldn't be easy, but I thought I could do it. If I didn't have the support of the Ravens, what did I have?

Ashton took a tentative step forward. "We've always known being in the Ravens was a risk. You've been in as long as me. We grew up together. You know the cost and the purpose."

Patrick stepped back, pulling me with him. "That's just it, Ashton. You and me, we never had a choice. A couple of orphans thrown in the mix. At least you have your magic. I have nothing."

Out of the corner of my eye I saw Ralph move next to Patrick. I didn't know Ralph very well. He was a trained sorcerer in his early thirties who had offered his help through Madame Lyndsey.

Ralph's eyes met mine. He didn't look as happy about this situation as Patrick sounded. He was the weaker of the two. I stared at him, wondering how he got involved in all of this. Had they seen something when they were out scouting? What was it that turned them away from helping me and the Ravens?

My stomach clenched. Maybe they never wanted to help me. Maybe they've been looking for a way to get rid of me since Max left. I was a fool to think I could step into this so easily. I didn't even know how to be queen.

"Let her go, Patrick," Ashton said.

I glanced back up at Ashton. He believed in me. I didn't have to do this alone. Even if I wasn't feeling strong, I needed to act strong.

Next to us, Ralph was fidgeting. I looked over at him. "Why are you doing this?"

Patrick pressed the dagger closer to my throat. "Shut up."

I pushed back against him, trying to get any distance I could from the blade. *There has to be a way out of this.*

"It's a valid question," Ashton said. "If you're scared, why not just leave? We wouldn't have stopped you. Why kidnapping?"

"Show him," Patrick said.

Ralph reached inside his robes and pulled out a piece of parchment. He unfolded it and stretched his arm out toward Ashton.

Ashton stepped forward and took the parchment from Ralph. He looked down at it and a scowl formed on his face. "You'd betray everything for this?" He crumbled up the parchment.

Patrick adjusted the blade in his hand. He was getting tired and he seemed focused on Ashton. This was my chance to get away from him. Patrick wasn't a sorcerer, but Ralph was. I didn't know what Ralph's alignment was or his level of ability. If I could get away from Patrick, I had to be confident in Ashton's ability to handle Ralph.

Ashton glanced at me and I flicked my eyes from him to Ralph then back again. He gave an almost imperceptible nod then cleared his throat, drawing the attention to himself.

"You do realize that there are other ways of getting money," Ashton said.

"None that come with the protection of the king," Patrick said. "I've been in hiding my entire life. I'm tired of living in filth. I want to have a warm place to sleep. A real roof over my head. I'm done with this life."

Ashton kept talking, but I wasn't listening anymore. Eyes closed, I took a few deep breaths to clear my thoughts. *Concentrate.* I had to get out of this without making Patrick press down on that dagger.

The dagger. I had been so focused on how I could escape, I didn't stop to think about the fact that if I could remove the dagger, I'd be safe. Master Flanders had spent the last few weeks working on summoning spells with me. I could call objects that were hidden from view as long as I had a good understanding of what the object was. I had to focus on the essence of the object. Opening my eyes, I glanced down at the silver blade against my neck. I couldn't see much of it from the angle that I was being held, but it was enough.

I called to the magic inside me, channeling it through my body, reaching out to the dagger. If I could get it out of his grasp, I could arm and free myself at the same time. It had to be done delicately, I didn't want to cause harm in the process. Using my magic, I reached out to the blade. There was a pull I felt inside when I made contact with the object I wanted to summon. I knew I was close. *There.* I could feel the blade.

Easing back, I reached inside for a different power, my arctic fire. I only wanted a little bit of it, just enough to startle him. The daily lessons with Master Flanders were paying off, the magic came quickly. I felt the icy sparks dancing on my palms.

As quickly as I could, I reached my hands up and touched the bare skin on Patrick's wrist. He jumped, moving the dagger away from me for a moment. I let go of the arctic fire and switched to the summoning spell, calling to the dagger.

The pulling sensation of the object came right away and I opened my palm. As the dagger slammed into my waiting hand, Patrick took a step back. He'd lost his weapon. I turned to face him. His mouth hung open, eyes wide.

I squeezed my hand around the hilt of the dagger and pointed it at him. "Now we'll see how you like having a blade put to your throat."

He raised his hands and stepped away from me. "Ralph!"

A gust of wind blew past me. Ralph was aligned with air. The temperature rose around me as Ashton launched flames at Ralph.

While my eyes were on the sorcerers engaged in battle, Patrick slammed into me, knocking me to the ground. I dropped the dagger. He had me pinned down with his knee on my stomach. I struggled to breathe against the weight of it.

He reached for the fallen dagger while holding me in place.

Anger rose inside me. I'd trusted these men, and was betrayed by them. They had promised to help me. They had lived with us for weeks, eaten with us, told stories around the campfire at night. A feeling I wasn't familiar with started in my stomach and grew. It was dark, twisted, and uncomfortable. I embraced it, using it to fuel my magic.

Patrick had reached the dagger and held it above me. "I should have killed you in your sleep. If the wanted poster hadn't asked for you alive, I would have."

The dark, twisted part of me had taken over. I narrowed my

eyes at him. "This is your only warning. Let me go, or I will kill you."

He laughed. "You, kill me? Your biggest weakness is that you're too nice. If you didn't always see the best in people, you would have noticed this a week ago."

Blue sparks crackled in my palms. "Wrong answer." I twisted to the side, knocking Patrick off balance. Then I reached my hands up toward his face and released the icy blue arctic fire.

Patrick dropped the dagger and the blade landed inches from my leg. He screamed and covered his face, blotting at the flames. I rolled away from him and stood, picking up the dagger as I did.

Patrick was on his knees now, the fire extinguished. His face was red and bleeding from where the fire had burned through the skin. I gripped the dagger in my hand. The dark feeling was easing and my breathing was heavy. *What had I done?*

Just as I was starting to feel guilty, Patrick charged me again. Without thinking, I lifted the blade in front of me. He ran right into the dagger, stopping only after the blade was lodged in his chest.

I let go of the dagger and stepped away from him. My heart was pounding wildly in my chest. Blood poured from the wound, spreading across his brown tunic. I looked down at my hands, they were crimson.

Patrick reached a hand up to me as he collapsed to his knees. My lower lip was trembling as I silently watched him fall to his side. His body twitched, then stopped moving.

I let out a breath I didn't know I'd been holding. Tears blurred my vision. Why did Patrick do it? I wanted the throne to save the people of Illaria, not kill them. Couldn't he see that? Everything would be so much easier if I had someone who could tell me how to be queen, somebody to teach me.

I dropped to my knees, whole body shaking as I stared at

Patrick's lifeless eyes. A lump rose in my throat. I thought he was my friend. I'd trusted too easily. I needed to be stronger if I was going to defeat the king. I tightened my jaw and looked down at my bloody hands.

A wisp of something dark found it's way inside me. For a moment, I let it in. It was easier to be angry at Patrick than feel sad. He deserved this. If I hadn't killed him, I'd be dead right now. Slowly, the anger gripping me subsided and the reality of yet another death by my hands crept in. My throat tightened as I realized that I wasn't any better than the king in this moment. Reaching out a hand, I closed Patrick's eyelids. He had been just as scared as me. Could I really blame him? This was the king getting into Patrick's head. Life was a struggle in Illaria. Everybody was scared and I hadn't done anything to change that yet. Saying you are the rightful queen isn't going to fix things. What had I done to prove that I was worthy of being queen? How could I expect these people to follow me? Something had to change.

4

I turned away from Patrick's body toward Ashton. I swayed on my feet, feeling the familiar wave of exhaustion that followed the use of my powers. Ralph was on his hands and knees, body heaving as he tried to catch his breath. Ashton stood over him, flames dancing in his palms.

I hesitated, wondering if I should run over and intervene or if I would be in Ashton's way. He didn't look like he needed me. He seemed to be handling Ralph just fine on his own. I took a few steps closer as Ashton extinguished his flames. He extended a hand to Ralph and helped pull him to standing.

My insides prickled. Ashton was showing mercy. A wave of guilt rushed through me. I looked over my shoulder at the dead body left in my wake. Could I have done something differently? My mind replayed the last moment of Patrick's life. He'd rushed me while I had the blade. There wasn't anything I could have done. Recalling the hesitation I'd had and Patrick's rally, a flicker of fear filled me. Ralph might do the same thing.

My heart raced and I ran toward them. Before I reached them, Ralph pushed Ashton to the ground. The older man lifted his leg above Ashton, ready to stomp on him.

I cried out. "No!"

Ralph turned to look at me, giving Ashton a moment to roll away from the attack. Moving quickly, Ashton launched a fireball at his assailant. Ralph screamed and dropped to the ground, rolling back and forth, trying to put out the flames. I stopped, unable to take my eyes off of the scene in front of me.

Patrick's warning about being too nice played in my mind. Were we being too trusting of those around us? Ashton was showing mercy to Ralph. He tried several times to send the men away before either of us fought them. Both of them could have left without harm if they had agreed to let me go. Would that have saved us, or would they have just come for me another day?

Ralph wasn't moving. The battle was over. Ashton walked away from the smoking sorcerer, eyes locked on me. "You okay?"

I nodded, closing the distance between us in a few steps. Ashton smoothed my hair away from my face and studied me. "You sure you're okay?" He looked behind me, probably at Patrick laying in the grass.

Taking Ashton's hand in mine I nodded again. "I'm not hurt. For now, that's going to have to be enough. We have to get out of here."

Ashton's jaw tensed. "We have to burn the bodies first."

"What?" I looked at Ralph and Patrick, lifeless on the ground, then glanced up at the king's castle. A shiver ran through me. If we left them here and the king found them, they could end up as undead soldiers.

Ashton let go of my hand and walked over to Ralph who was still smoking. My stomach lurched at the sight of his blackened body. I looked to the woods for a moment, not wanting to watch Patrick's body go up in flames, then thought better of it. Smoke stung my eyes and I turned back to face the fire. He was dead because of me and I needed to see that the deed was done. While I watched the flames consume his body, I felt numb.

"Come on." Ashton walked away from the castle in the direction of the woods, I followed close behind. His hands were by his side, but he didn't reach for me. I noticed the sleeves of his tunic were singed and wondered how warm his touch was after he used fire. Looking away from his hands, I focused on the ground as we walked. I didn't want to think about fire right now or the bodies we left behind. All I wanted to do was get back to camp.

"We need to teleport somewhere safe," I said.

Ashton hesitated, but kept walking. "I can't teleport anywhere. I probably shouldn't have even come with you."

We had reached the tree line and were hidden from view. I stopped walking and tugged on Ashton's hand. His green eyes locked on mine.

"Explain," I said.

"I may have a tracing spell on me." Ashton let out a breath. "When I was fighting against the king and his Reapers, I ended up teleporting away before we finished the battle. It's possible the king traced my teleportation. I didn't go straight to camp to make it harder if he had, but I don't know if it's safe for me to teleport at all."

"How long do those spells last?" I hadn't heard of magic like this before but I was still so new to the world of sorcery that nothing really surprised me.

"I don't know. I planned to talk to Master Flanders in private. I didn't want to scare everyone at the camp." He shook his head. "I'm sure they are all afraid after what happened."

It was my turn to let out a breath of frustration. "Things haven't been going so well at camp."

Ashton's forehead creased in concern. "What do you mean?"

"We lost a lot of people. And I've heard some talk. Saffron and the others try to hide it from me, but I've heard it."

Ashton put his hands on my arms. His touch was warmer

than usual after using his fire so recently. In the cool early morning air, the contrast caused goosebumps to rise on my arms and a shiver ran through me. He slid his hands up and down my arms, trying to warm me up. "You can tell me."

"Ashton, they don't think I can do it." I bit down on my lip, feeling shame. I hadn't said the words out loud before but in the last couple of weeks my confidence had been stolen from me. The people who left the Ravens did so because they didn't believe I could defeat the king. Whispers around camp questioned why I had sent Max away. Others talked as if we had already lost.

"That's not what I've heard." Ashton pressed his hands against my upper arms. "There are people who believe in you. People who have been waiting for you, counting on you. Not everybody wanted Max. Some people were happy to see him go. You're just starting. You'll show them."

"How?" I had spent a lot of time thinking about this while Ashton was gone. When I stepped up to claim the title, I wanted Max by my side. I wanted his help and his support while honoring my family name. After he'd left, I was no longer sure what I was going to do. I didn't know anything about how to be a queen. If he really had joined the king, did we even stand a chance? I didn't want to think like that, but it was hard to be positive while standing in the middle of the woods after being so easily kidnapped.

"You'll find a way to prove yourself to them. Soon. You'll see." He planted a gentle kiss on my cheek.

His words helped but his presence helped more. Having somebody who believed in you by your side made it possible to endure the difficult times. "Thank you."

Ashton dropped his hands from my arms. "Now, let's see about getting back to our camp."

"Any ideas on how we're going to do that?" I asked as I followed him between the trees.

"I suppose we'll have to walk. There's a safe house outside of Greenville. We should be able to avoid the city by going around it. Then we can request horses or send a message from the safe house."

Why did everything seem to revolve around Greenville? Maybe I should have insisted on going there myself to find Annalise after Sir Edward's note. I'd wanted to go myself, but my friends worried for my safety. "We have scouts in Greenville. Could they help us?"

"We'd never find them, it's the biggest city in Illaria. It's easy to get lost there, hard to find somebody who doesn't want to be found."

"That's probably why we haven't heard from the scouts yet," I said. We'd sent two scouts to Greenville before we even moved the camp. Master Edward's hidden letter had been a priority for me. I felt like I owed it to him to find the girl whose name he had left for me. Whoever Annalise was, I wanted to find her. But if she was in hiding, who knew how long it would take.

"The men we sent are good, they'll find her. It will just take some time," Ashton said.

I wondered if she was even alive. Why had Sir Edward sent us after a girl without any explanation or warning? Was it even a person we were looking for? What if it had been a code that none of us understood? Greenville was a huge city. It would be a good place for somebody or something to hide.

I thought about the time I'd been to Campari, the port city near my village. It was the largest city I'd ever been to, and it was supposed to be small when compared to Greenville. When I was in Campari, nobody had noticed a young girl and her grandmother. We could have walked anywhere we wanted without a single person noticing us. People were busy, they had their own things to do. Was Greenville even more crowded and busy? "Maybe we could hide in Greenville. Maybe it would be safer there where we can blend in. Out in the open we are easier to spot."

The sun was rising now, casting an orange glow through the trees. I could read Ashton's anxiety easily. He was hiding something from me. "What is it?"

"I don't think you're going to be safe anywhere." He shook his head. "Not even in the Raven camp."

"I know there's lots of talk, but you can't think that more of the Ravens would turn on me?" I was hurt. After being on the run for weeks, all I wanted was a place I could go to sleep at night without worrying about my safety. I wanted to believe Patrick and Ralph were the exception, not the rule.

Ashton reached into his pocket and pulled out the crumpled paper he'd taken from Patrick. He smoothed it out and handed it to me.

I took the paper and my mouth dropped open. I was looking at a drawing of myself. My eyes found the words on the bottom of the page. *5,000 soldi. Wanted Alive.* The king was going to turn my own people against me. They were struggling to survive in the ruin he had inflicted upon the kingdom. That much money would keep a family fed for years. How could anybody turn down that kind of money?

My whole body felt like I had just jumped into an ice cold pond as my breath was knocked from me. The king was hunting for me but something had changed since we met. He wanted me alive.

My heartbeat quickened as I recalled our meeting at his castle. He'd wanted me to marry him and use my power to help him control the kingdom. A creeping feeling ran through me, as if I were being watched. I glanced behind me, almost expecting to see him lurking in the woods. We were alone, but the feeling remained.

I took a deep breath and crumpled the paper back into a ball, then handed it to Ashton. "Now we know why they were so quick to turn me in."

He pocketed the paper. "As long as we stay out of sight, you should be safe."

Saffron and all the others I'd added to my personal council had insisted I stay locked away at the camp for my own safety. Yet here I am, wandering the woods after being kidnapped by one of our own.

I shook my head. "I'm never going to be safe. Not while the king lives. I can't hide. We have to get back to camp. We've got to figure out a way to defeat the king."

5

MAX

King Osbert sat with his arms crossed over his chest. He wore his usual bored look, the one he seemed to reserve for his lessons with Max.

Letting go of the spell, Max shook out his hands and blew out a breath of frustration. He glanced at the king again, hoping for some glimmer of approval, and found none. Max tried to tell himself he didn't need the king's praise. After all, he was here to steal the throne away from him, but Max wasn't used to being treated like a nobody. He was used to inspiring fear or adoration. The lack of any emotion made the king too difficult to read. It was unsettling.

Max steadied his breathing and lifted his arms, determined to make the spell work. He'd been practicing dark magic with the king for hours every day since Nora had arranged for the meeting. Max lowered his eyes and let out a long breath. Raising his hands in front of him, he called to the Darkness. He'd been trying to channel it directly from the source but it was harder than it should be. As if it resisted him. Max cursed under his breath. He pressed his palms into his temples trying to ease the pounding that had started in his head. Magic had always come easy to him. Why was this so much harder?

"Stop." King Osbert's heavy cloak rustled over the stone floor as he walked toward Max. "Wanting to connect to the Darkness isn't enough. You are going to have to do something drastic to make it happen."

Max narrowed his eyes. The king made it seem so easy. He had to be leaving out a step. "I'm doing everything you asked me to do."

King Osbert sighed. "Yes, you are, but it's not enough. It might be time to open a more permanent channel."

"How?" Max dropped his hands to his side. He'd been struggling to find ways to open channels to the Darkness, but they never lasted long. It was difficult to sustain a temporary opening to the underworld while also performing spells. It was the key to the king's ability to raise the dead. And Max was learning it, but was nowhere near as strong as the king. If there was a way to leave the channel open, a way to spend all his energy on the spells, there was no limit to what he could do.

"There is a way to create a bridge, a sort of portal to the underworld." King Osbert reached for the black stone that hung around his neck. "It isn't much different than how the power stones were created."

Max locked his gaze on the black onyx around the king's neck. He'd learned that the stone was what had given the king the power to take away other sorcerer's magic. He also knew that the stone's magic didn't work on his sister. His stomach twisted at the thought. He had a feeling he knew where this was going and a wave of guilt rushed through him. He pushed it away and tightened his jaw. When he left the Ravens, when he'd joined the king, he'd made his choice. It was time to follow through with that choice. "What does this have to do with my sister?"

King Osbert smiled. Max had learned to mask his reaction to

the king's smile. It was far too sinister an expression for any man to wear.

"Your sister will be our bridge. She is the key to opening a permanent channel to the underworld. The key to bringing the Darkness back so we can use it to its full potential."

Max's stomach knotted. He knew that when he made his alliance with the king, he was sacrificing his sister. He'd tried to marry her off and send her away. He should have pushed harder. He didn't know what turning her into a bridge between the realms would do to her. It might have been better if the king had killed her. What would the Darkness do coursing through her? Would she be able to control it or would she end up succumbing to it?

Max wasn't opposed to using Dark Magic if it meant he could win his kingdom, but he wasn't fond of the king gaining even more power before he was able to make his move. If Etta stayed hidden in the Raven camp, everything would be much easier for Max.

A knock sounded on the door. "Enter," King Osbert called out.

The door swung open revealing a guard wearing black leather armor, the flaming phoenix practically glowing on his chest. "Sorry to bother you, your majesty. But your tracing spell was activated in the woods. Scouts reported a fight involving a few sorcerers near the castle. Two sorcerers left the fight after setting fire to the bodies of the fallen. One of the sorcerers was a girl who matched the description of the princess. The other was a young man with blonde hair."

"Ashton," Max said before he could stop himself.

King Osbert glanced at Max. "It seems he was a good target for a tracing spell. We can follow his trail right to your sister." Then he turned back to the guard. "Ready the undead."

The man bowed then left the room, closing the door behind him.

Max squeezed his hands into fists. He wondered why things couldn't go as planned. If they turned Etta into a bridge between their realm and the astral realm, Max was going to need a lot more than a group of fire sorcerers to challenge the king.

He turned to look at Max. "You still think Ashton is the way to break her?"

Max nodded. "It's her greatest weakness. She'll do anything for her friends, even more for Ashton."

The king ran his hand over his close-trimmed dark beard. He studied Max, eyes narrowed. "This could be our chance to open that channel for good. How has your practice gone with removing a person's essence?"

Max took a deep breath. Of all the things the king has asked him to do, removing a living person's essence from their body was the one that made him cringe the most. He knew there were very few ways to return the essence to the body, none of which the king had taught him. All of his victims had died, their essences were trapped in the Astral Realm for days or weeks before their physical bodies gave up. Despite not enjoying the practice, he was good at it. "I haven't made a mistake in weeks."

"Good." King Osbert walked toward the large, wooden door. "Prepare for a trip to the woods. You'll be practicing on your old apprentice."

6

W e walked through the woods as the sun rose higher in the sky. We'd have to leave their cover soon and my stomach was in knots at the thought. Would we make it safely to the house before somebody found us?

I realized I was less concerned about being overtaken than I was about having to kill somebody else. My mind kept replaying the deaths of the men I'd killed over the last few weeks. How had I become this person? I tried to find guilty feelings for killing Patrick, but they wouldn't come. When I thought back to his unmoving body, I was filled with anger. I didn't even flinch as I watched Ashton set his body on fire. We told ourselves it was the right thing to do, that we didn't want them to suffer as undead soldiers in the afterlife. Neither of us said it out loud, but I think we were both more concerned about seeing a familiar face coming after us at the bidding of the king.

There hadn't been much in the way of conversation as we stepped over fallen logs and wove our way around the large trees. The birdsong was out of place here, so close to the king's castle. It was almost peaceful. As if the king's evil hadn't reached the woods. It reminded me of home. How my little village had been untouched by the violence of the king and his undead until they came for me. Yet, I'd seen the damage he could cause in the gallows and empty towns I'd passed through. Had his reach traveled beyond the cities? Was there anywhere safe in Illaria? I stopped walking again. "Ashton?"

He turned to look at me. "Yes?"

"What's it like out there? Those posters. The Darkness. What's happening?" Maybe things weren't any different than they had been. Maybe we were being overly cautious.

Ashton frowned. "It's getting worse. Any city where the king thinks they may support you is punished. He sends guards to attack them or cuts off supplies. The people say it hasn't been this bad in a long time. It's like when he first rose to power, as if he's building an army again."

A chill ran through me as I recalled the empty city in Redding. All those people, gone. Probably now hidden away somewhere as undead soldiers, just waiting for a command from the king. It was terrifying. Suddenly, I felt exhausted and overwhelmed. "How are we going to do this? How are we going to defeat him?"

"That's what we were working on. When we get back to camp, the other scouts should be back. We'll make a plan. We're going to beat him, Etta."

I shrugged off the prickle I still got from him using my new name. Hearing the name I'd taken when I accepted the role as queen coming from him reminded me of how important all of this was. There had to be a way to win, it just seemed less clear than it had a few weeks ago.

The lack of support from the Ravens and the reward for my capture were making it difficult to sustain hope. The king was turning my own people against me. If the posters had worked to convince a member of the Ravens, how would they be received by regular people?

Ashton stopped walking and turned to me. "I know it's a lot. But we can do this. We have to."

I nodded. He was right. Somebody needed to step up for the people. Somebody needed to end the suffering. "I know. It just seems so much bigger now. Everything is getting more difficult. And Max. Do you think?"

I couldn't even say it out loud. Ann had given me no reason to doubt her, but I didn't want to believe that Max had joined the king.

Ashton took a deep breath. "We'll face that when we have more facts. For now, we have to accept that it is a possibility."

"Could the king be controlling him?" A jolt ran through me. I'd never seen an undead soldier before and I didn't know if it was obvious they were dead. "Is he, could he be?"

"No," Ashton said. "I know what you're thinking. But if it was Max, and he was using his magic, he's not dead. In every story I've ever heard, if a sorcerer is killed and brought back, they don't retain their power. They can't perform magic."

My heart sunk but it was quickly replaced by a feeling of relief that surprised me. While I would have liked to be able to claim that Max was being controlled by the king, I wasn't ready for him to be dead. My insides twisted in conflict. I didn't want to have to fight against Max, and I certainly didn't want him fighting with the king, he was the only family I had.

We stood in the woods, silent for a few moments while we both thought about the things that had passed. I didn't know Max the way Ashton did, but the more I tried to reason a way out of him working with the king, the more I convinced myself that what Ann saw was probably the truth. "We've lost him, haven't we? He's not coming back."

Ashton pulled me into a hug. "No, he's not."

We didn't need any more words. We both knew Max had joined the king but neither of us could say it. I rested my cheek against Ashton's strong chest and let myself relax in his embrace. How I'd missed being close to him while he was away. Just being in his presence had a way of helping me believe everything was going to work out. He calmed me. I breathed him in and reached my arms around his waist, holding him close. We needed more moments like this. More time to be together. What would I do without him?

If he hadn't grabbed hold of Ralph while they teleported away, I'd be in the hands of the king right now. I pulled away from the hug. "I never thanked you for saving my life."

He brushed the loose curls away from my face. "You don't have to thank me. You know I'd do anything for you."

I stood on my tip-toes to bring my face closer to his. "And I'd do anything for you."

He reached around me, pulling my body next to his, and leaned in to kiss me. As soon as our lips met, my mouth felt like it was on fire. My body reacted without effort, bringing ice from deep within the pit of my stomach, up through my chest, and into my kiss. Sparks danced around us and the hair on my arms stood on end. He pressed his lips harder into mine and I matched his intensity. My fingers worked their way through his blonde hair as his traveled up my spine. I never wanted this moment to end.

A rush of cold descended upon us and I pulled away from the kiss.

Ashton's face was flushed. "Everything okay?"

"That cold didn't come from me," I said.

We both stood frozen in place, eyes searching the woods around us. Something wasn't right. Suddenly, my fingers filled with the tingle of magic and it spread without warning into my arms. My whole body tensed. I lowered my voice to a whisper. "Ashton?"

His face looked pale. "I feel it."

My heart pounded in my chest as I scanned the trees around us. I hadn't felt magic like this since our last contact with the Reapers. The temperature felt like it had dropped and I shivered. "Do you see them?"

Ashton turned, his back to me. "Not yet."

We stood back to back, waiting. The seconds dragged on, feeling like hours. Then, out of the corner of my eye, I noticed movement coming through the trees. My stomach was full of knots and my breath came out too quickly. I swallowed back my fear as a hooded figured drifted toward me. "Ashton."

"I'm here," he said.

A second Reaper drifted from the opposite side, closing in on me. "Two of them."

"Same over here," Ashton said. "We can do this. You can do this."

I took a deep breath, calling on the strength I knew I had. I'd done this before. I could do it again. Jaw set, I squeezed my hands into fists and reached inside myself to find my magic. The arctic fire was getting easier to control, but it still took focus. I found the flicker of the spark in the pit of my stomach and pushed it through my body, filling my veins with ice as it spread through me. Opening my fists, I could feel the popping of the blue sparks that danced in my palms.

"On the count of three," Ashton said.

I nodded, then realized he couldn't see me. "One, two, three." Lifting my hands in front of me, I aimed at the Reaper on my right. The creature moved faster than I'd seen them move in the past, making me leave my position next to Ashton as I pursued him.

The hair on the back of my neck stood on end and out of the corner of my eye, I saw the second Reaper closing in on me. I turned toward the greater threat and pushed my icy blue arctic fire toward him. As I did, the first Reaper moved closer. I divided my hands, aiming blue flames at each of them, but they weren't backing down. For some reason, my powers weren't having the same effect on them.

Heat rose inside me as frustration gave rise to anger. There was strength in it, mixing with the ice flowing through me. I felt my powers wrapping around it, pulling from it, using it. I let the anger grow, fueling me. My hands burned as the blue flames glowed bright white. I closed my eyes against the blinding light flooding through me. This wasn't my usual arctic fire, this was something different. As I pushed the power from my hands, I let out a scream. It was as if the power itself had taken over, acting without my permission. Then, as abruptly as it had started, it stopped.

I dropped my hands and blinked open my eyes. The Reapers in front of me were gone. I turned to find Ashton. Instead, I found myself alone in the woods. No Ashton, no Reapers, nothing. The Reapers had managed to separate us while we were fighting them. Had they taken him? I didn't want to consider that possibility. He had to be close, I didn't remember going very far. I turned in a circle, looking for footprints or signs of where he might be.

Then I heard him. Ashton let out a cry that caused a ripple of fear to run through me. Without hesitating, I ran right for him. I wasn't going to let anything happen to him. Branches caught on my sleeves and skirt as I ran through the woods. I tore the fabric away, not caring what damage I did to the dress or myself. All I wanted to do was get to Ashton. His fire could keep Reapers away, but it wasn't as strong as the arctic fire I could wield. I had to find him.

7

The world spun around me as I ran. I'd used too much energy when I fought off the Reapers and though I was stronger than I had been, it still took a lot out of me to use my magic. I stopped for a moment to let the ground stop moving and listened. I needed to make sure I was going in the right direction and so far, all I'd seen were more trees. Where was he?

The birds had stopped singing. Even though I couldn't feel them, the Reapers had to be near. They scared away all life. Stepping slower so I could listen for signs of Ashton, I crept through the woods. Snap.

I turned around at the sound and let out a scream. I'd never seen the undead soldiers that the king had at his command, but nobody needed to tell me that's what was coming after me now. Hundreds of them. Men, women, children. Their faces were ashen, eyes milky white. Some of them wore torn and rotted clothing, others were in silk and fur. A few of them looked like skeletons with rotting fabric hanging off their bones. They moved with forced, stiff movements. They weren't fast, but they were all coming for me.

For a moment, I was frozen in terror. These were normal

people, people who had been taken from their lives to be used by the king. They had no control. My heart was pounding in my ears as I stared in shock at the undead coming after me. What was I supposed to do?

Run. There were too many of them. I turned and ran.

My mind reeled as I ran. What did I know about the undead? How could they be stopped? They were already dead. How did you kill them? How did you hide? What made them go away? My breaths came out shallow and fast. My muscles burned, my lungs on fire. I'd never run so fast in my life.

Ahead, the forest broke and I could see the road. Maybe I'd be able to find someone to help me. Or maybe I'd be leading a whole group of undead soldiers into a village or a town. My head was still spinning, I was only able to keep going on pure adrenaline. I had to do something. I couldn't run forever.

The slippers on my feet weren't meant for running and one of them flew off. I kicked off the other as I reached the dirt road that cut through the woods. I took a few more steps, then stopped, barely able to breathe.

Turning, I looked behind me to see that the horde of undead creatures making their way through the woods. I could possibly outrun them. They weren't as fast as I was, but they wouldn't need to rest. Eventually, my body would give out.

I leaned over, resting my hands on my knees, desperately trying to slow my breathing. *Think.* How do you get rid of the undead? I didn't think I had enough energy to use my arctic fire on this scale. The last thing I wanted to do was to end up unconscious after only taking out a few of the hundreds of bodies that were going to break through the tree line any minute.

I had two choices: I could run or I could fight. Neither was ideal. All I wanted to do was find Ashton and get back to our camp. I took a deep breath as the trees moved in front of me. They were here. It was too late to run.

I called to my magic, filling my insides with the familiar cold sensation. I thought back to my last few weeks of lessons with Master Flanders. There were other things I could do, spells that weren't as tiring as using the arctic fire. Reaching out with my magic, I called to water. If there was a stream or a river nearby, maybe I could bring that water to me and use it to push back against the undead.

A rush of cold made me gasp as water found its way to my hands. It wasn't much, but I had to try. Sweeping my arms through the air, I moved the water past me, it surrounded me, without getting me wet. It took all of my concentration not to drop the flow of water as I sent it in a stream toward the creatures coming through the woods.

Behind me, a huge gust of wind pushed the water and me ahead. I lost my balance and dropped my arms as I struggled to maintain my footing. The water came crashing down around me. All I had accomplished was getting the first group of undead wet but the wind had knocked a few of them down. Where had that come from? I shook out my hands and glanced over my shoulder.

Relief flooded through me. Master Flanders, Madame Lyndsey, Saffron, and Celeste were standing behind me.

"Etta, back here," Saffron called.

Without question, I ran behind her. I was tired and weak. I would make their work harder for them if I passed out in front of a hoard of undead. Saffron unsheathed her sword and extended it toward the oncoming foes. Her jaw tense, knuckles white as she gripped the hilt. She glanced at me. "Stay here."

I nodded and stared at my defenders. How were they going to face them all?

"Wait," Master Flanders called. He knelt down and rested his hand on the ground. A second later, the whole ground rippled like waves rolling away from him. The undead monsters wavered and fell to the ground. "Now!" He charged into the fray, arms extended in front of him.

Madame Lyndsey's hands erupted into flames. She launched a fireball at the creatures, then followed Master Flanders.

Celeste hesitated for a moment, looking around, then turned to me. "Where's Ashton?"

A lump rose in my throat. "I don't know, we got separated."

Celeste let out a long breath and nodded once. "Don't worry, we'll find him." Then she ran into the oncoming creatures, arms extended. She used wind to knock them down with one hand, then stabbed them in the chest with a dagger I hadn't noticed before.

I felt weak and useless. Pushing up my sleeves, I took a step forward. I wanted to help.

Saffron took a few steps in front of me, sword extended. "You need to stay here. They're here for you. Let's not make their job easier."

I opened my mouth to protest, but I knew she was right. The king was after me and he wanted me alive. I didn't want anything to do with him or his plans for me. Balling my hands into fists, I watched the slaughter taking place in front of me.

Master Flanders was raising and lowering the ground to send the undead toward Madame Lyndsey, who would burn them as they approached. Celeste continued to stab any that came her way. They were making quick work of the hundreds of undead monsters, but the onslaught of them coming from the woods didn't seem to have an end.

It wasn't long before some of the undead broke through the magic that Master Flanders and Madame Lyndsey were using on them. A gray-skinned man with patches of what used to be long, dark hair charged at us. I stepped back, calling to my ice, willing it to rise from within so I could help.

Saffron was fast. With ease, she swung her sword, removing

the creature's head. Then she jabbed the blade through his heart. The body collapsed in a heap on the ground as if it were nothing more than a pile of blankets. There was no scream, no blood. Just a lifeless, gray form in a heap on the ground. I looked away from the body to Saffron.

She looked at me briefly before turning back toward the woods, sword raised and ready to fight. My eyes traveled from Saffron to the sorcerers in front of me. As I watched them, I realized that fire was the most efficient way to eliminate them. Lips pursed in concentration, I tried to call fire. Not arctic fire, but real fire. The kind that Ashton used, the kind that Max and the king used. Master Flanders had been working with me to channel the other elements, but so far, the only time I had successfully called fire was the accidental incident the night Max left.

Frustrated by my inability to do something that most sorcerers could do, I shook out my hands and decided to try something else. Wind. I could call wind. It was the only other element that I had been able to master aside from water and it took little energy for me to bring it. Maybe I could help that way.

Four undead stumbled over the undulating ground and crawled on their hands and knees toward the place where Saffron and I stood. Reaching inside, I felt the place where my magic was waiting for me. I called to it, forcing it through my veins. A chill ran through me as I pushed a gust of wind from my hands at the creatures.

In a cloud of dust, the bodies slid away from us, back into the woods. I knew it wasn't good enough. All I'd done was send them away, I hadn't destroyed them. A flicker of panic rose inside me as I realized I may have sent them too close to the sorcerers fighting in the woods.

Just then, I saw Celeste approach the dazed looking creatures as they tried to stand. She called out to me without breaking her focus. "Nice wind!"

I smiled despite the scene in front of me, happy I could find a way to help. I didn't want to be the girl that stood by while others fought the battles.

An undead man with short, white hair had managed to regain his footing and lunged toward Celeste. She reacted with lightning speed, pushing her dagger into his chest. His empty, white eyes widened for a moment, then closed as she pulled the dagger out of his ribs. The creature tensed, then fell face first to the ground, unmoving. Celeste continued her assault on the group, using her dagger to wound each of the creatures. Each one fell to the ground with little to no reaction at having been stabbed in the chest. I wondered if this time the dead would stay dead.

Saffron moved her sword from hand to hand as she paced back in forth in front of me. I could tell she was feeling just as antsy as me. She probably wanted to be out there in the thick of the battle. For every creature that met its death at the hands of one of my friends, a new one seemed to appear. My heart raced in my chest. We were being overrun.

She took a few steps closer to the woods and I dropped into my sorcerer stance. They'd be breaking through the tree line any second. There were just too many of them.

A long shriek emitted from one of the undead and all the others joined in on the cry. I covered my ears with my hands, eyes streaming. I'd never heard anything so terrible in all my life. In front of me, Saffron dropped her sword. It took her several seconds before she picked it back up.

The creatures were frozen in place, screaming. They weren't advancing on us anymore. Something had stopped them.

Then the screeching stopped and the undead started to dissolve back into the woods, away from us. We were left breathless and confused. The only sound I could hear was the ringing of my ears. Saffron's mouth moved, but I couldn't hear what she was saying.

Master Flanders, Madame Lyndsey, and Celeste joined us on the road. They were all haggard from battle. Master Flanders' long hair was free of its usual tail, gray strands blowing around his face, sticking to his damp skin. Madame Lyndsey wiped blood from her mouth and rolled up charred sleeves. Wielding fire had a tendency to destroy clothing.

Celeste walked up to me. Her chest was rising and falling in quick breaths. Her brown curls formed a wild mane around her face. She said something to me, but I shook my head. The world was still wrapped in silence.

Celeste's brow furrowed in concern and she placed her hands on my cheeks. She spoke again. This time I read her lips. I think she asked me if I was okay.

I nodded and mouthed that I couldn't hear. At least I think I mouthed it. I might have said the words. It was impossible to tell.

The little group gathered around me. They were all speaking, or at least their mouths were moving. Panic started to well up inside me. Was I the only one who couldn't hear? Would I ever be able to hear again?

A huge bang answered that question. We all turned our heads in the direction of the noise. Suddenly, the ringing was cleared from my ears as if it had never happened.

"What was that?" I asked.

Everybody turned to face me.

"I couldn't hear anything for a while," I said.

"Silencing spell," Celeste said. "Somebody didn't want you to hear them."

"What did I miss?" I asked.

She swallowed and looked at the older members of the

group. There was a heavy silence among all of them. I noticed Saffron nod to Celeste.

Celeste looked like she was in pain. Whatever it was, she didn't want to say the words. "We heard something terrible." She winced. "We think it was Ashton, he was being tortured. We could hear him screaming."

8

I screamed as loud as I could. "Ashton!" If he was close enough they had heard him, he could hear me.

"Etta!" Saffron said. "You're going to let them know where we are."

My whole body was shaking. "I don't care. If somebody is hurting him, let them find me." Heat formed in the pit of my stomach and rushed through me. Sparks formed in my palms and I squeezed them shut. I took a deep breath. Whoever was torturing Ashton would feel my fire, but I needed to maintain control so I could save my energy for them.

Saffron rested her hand on my shoulder. "Etta, it's going to be okay."

I shrugged away from her. The anger I had felt was melting into fear. I wanted Ashton back with me. I wanted him safe. "How can it be okay? Somebody explain this to me. Where did the sound come from? And why couldn't I hear it?"

Madame Lyndsey took a step forward. "I think Ashton may have cast that spell. He didn't want you to hear him."

I shook my head and looked down the road. He knew I'd do

anything to help him. "Why would he do that? Why not fight back?"

"He probably couldn't fight back. Whatever has him, he was trying to keep you from following him. It's probably a trap," Celeste said.

"Does it matter?" I looked at Celeste. "It's Ashton. We're going after him."

Master Flanders cleared his throat. "I'm sure it's a trap. To find it, we have to go this way." He started walking.

Without waiting for the others, I followed him. "Thank you."

He smiled, then his expression grew serious. "Given the monsters that were sent after you, there is only one person who could have done this." Master Flanders fell silent.

A chill ran down my spine. *The king.* He sent the undead after us and he took Ashton. He tortured Ashton, knowing I'd come after him. Would he leave Ashton alive? He'd let him live once before. Would he do it again?

Celeste caught up to me and walked silently next to me. I was grateful for her company. Everybody in this group knew Ashton. He'd been friends with Celeste for years. Saffron had known him since he was a child. Master Flanders and Madame Lyndsey had both been involved with the White Ravens long enough to have some history with him. I couldn't choose a better group of people to face down the king and get him back.

I whispered to Celeste, unsure if we were trying to stay silent on purpose or if the tension of what we were doing was keeping everybody silent. "How far away do you think he was?"

"Can't be too far," she whispered.

"No need to stay quiet," Master Flanders said. "The king already knows we're coming. In fact," he slowed his steps, "I would wager he's already here."

He stopped and stood, hands clasped in front of him. He looked peaceful and relaxed. Probably the opposite of how I looked. My heart throbbed in my ears and my hands felt sweaty. I squeezed them into fists and lifted my chin. If I was going to see the king again, I would remain strong.

A huge gust of wind sent a cloud of dust rising over us. I covered my eyes with my forearm as dirt pelted my face. As the wind died down, I lowered my arm and blinked the debris from my eyes.

Standing in front of us was the king. On either side of him stood two Reapers. Behind him were at least a hundred rotting, undead. They stood still, watching us. I clenched my jaw, trying to look braver than I felt.

The king waved his hand and in a smaller cloud of dust, a prone form appeared on the ground in front of him. It was Ashton. He wasn't moving.

My heart stopped for a second and a lump rose in my throat. I felt like my whole world had come crashing down around me. All I could see was Ashton, almost forgetting the king was even there.

Laughter brought me out of my single-minded focus on Ashton. I looked up to see the king laughing. He wore a wide grin, showing his straight, white teeth. He crossed his arms over his chest and nodded to me. He was asking me to come to him.

The king had faced me before and he had let me go. His posters said they wanted me alive. For some reason, the king wasn't willing to kill me. I stepped forward.

Fingers grasped my upper arm, stopping my progress. I turned to see Saffron. She shook her head at me, eyes pleading for me to stop.

"It's Ashton," I said. For him, I would face death itself.

Saffron let go of my arm and I swallowed. As I stepped forward, I straightened my posture, trying to look like the queen I claimed to be.

The king's eyes found mine and didn't waver. He didn't even

blink. I held his gaze, trying to show him I wasn't afraid while my insides were crying out to turn back. Dropping my eyes, I looked to Ashton. He was all the motivation I needed.

I stopped walking a few steps away from Ashton and the king. Every piece of me wanted to run the rest of the way, to drop down to the ground and see if Ashton was alive. It took all of my willpower to stand there, chin held high, staring right into the king's dark eyes. "I've come for my friend."

King Osbert used his toe to push Ashton's body over so he rolled onto his back. "This friend?"

I gritted my teeth. "Yes."

"He's important to you, isn't he?"

"You know he is," I said.

"Really, my dear." The king stepped over Ashton so he was only two steps away from me. "I'm doing you a favor. Having people you care about is a weakness. Look how easily I was able to bring you out in the open with a threat on his life. Keeping him around is going to lead to your doom."

I shook my head. "You're wrong. Having people to care about is what makes life worth living."

King Osbert let out a long, drawn out sigh. "You're still so young. You have so much to learn."

"Why are you doing this?" I was getting tired of his games. He'd drawn me into his castle once by threatening all of my friends and now was trying the same thing again. He was right, the people I cared about were my weakness but they were also my strength. Without their support, I wouldn't have the courage to stand up to him.

"Etta, my love. We've discussed this before." He wore an expression caught between a sneer and a smile.

My insides squirmed. His words made me feel like I had spiders crawling under my skin. I clenched my teeth. "I'm not *your love.*"

"Not yet, but I haven't given up yet. When I give up, you'll know. Because you'll be dead." He snapped his fingers and the pallid soldiers behind him began walking toward me. Their movements were stiff and forced. As if they didn't want to follow his orders. Their blank eyes were pure white. I took a few steps backward.

The king laughed, bringing me back to my senses. I didn't want to show fear in front of him, but he could see it written all over me. My eyes darted from the king to my friends behind me. I didn't want to turn around to look at them, but I could catch a glimpse of them. They were all standing there, waiting.

The king followed my eyes. "Your friends?"

"Leave them out of this."

He lifted a chain on his neck, showing a black stone that glittered when it caught the sun. "You know what this is, don't you?"

My brow furrowed. Why was he showing me a black rock? I looked back at him. "Should I?"

"They really have kept you in the dark," he said. "I wouldn't do that to you. They keep you ignorant so they can manipulate you. You think they're your friends, but they hide so much from you."

"You don't know anything," I said.

He held the stone up again. "This, my love, is how I took away all of the magic that first night we met. Right now, if any of your friends tried to use magic, they'd find they couldn't."

I stared at the stone in disbelief. "How is that possible?"

"Like I said. There is much you don't know but it doesn't have to be that way. When you are my queen, I will hide nothing from you."

My upper lip curled in disgust. Just the thought of being around the king made my stomach churn. He was evil. He'd killed my parents, my grandmother. How could he ever think I'd agree to help him? "You know I'd die first."

He shrugged. "That can be arranged. You'll make a fine undead queen. Though I'd rather have you alive. You see, one thing I haven't mastered yet is how to allow sorcerers I kill to keep their powers once I bring them back from the dead. That'll change soon enough. Next time we meet, I have a feeling you'll see things my way."

I shook my head. "There is nothing that would ever make me want to join you."

He stepped closer to me so we were only inches apart. The hair on my arms stood on end. He reached out and lifted my chin with his finger so I was forced to look him in the eye. "It's a shame your defiance can't be controlled with ambition. Very different than your brother."

I turned my face away from him, and swatted his hand away from me. My skin crawled all over again from his touch. My heart pounded in my ears. *Is he controlling Max?* "What have you done to my brother?"

He raised an eyebrow, and a wicked smile filled his face. "Nothing. He came to me."

"You're lying." My nostrils flared and my hands trembled. I didn't want to hear any more. I was worried that the last thread of hope would break.

"You'll see, soon enough, you'll feel the pull from the Darkness." King Osbert's smile was gone and he studied me for a moment. His gaze was almost a challenge. I felt my temper rising and for a moment, I wanted to lash out at him. *That's what he wants.*

I focused on slowing my breathing and keeping my voice steady. "If you aren't going to kill me, you should go."

The king clapped his hands and the undead broke away, heading toward the trees. His Reapers still hovered a few feet behind him. He turned and walked a few steps away, then stopped and faced me again. "If and when I decide it's time for you to die, I will do it myself. That spell can't protect you forever. Besides, I know your weakness." His eyes traveled to the ground where Ashton still lay, then behind me where my friends waited for me.

"You leave them alone." Ice was filling my veins as I stared at the king. I wanted to claw the smirk off of his face. Blue sparks began to crackle in my palms.

He looked down, noticing the magic. "There's darkness in you. I'll see you sooner than you think."

I squeezed my hands into fists, fighting the urge to challenge him. I wasn't anything like him. I wasn't anything like Max. Nothing would cause me to use Dark Magic they way they had.

A gray cloud of smoke rose around the king, enveloping him and his Reapers. I dropped to the ground and threw my body over Ashton. There was no way I was going to let him take Ashton away from me. I clung to him, worried that if I let go, I'd never see him again.

9

When the smoke cleared, my hands found Ashton's chest. I rested them there, waiting to feel the beat of his heart. A weak rhythm played in his chest and I let out a small sigh of relief. He was alive, for now. How had this happened? How did we end up separated? Why was the king doing this to me? Why Ashton? My mind reeled and my throat tightened. *This is my fault.* I was causing this harm to everybody that I loved, to everybody who loved me. *I am dangerous.* This was my fault and I had to fix it, no matter the cost. Hot tears streamed down my face as I studied the slow rise and fall of his chest. *I am not going to let you die.*

Brushing his honey-blonde hair away from his face, I felt his forehead. He was so cold. I lowered my face to his, kissing his mouth. His lips were like ice. What had the king done to him? I whispered in Ashton's ear, "I can't lose you. Do you hear me?"

Celeste knelt down next to me and I turned to look at her. I was sure her worried expression mirrored my own.

"Celeste." My voice was high pitched with panic and I was speaking too quickly. "What do we do? How do we help him?"

She shook her head. "I don't know."

I looked behind me. "Master Flanders!"

The old man's knees cracked as he sunk down next to us. His fingers moved over Ashton's face, down to his neck. "He still has a heartbeat, he's still breathing."

Saffron sat down next to me and wrapped an arm around me. "It's going to be okay, Master Flanders will figure it out." She pulled me in for a hug.

I looked at Saffron and saw the worry drawn across her face. She'd thought of Ashton like a little brother since he was a small child. This had to be just as hard on her, yet she was comforting me. I squeezed her hand in mine. "Whatever it takes, I'm going to fix this."

Saffron smiled at me but it faded quickly. "I know."

My heart ached for her. She was probably thinking about Max. In the few weeks since he left, I'd heard whispers about them. She seemed to get more questions than I did from people who thought their conversations were private. People wondered how she could be trusted after years of being inseparable from Max. Others were taking bets on when she would find him and kill him for his betrayal.

I hadn't seen them together when their relationship had been out in the open, but I knew they'd been through more than two people ever should. I wanted to say something comforting to her, but a dark look crossed her face. I wondered if she was thinking about what the scouts said about Max working with the king. Before I could figure out what to say, Master Flanders cleared his throat and I turned my attention to him.

"There is Dark Magic at work here." He reached a hand out, resting it on top of mine and Saffron's hands. "I'm afraid the king has sent Ashton's essence from his body."

"What?" I pulled my hands away. How was that possible? Everybody knew that after you died, your essence went to the astral realm where you would be judged by Vraga, the Goddess of the Underworld. I blinked a few times, trying to make sense of his words. If Ashton's essence had left his body, did that mean he was already gone?

My eyes filled with tears that I couldn't contain. I felt like a part of me was being ripped from my body. *This can't be happening.*

I leaned over him, resting my palms on his chest. It rose and fell slightly and a light beating could be felt from his heart. Flutters of hope filled my chest. "He's still breathing, he's still alive."

Master Flanders took hold of my hands and gently moved me away from Ashton. "Etta, he's alive for now. His essence is near. When this happens, the essence hangs on to the body by a thread."

I looked around as if I would be able to see a transparent Ashton floating nearby. "How do we get it back in? Will that bring him back?" There had to be a way to save him. I wasn't going to lose him. "Ashton? Can you hear me? Come back to me!"

I looked at Ashton, my vision blurred with tears. His face was even more pale than it had been. He didn't look good. I wasn't an expert on anything that had to do with magic. I was still learning, but even I could tell that he didn't have much time. If there was something that could be done, it had to be done quickly. I didn't even want to consider what my life would be like without Ashton.

"We have to save him." I looked up at Master Flanders.

"If we return his essence to his body, it will bring him back," Master Flanders said.

I lifted my chin and took a deep breath. "Tell me what I need to do."

"I'm afraid it isn't that easy, Etta." He glanced at the group of people around us. Nobody else spoke.

"Just tell me," I said. The tears were gone now. Replaced by an energy I'd never felt before. I was more alert than I'd ever been in my life. This was the most important thing I'd ever had to do. Whatever the cost, I would save Ashton. "I don't care what it is. I'll do anything."

"Master Flanders." Madame Lyndsey's voice behind me made me jump. I turned to look at her. Her eyes darted from one side of the road to the other. "Can we finish this back at camp? I don't think this road is safe."

A loud cry from a bird reminded me that we were on a road in the middle of the woods, near the king's castle. We were completely exposed. A shiver ran through me. What if those undead returned? What if the king came back for us?

"What about Ashton?" I leaned in over him protectively. I wasn't about to leave him or his essence behind.

Master Flanders' groaned as he rose to standing. "We'll bring him with us, of course."

"And his essence?" I asked.

"It's in the Astral Realm. It can move freely, but is still attached to him by that thread. It will follow us." He produced several red coins and handed one to Madame Lyndsey and one to Celeste. The coins were the only way we could teleport directly in or out of our camp. Only a few people had such coins. Each of our scouts had one, and if a member of my council left camp, they could get one from Master Flanders. He was the keeper of the coins and the only person in camp who knew how to make them.

"Madame Lyndsey," Master Flanders said. "Can you please bring Ashton with you?"

I hesitated as she approached, not wanting to let go of him.

"I'll be careful with him," Madame Lyndsey said. "We'll be waiting for you at camp."

Reluctantly, I lifted my hands away from Ashton and stood.

Madame Lyndsey gently slid her arms under him as if he

were a baby, but rather than lifting, she stayed on her knees in front of him as gray smoke rose around her. She'd land at camp with him in her arms.

My throat felt tight and my mouth was dry as I watched him vanish in front of me. I stared at the place where he had been until all of the smoke cleared. A hand touched my shoulder and I tuned to see Celeste. "Want to go back with me?"

Forcing a smile, I nodded. I'd started to learn the basics of teleporting in my lessons with Master Flanders, but hadn't yet tried it on my own. Until I could master the skills, I'd have to have somebody else take me with them. Celeste clasped my hand, and as the smoke rose around us, I saw Master Flanders and Saffron enveloped in their own cloud.

A CROWD HAD ALREADY GATHERED around Madame Lyndsey as my feet touched down on the ground at Camp. People rushed to me asking questions and checking to see if I was harmed.

"I'm fine, really, thank you." I stood on my tiptoes to try to see Ashton over the crowd. More people surrounded me, blocking my route to him. "I appreciate the concern." I used my best polite responses as I weaved my way around people, doing my best to smile and not show the fear on my face.

Saffron pressed against my side and I relaxed a bit knowing she was next to me. Despite my hope that there were no other threats against me at camp, my heart was racing in my chest. "The queen is safe, but she's been through a lot. Please give her some space so she can recover."

Saffron stepped in front of me, arms extended to move people away from me. I'd never tried to separate myself from the rest of the Ravens. It was something I prided myself on, yet at this moment, I wanted them to leave me alone. My skin crawled at the thought of people getting too close to me. I bit down on the inside of my cheek, trying to hide the irrational fears rising inside me. I didn't want to be afraid of the people who were trying to help me defeat the king. They were supposed to be loyal to me, believers in the same cause.

At Saffron's urging, the crowd backed away, allowing a clear path for me to reach Ashton. Without worrying about decorum, I ran to him. I could feel the eyes of all those who had gathered. Whispers surrounded me. I ignored them as I dropped to my knees at Ashton's prone form. I leaned my ear over his mouth, listening and feeling for breath. Finding it, I sat back, a wave of relief rushing through me.

"Jonathan, Michael," Saffron called out. Two men who had been with the Ravens as long as Saffron stepped forward. They were about ten years older than her, both had grown children who had been raised in the Raven camps. Saffron trusted them and I trusted her.

I stood and faced them. Both men inclined their heads to me. "Your highness."

I nodded.

"Can you two help us get Ashton to the barn?" Saffron asked.

Without a word, the two men lifted Ashton and walked through the crowd. Murmurs and gasps followed them as they cut though the crowd of people. Madame Lyndsey, Master Flanders, and Celeste followed them. I watched them walk away for a moment before I started moving. A tapping on my shoulder stopped my progress.

"What happened to him?" I recognized the woman who approached me as another long time member. Her forehead was creased in concern.

I spoke loudly so all of the onlookers could hear me. I wondered how many of them didn't believe in me. I took a deep breath. It didn't matter. I would earn their trust eventually and that would start by being honest with them.

"We were attacked by the king and Ashton was injured. This changes nothing. If anything," I looked around at the eyes fixed on me. The whispers had stopped. "This makes it even more important for us to find a way to defeat him. We are going to defeat him."

I turned and walked away from the stunned silence. The fear I had been feeling since Ashton was injured was being replaced by anger. I wanted the king to hurt just as bad as I did.

10

I slid the rotting wooden door closed behind me as I entered the dim barn. Light fell in patches across the dusty floor from the missing pieces of the thatched roof. It wasn't much, but we were thankful to have a large place we could meet in.

Ashton was lying across the table in the center of the room. Johnathan and Michael had already left, only the group who had fought the king in the woods remained. They stood around the table watching as Master Flanders held his hands over Ashton's face.

I moved slowly toward the table. My hands trembled and my heart raced in my chest. Seeing him sprawled out across the table reminded me of the funeral piers erected to burn the bodies of the dead.

Master Flanders looked up as I approached. He shook his head and dropped his hands. "I'm afraid it's getting worse."

It felt like someone was sitting on my chest, making it hard to breathe. This shouldn't be happening. Ashton shouldn't be going through this. The king only hurt him to get to me. I knew that whatever needed to be done, no matter the cost, I would save him. "How do we help him?" I stopped in front of the table and looked down at Ashton. My heart felt like it was breaking. *I have to fix this.*

Master Flanders waved his hands in front of him and five golden glowing spheres appeared before him. They were smaller than an apple, maybe the size of a small stone. I pressed my brows together as I studied the golden lights. I glanced at my friends, they were all just as fixated as I was on the spheres.

Master Flanders lifted a hand, palm up under the first sphere. "These represent an old story, one that many have attributed to myth. It's one of the most highly protected secrets in Illaria."

I watched him trace his fingertip over each of the spheres, wondering where he was going with this.

"There have always been sorcerers who use dark magic. This magic can be amplified by channeling the Darkness. When the Darkness is nearer, it's easier to channel. Last time the Darkness came to Illaria, it was brought here by several sorcerers who used it to create what we call power stones. The creation of these stones caused the rift between the world we live in and the astral realm. They brought the darkness to us and weakened the barrier, making us more at risk than ever before for the return of it." He waved his hands over the stones and the colors changed. "Right now, the Darkness isn't our concern, these stones are."

He cupped his hands around the first sphere. It glowed bright orange. "The first of these stones is the Stone of Morare, the stone that controls the Reapers. King Osbert was able to find its location from his research. Part of the reason he destroyed all of the libraries is that he didn't want anybody else to find the other stones."

His index finger touched the second sphere. It changed to black. "The second stone is the Black Onyx. This stone is said to be able to remove magic for all except for the holder." He glanced at me. "He used this the night of the battle outside of Luxor."

The next stone began to glow a deep blue. "The third stone is the Skystone, said to have been made by a high priestess of Taivas who wanted to find a way to be closer to the sky god. This stone is said to amplify the powers of the user, making their magic a hundred times stronger than it would be without the stone."

He placed his fingertips under the next orb and it glowed red hot like the ember of a coal, then turned to black. "The fourth stone has a troubled history. Some say it no longer exists. That it died out with the last dragon."

The hair on the back of my neck stood on end at the mention of dragons. As a child, I'd read stories about the ancient beasts that had once roamed our land and flown through our skies. But they were long gone. A traveling circus had once brought the skull of a dragon through the village. It was a gruesome looking thing with massive empty holes where eyes should be and long, sharp teeth. In the weeks since joining the White Ravens, the long-dead creatures had been brought up too many times to be coincidence.

Celeste stepped closer to the glowing red light. "The fourth stone has something to do with dragons?" She sounded like she was trying to mask her excitement. She'd been working with a dragon egg on a healing orb and she knew more about dragons than anybody I'd ever met.

Master Flanders nodded. "They say it can control dragons. There's no record of what the stone actually looks like but we think it was made from the volcanic rock of the Belaur Islands. Most scholars refer to it as the Belaur stone or the Dragon Stone."

I looked at the glowing spheres hovering in the air in front of me. I felt hot and pulled on the collar of my dress as if it were suffocating me. I didn't understand how any of this was supposed to help Ashton. If anything, it was making me feel worse. The king knew obtaining these stones would make him impossible to defeat. I glanced at Ashton then looked back at Master Flanders. "Why are you telling us this?"

Master Flanders took a step to move in front of the last sphere and with a wave of his hand, it floated over to me. The stone changed color, glowing a silvery-white. It resembled a full moon. I passed my fingers under it. "What is this one?"

"The astral projection stone." Master Flanders was silent as the weight of his words sunk in.

I looked up at him. "If we had this stone, could we give it to Ashton? Would it help his essence find his body?"

"Not quite," Master Flanders flicked his hand and all of the spheres vanished. "The person who has this stone can enter the astral realm at will. Then, that person could see Ashton or any others who are in astral form and could guide them back to their physical forms. You see, the problem with what the king did is that he sent Ashton's essence out of his body without his consent. When the essence is thrown off like that, it can't find it's way back. But if you leave of your own free will, you can return."

I stared at the place where the sphere had been. That stone was the only way to save Ashton. I didn't care what I had to do, I needed this stone. "Where is it? How do I find it?"

"Oh no," Saffron stepped in front of me. "You're not going on some quest to find a magic rock. It's not safe out there for you."

My voice choked as I spoke. "Don't you tell me what I can and can't do." My nostrils flared. I felt like I had lost control. "This is Ashton. If that stone is out there, I'm going to get it and save him. All of this is my fault. The king is trying to hurt me. Ashton didn't do anything to cause this."

"He knew what he was risking. Probably more than anybody in this room," Saffron said. "He's been a Raven since he was a child. He was raised to fight the king. He made his choice and I'm not going to lose you, too."

"You know I'm going to do this." My voice grew small. I didn't want to hurt Saffron after all she'd been through, but she should know that I wasn't going to back down on this. "I have to do this. If there's any way to save him, I have to try."

"Send somebody else," she said. "It's not safe for you to go on a quest."

I walked over to Ashton and ignored the gasps around me as I reached into his pocket. Smoothing out the paper, I turned and held it in front of me. "See this? This is why they took me." I handed the paper to Saffron. "I'm not safe anywhere."

Saffron took the poster from me and looked from the drawing to me, then back again. "Where did you get this?"

"Ashton brought it back with him. They're probably all over the kingdom. Patrick and Ralph must have seen them. Who else will think it's a good idea to turn me in? For that kind of money, who's to say somebody wouldn't turn the whole camp over to the king."

A shadow crossed Saffron's expression and she pressed her lips together. "A few weeks ago, I would have said that I trust the Ravens without doubt. After Ma-" she paused, unable to say his name. "After what's been happening, I'm not so sure, anymore."

"Etta should go and get the stone. She'll be safer on the road for now. She'll only be gone a week or so. It will give us time to find out if we have any more traitors here at camp," Master Flanders said.

"I'll go with her." Celeste moved next to me and linked her arm through mine. "We worked together well in Luxor. We can do it again." She smiled at me. "Nothing like a couple of friends on an adventure."

"I should go with you," Saffron said.

"No, you can't." I shook my head. "I need you here. You know the Ravens. You're the only one who can run this camp for me while I'm away."

Saffron sighed. "I don't like it."

"Saffron, you have to let Etta do this," Master Flanders said. "She'll have help."

"Help?" I didn't like the idea of having people I didn't know accompanying me on a trip somewhere. It was hard enough to trust people with everything that was happening, and I was just starting to realize I had a tendency to trust people too easily. Sir Henry's warning flashed through my mind. After our diplomacy and geography lessons, he'd told me not to trust anyone.

"They'll go to the Oracle at the Black Tower, she's the keeper of the Astral Stone," Master Flanders said.

All good feelings flowed out of my body, replaced by the icy feeling of dread. I'd heard stories about The Black Tower. It was located on an island and had once been a thriving ancient city. Over the centuries, it had been abandoned and was rumored to be a cursed place, full of sickness. The tower was said to be the only thing on the whole island that was spared because it was a direct link to the gods. It had become a place to go to pray if you were on death's edge and had not led a good life. It was the last resort of those who feared they would not be treated with kindness when they met Vraga in the Astral Realm. "They say nobody returns from there."

"Those who travel there are already on borrowed time," Master Flanders said. "Delphina will make sure you are safe while inside the sacred city."

I bit down on the inside of my cheek, trying to hide the fear I was feeling.

"It may be the safest place for you," Saffron said.

I turned to look at her, surprised she was reacting so calmly to me visiting the tower. "I've heard stories about the Oracle and the island. Nothing about them suggest safety."

Saffron shrugged. "They're just stories as far as I can tell. Rumors and superstitions I suspect. The king is superstitious enough to likely avoid the island altogether."

"He won't go there himself," Master Flanders said. "He's afraid of the Oracle, of what she might say."

My forehead creased in confusion at his words. "Why would he be afraid of her? Are the stories they say true? Was she really born of a Dragon? Or does she eat the bones of the dead?"

Master Flanders pressed his mouth into a tight line, then shook his head. "People misunderstand the Oracle. She has a gift, it's unfamiliar and rare magic. Some people fear that she can control the future when all she can do is see visions of what might come to pass. Delphina would never hurt anybody."

I thought about how magic was treated in Illaria. It was regulated by the guild and only allowed to be performed with an instructor present until you passed your trials. People were afraid of magic. It was everywhere, and inside of everybody, but unless you could channel it, it sat dormant. I wondered if the Oracle's magic was something that was learned like I was doing with my own lessons. I felt a twinge of pity toward her. She lived alone, feared by all because her magic looked different from the norm.

I glanced at Celeste then looked at Saffron and Master Flanders. "Okay, how do we get to the Black Tower?"

The journey to the Black Tower required us getting to Campari, the port town near my old village. From there, we'd have to find a boat willing to get us to the Sacred Island. My eyes rarely left Ashton as the others discussed the best way for Celeste and me to get to the tower. I kept hoping he'd sit up, that it was all a mistake.

I rubbed my eyes and turned away from him. Saffron and Master Flanders were in a disagreement over the best way for us to travel. Saffron wanted us to teleport as close to the tower as possible, Master Flanders didn't think that was a good idea. The problem arose from the fact that I couldn't teleport myself yet, let alone anybody else, and that Celeste hadn't been to many places in Illaria. It's impossible to teleport to a place you've never been. We'd either have to ride horses to where we needed to go or somebody who had been there would need to teleport us.

"Please, stop arguing." I was tired and the only thing I wanted to do was see Ashton's essence safely returned to his body. "Master Flanders, how much time does he have?"

Master Flanders shook his head. "It's impossible to know that. Could be a couple of days, could be a couple of weeks."

I took a deep breath and let it out slowly. "We need to get this stone as quickly as possible. Why can't you teleport us?" I looked at Master Flanders and Madame Lyndsey.

They looked at each other, a moment of understanding passing between them before they spoke. Master Flanders looked at me. "I don't think teleporting anywhere is safe right now. Teleporting leaves a marker at the place where you leave from and the place you arrive at. Any sorcerer who is looking for you would sense the marker. It's probably how the king got word of you when you arrived near his castle. You can teleport away from the island, though. There aren't any sorcerers there to track you. That will help make the trip shorter."

Madame Lyndsey took the poster from Saffron and held it up. "With this out there, you have a lot more enemies than you used to. The king has been notoriously hard on sorcerers over the years, especially those who refuse to work for him. If somebody thinks it can give them a reprieve from his wrath, they'll likely turn you in. They may even be out searching for you."

"I didn't know that," Saffron said. "Sometimes I hate being the only non-sorcerer."

"I know how hard this is for you," Madame Lyndsey said. "All of us, our hearts are breaking for you."

Saffron nodded once. "Any news from the Order?"

Madame Lyndsey shook her head. "I resigned from the Order of the Dragon when Etta claimed the throne. None of them speak to me anymore." A flicker of pain crossed her face.

"You were in the Order of the Dragon?" I asked. That meant she might have been friends with Max. How close had they been? There was still so much I didn't know. One of these days, when I wasn't running for my life, or for the life of somebody I loved, I wanted to sit down and ask questions of all of my friends.

Madame Lyndsey forced a smile. "I was, as many fire sorcerers are, but that's not who I am anymore."

Saffron frowned. "We have no way of knowing what the Order is up to. They could be hunting you. I don't think it's safe for you to teleport."

"How do we get to Campari?" Celeste asked.

"You'll ride," Saffron said. "Go to Sir Henry's first. Three days ride from here. Then you can go to Campari from there."

"Excellent plan," Master Flanders said. "You should leave today. Before the rest of the camp knows you're here."

"What will you tell them?" I looked from Master Flanders to Saffron.

"Nothing," Saffron said. "You're queen. You don't ask permission. You grant it."

11

S affron's words sent a chill through me. I'd stepped up to the role, told everybody I was fighting for the throne, but I still didn't feel like a queen. It was true I didn't need to explain myself. How often had Max left and only his closest advisors knew the reason?

I lifted my chin. *I'm not Max.* There was a reason why people were whispering about me. They didn't see the same strength in me they had in Max. But he earned that through fear. I looked down at my too-thin body and small hands. Max had looked the part of a king. I still looked like a poor peasant girl. Aside from the magic I could create, there was little I could do to draw that sort of respect through fear. Even if I could, I didn't want to. I was nothing like Max which was a source of pride for me. I looked up at Saffron. "No, I won't run away. Call a meeting."

"What are you going to say?" Celeste asked. "You can't tell them the truth. What if the word gets back to the king?"

"I have to tell them something," I said. "Saffron, you're right. I'm the queen. I need to start acting like one."

A small smile crossed Saffron's face. "As you wish, your majesty."

I shook my head. "No, that's too much. The king uses that title. Save that for when we win."

She nodded. "Your highness it is, then." Saffron turned and headed toward the door.

"I'll prepare some supplies and horses for you," Madame Lyndsey said. "See you at the stables when you're ready."

"Thank you." I watched both women leave then walked back to Ashton. I ran my fingers through his hair and leaned down so I could whisper in his ear. "Hang in there for me. I promise I'm going to save you. You know I'll do whatever it takes."

I kissed his cold forehead and brushed my fingers over his cheek before turning away from him. "Master Flanders, you'll take care of him while I'm gone, right?"

"You know I will. Don't you worry about us while you're gone." He placed a hand on my shoulder. "You can do this. Go, talk to the Ravens, then ride. Find the stone."

I wrapped my arms around him. Master Flanders had been a constant in my day over the last few weeks. Though I often struggled to understand his cryptic teaching methods, he had never let me down. If he thought I could do this, I would go. "I'll be back soon. Keep him alive for me."

Master Flanders squeezed me, then let go of the hug. With one more glance at Ashton, I left the barn. I knew we were on a tight timeline. The sooner we could leave camp, the better our chances of saving Ashton. While it was a risk to leave the safety of the wards and ride past towns that might have posters up offering money in exchange for my capture, I couldn't let those things scare me right now. They didn't matter. What mattered was finding that stone and saving Ashton.

I SMOOTHED out the torn and dirty dress I was wearing and

tucked my hair behind my ears. I was sure I looked like a mess, but I didn't really care. The Ravens needed to feel like they could trust me. They needed to know that I would fight for them and keep them safe. They needed to know that we could win.

Two-hundred people called the camp their home. Most of them were standing around me in the outdoor area we used for meals. I climbed on top of a table so I wasn't lost in the crowd. Everybody stopped talking to watch me. A baby cried somewhere in the back of the group and a few children could be heard giggling or talking. Their voices reminded me of why we were doing this. I took a deep breath.

"Before we begin, please join me in a moment of silence for our lost brother. Nathan has entered the Astral Realm and will join his family in the Underworld."

Silence hung in the air, heavy around us. The mood of the crowd seemed to shift as I waited. Nathan had been well liked and his loss reminded us all of the weight of what we were up against. But I didn't want this speech to leave the Ravens feeling defeated. I wanted them to feel like we were moving forward, and finding a way to honor the sacrifices of those who had died for our cause.

"Today, the king asked me to join him, something I'd never do. To punish me, he sent Ashton's essence from his body. I refuse to let the king win. I will travel to the Black Tower and ask the Oracle for help in saving him."

Heavy silence still hung around me. I took a moment to look around the crowd. Were there people standing here who wanted to see me gone? Were there people here who would be willing to sell me out for 5,000 *soldi*? How did I convince them that I was worth following?

I lifted my chin and looked out at the crowd. "I know things haven't been easy the last few weeks. We lost friends, we lost a leader, we lost our home. Things have changed not only for the Ravens, but for all of Illaria. You don't know me as well as you knew Max. You don't know if you can trust me or what I'm capable of.

Let me tell you what I believe. I believe that Illaria is worth fighting for. I believe we deserve to be happy, that we deserve peace. I believe in honesty and earning your trust. The Ravens are a family, and family supports one another." My voice choked as I realized what I had said. Max was supposed to be my family. He'd turned his back on us all.

I cleared my throat. "Let me tell you what I am not. I am not Max. I will not turn my back on my family. No matter the cost, I am a Raven. Together, we are going to fight and we are going to win."

Somewhere in the center of the crowd, a fist shot up into the air and a few whoops grew into applause. I smiled and waited for them to quiet.

"While I am away, Saffron will be in charge. It is important that we continue to build our resources and gain strength. When I return, we will begin the real work. We will prepare for the final battle, the battle where we take down the king."

Cheers broke through the silence. Celeste offered her hand to help me jump down from the table. A few of the people who were closest to me wished me luck or offered to pray for me. I thanked them as I walked toward the stables, Celeste next to me.

I couldn't shake the feeling that I was doing everything wrong. There was no book to teach me how to be a queen. Nobody I could ask for help. It was times like this when I really missed the parents I had never known. I reached for my pendant, sliding it up and down the metal chain.

"You did good," Celeste said.

I dropped the pendant. The two of us had spent a lot of time

together over the last few weeks. She could tell how I was feeling. "Thank you."

"We're going to find the stone, you know," she said.

I nodded. My mouth felt dry as I pictured Ashton hardly
breathing sprawled out on the table in the barn. If we didn't find
that stone, if I lost Ashton, I didn't know what I would do.

Max stood in front of the roaring fire in the sitting room at the Dragon's Keep. It was a warm day, but there was something about staring into a fire that calmed him. The events of the last few hours played over and over in his head. The look of shock and betrayal on Ashton's face was burned into his mind forever. Max's insides twisted as he tried to force the memory from his mind. He could almost feel Ashton's presence with him, judging him. He deserved it. Max had taken Ashton under his wing. He'd taught him everything he knew about sorcery. Until today, Max had thought Ashton might still tire of Etta and join him. That would never happen now.

How had things come to this? How much longer would he need to pretend at being the king's sidekick before they could remove him from power?

"They told me you'd be here." A silky, smooth voice carried through the large stone room.

Max turned to see Nora leaning against the doorframe. He turned away from her, back to the fire.

"They also told me what you did." Her footsteps sounded

over the stone floor. She stopped behind him. "I know how hard that must have been for you."

Max glanced at her but didn't respond. She had no idea what he was feeling. He could hardly explain it himself. He wanted the power, the title, the throne. But the deeper he got in with the king, the more he began to question everything.

She slid her hand across his shoulders. He shrugged it away and looked over his shoulder at her. "Not now, Nora."

She smirked, an expression she used often. It was as if this was all a game to her. "Have it your way. I just thought you'd like a little distraction before my father arrived for dinner." Pausing in front of the door, the smirk faded. "He's testing you. He wouldn't have made you do that to Ashton if he trusted you."

Max's expression soured as he watched her leave. He'd been thinking the same thing. King Osbert was an intelligent man. He had to have his doubts about Max. Taking a deep breath, Max wondered if he was making the right choices. Was it going to be worth the cost of the crown in the end? He leaned his forehead against the fireplace mantle, feeling the heat of the flames give him strength. After a few deep breaths, he left the room.

As he walked through the dark, damp hallways he flinched at every sound. Every creak, every groan, every drip of water. He hadn't slept in days and though the king had welcomed him into his group of devoted sorcerers, he'd been unable to shake the idea that the king was on to him.

The tingle of magic rose to his hands just as the scent of death filled his nostrils. He stopped walking and turned slowly to face the Reaper that was following him. Up close, he could see the paper-thin skin pulled over the skeletal face of the creature. Its nose and eyes had rotted away long ago, leaving gaping holes in the head. Nothing about it was natural.

The Reapers were like something out of a nightmare, but Max had grown used to them over the last few weeks. He could even see the appeal in having them around, as long as you were the one who controlled them. Every time he encountered the Reapers, he regretted his fight with Master Edward. The old archery master was said to know the location of the Stone of Morare, but he took that secret to his grave. Max narrowed his eyes at the creature. "What do you want?"

The Reaper didn't respond. It floated in place, the dark fabric of its cloak blowing as if there were a breeze. Max let out a long breath and turned back in the direction of his quarters. As he walked, he was acutely aware of the silent being following him.

After washing and changing quickly, Max left his room to find the Reaper waiting for him. The hair on the back of his neck stood on end. Was it going to start following him everywhere? Max looked past it, trying not to breathe in through his nose as it followed him down the hall, toward the dining room where the king would be waiting for him.

13

Our route took us over rolling hills in unsettled countryside. The wind blew the scent of sage and the crispness of the coming fall. I pulled my hood over my head and focused on keeping up with Celeste.

She was an experienced rider and kept us going at a pace that was safe for the horses and not too taxing on us. We took few breaks, keeping them as short as possible. We were both tired from the long night but wanted to put as much distance between us and the camp as we could. Any time I felt like slowing down, I thought about Ashton. I didn't know how much time we had to save him and I wasn't about to waste a minute.

The temperature dropped as the last rays of sunlight faded away. Stars were beginning to appear in the sky. We had moved quickly and hadn't come across any other travelers. I pulled up on the reins, stopping my horse. Celeste stopped alongside me. "It's probably a good time to stop for the night."

I pointed to a grove of slender trees a short ride from the road. "We can make camp there."

Riding through the grass, we dismounted before we entered the grove. After making sure the horses had food and water and were settled for the night, we found level ground to set up our bedrolls. Upon digging through our bags, we found that Madame Lyndsey had packed provisions so hunting wasn't necessary tonight.

I took a bite of an apple and pulled my cloak tighter around me. Celeste was staring up at the sky. I looked up and caught a glimpse of the moon through the trees. It was surrounded by thousands of glittering stars, a tapestry of light. I tried to think of the last time I was able to look up and admire the beauty of the night sky. A shooting star crossed the sky and I smiled, thinking of the tale my grandmother had told me about them. She said they were a gift from the sky goddess, Taivas. If you could find the place where the fallen star landed, you'd be granted any wish you could dream of. *Maybe I should start chasing the stars.*

"Etta?"

I turned to Celeste, only able to see her outline in the dark. "Yes?"

"You and Ashton," she paused, "you love him, right?"

I finished chewing and swallowed. My chest felt tight thinking about him so far away from me. Was he still doing okay? "Yes, I do."

"How did you know? I mean, I've heard the stories. You were supposed to be married off to some prince. You chose Ashton instead."

There was an edge of hurt in her voice and I thought back to when I first met Celeste at the Trials. I had thought she and Ashton were more than friends at first, but they made it clear there was nothing romantic between them. I wondered if it had always been that way. "Celeste, did you and Ashton?"

"No!" Celeste's voice was high. "No, we've only ever been friends. I only ask because, well..."

"What?"

She sighed. "I don't know if I should say anything."

"Come on, now you have to tell me." I nudged her with my elbow.

"There's this guy at home, in Gallia. We went to the Academy together. We've been out a few times, but I don't know, it's complicated."

A wide smile filled my face. Celeste and I had talked often over the last few weeks, but I'd only gotten bits and pieces of her life in Gallia. She kept a lot of it to herself. "What's his name?"

"Armando," she said.

"How'd you meet?" I asked. Talking about something normal, something that wasn't about ruling a kingdom or staying alive was a welcome distraction. I started to relax.

"We were in school together and we were both accepted into the teaching apprenticeship program. He's a year older so he got to do his trials three years ago, I had to wait. He's already a full teacher now."

Every time she mentioned the Sorcery Academy, I soaked up every word. It must have been so amazing to learn magic from such a young age. To live in a place where sorcery is celebrated. "So he's still there?"

"He'd never leave. He loves that school," she said.

"Celeste, you know I am happy you are here, right?"

"Yes."

"Why are you here when he's so far away?" I knew she believed in our cause and that she was Ashton's oldest friend. However, it didn't explain why she was putting her life in danger so often to help me.

"I believe in you and your cause," she said. "And you've grown to be a dear, dear friend, which is reason enough to help. But my original intentions were a bit selfish. I wanted to do something great. Be a part of something bigger than me. Prove that I'm somebody special."

I knew how she felt. Every day since finding out who my

parents were, I felt like I had to live up to impossible expectations. "You're amazing, Celeste. I wouldn't be here without you. You don't need to prove yourself to anybody."

"Yes, I do. Family is everything in Gallia. If your great-great grandfather did something crazy, you'd still be answering for it long after he was gone. There's a lot in my family that makes people question me."

"Is this somehow related to Armando?" I asked.

She adjusted her position. "He's from a very old, noble family. I am not. While my family has moved up, it has only been in the last generation. His parents would never accept me. If he wanted to be with me, he'd have to give up everything. I can't ask him to do that. So I thought maybe I could prove myself."

I leaned over and pulled her into a hug. "You are incredible. Anybody would be lucky to have you."

"Maybe after you're queen, you can tell that to Armando's parents." She laughed.

"I'd be happy to."

In the distance, an owl hooted and I was reminded of how late it was. "Why don't you get a few hours sleep? I'll take first watch."

MY EYES WERE GROWING heavy as I watched the moon travel across the sky. Thankful for the peaceful watch, I whispered to Celeste. "Wake up, your turn."

She stirred a little and I gently shook her to wake her. She stretched. "My turn?"

"Yes, quiet so far." I covered a yawn. "Wake me if you need me."

The sky was streaked with gold and red when I woke.

Celeste was already preparing the horses for the day's ride. I sat up and rubbed the sleep out of my eyes. "Morning."

"Good morning." She walked over to me and sat down next to me. "You were talking in your sleep."

I blinked a few times. I'd never talked in my sleep before. "Really?"

Her mouth twisted to the side. "Had me a bit worried. Did you have bad dreams?"

"What did I say?"

"It came in spurts. Lots of yelling, telling somebody to stop, asking somebody to stop hurting someone." She stood and offered her hand to me. "I suppose it makes sense, you've been though a lot."

I took her hand and let her help pull me to standing. "I don't remember anything. I don't even remember dreaming."

Celeste leaned down and rolled up my bedroll. She stood, holding it in her arms. "That's good, at least. We're going to need to be extra vigilant today. The chance of seeing others on the road today is very likely."

I took the bedroll from her and walked over to my horse. "We'll be fine. Nobody knows to be looking for us."

"Except the king," she said.

Goosebumps rose on my arm at the memory of hundreds of undead flooding the woods. I looked around, feeling suddenly weary. I've had enough of those monsters to last a lifetime. "Let's get out of here. We've probably already stayed too long in one place."

The road was the fastest route to follow and as long as we kept going and didn't draw attention to ourselves, we should be fine to use it. I tightened my grip on the reins as we picked up the pace. I hadn't prayed in years, but as we rode into the sunrise, I asked the gods to watch over us. All I wanted was to find the stone and return to Ashton. Nothing else mattered.

As Celeste had guessed, we started to see other travelers on the road. None of them seemed to care that we were there. Sometimes people nodded or lifted their hats in greeting. Others ignored all other travelers. Most of the people we passed were pulling wagons with goods. There were few single riders on horseback and even fewer groups like us.

One of the rare single riders was a young man a few years older than us. As he approached, he slowed down and matched pace with us. Surprised to see two women alone, he offered to accompany us to the next town. Rather than draw attention by sending him away, we agreed to his company. Celeste positioned herself between me and the newcomer.

"The name's Wiley, I'm making my way to Yorktown. A friend is holding a job for me there. How about you, ladies?" He smiled at us.

We hadn't discussed what we would say if we were asked questions from strangers. I wasn't sure what to say. Do I make up a name? Do we make up a story? Celeste spoke before I could decide what to say. "I'm Celeste, this is my friend Wilona. We're going to visit our uncle."

Wiley narrowed his eyes and looked at the two of us. We didn't look related. We both had dark curly hair, but that's where the similarities ended. She had beautiful tan skin while I looked more like a ghost. Her dark eyes were large with long, dark lashes. My eyes were bright blue. Not a color I've seen on many people. It was something I had grown to dislike about myself since it made me stand out so much from everyone else.

After a minute of looking at us, Wiley shrugged his shoulders. "You two have the same nose, did you know that?"

I laughed. I hadn't spent a lot of time looking in the mirror, or at Celeste's nose, but I had a feeling mine looked nothing like hers. "We hear that all the time," I lied.

We stopped at noon to rest the horses. We sat under the

shade of the only tree for miles and shared our food supplies with Wiley. He told us stories about growing up in the mountains at the edge of Illaria. He'd been riding for months to reach a city where he could find work. He told us of the hardship he'd known growing up. "My older brother left a few years ago. I stayed to help my mother. When she passed into the Astral Realm, there was nothing keeping me there, so here I am."

"I can't imagine being on your own like that for so long," I said.

"I've made friends along the way," he said. "Like you two."

We finished our food, and listened to Wiley tell us about his travels. Soon, it was time to go again. We rode for another hour before the road split into a fork, one would take us toward Sir Henry's, the other, toward Yorktown. We said our goodbyes and went our separate ways.

"He was nice," Celeste said. "See, there are still good people in the world."

"That's true." I smiled. Maybe I wouldn't have to be as worried about those posters as I thought.

The road was lined with tall yellow grass. We rode alone, quiet in our own thoughts. The silence didn't last for long. From behind, I heard hoof beats approaching. I glanced behind me to see a cloud of dust that signaled multiple riders. My heartbeat quickened. Whoever they were, they were traveling fast. "What do we do?"

Celeste looked tense. "Get in front of me so they can pass. Keep riding like normal. Don't look back, don't draw attention."

I took a deep breath and tried to steady my shaking hands as I pulled my horse ahead of her. Whoever they were, I hoped they would pass us without notice.

My fingernails bit into my palms as I tightened my grip on the reins. It took all of my willpower to keep my eyes forward as the thundering sound of horses drew nearer.

As they approached, we were engulfed in their dust cloud. I coughed and waved my hand in front of my face, trying to clear the air. Without warning, my horse reared up, nearly throwing me. I reached with my hands, desperately grabbing at her mane and squeezing my legs tight around her. I managed to hang on, but she had stopped moving. As the dust settled, I saw the riders. The red phoenix of the king's crest bright against their dark armor. They had us surrounded.

14

I glanced behind me to make sure Celeste was still with me. She stared back at me wide-eyed. I coughed again, and wiped my eyes to clear the dust from them. My heart pounded in my chest as fear gripped me. We hadn't even made it to Sir Henry's yet. How were we going to get to the Oracle if we couldn't even manage to make it a few days on the road?

"What do we have here?" A fat man with a pock-marked face leaned toward me. Then he turned to the other men with him. "Looks like we found her, boys."

I counted twelve riders around us. My breath caught. How would we fight twelve at once? Could we? Focusing on the sound of my own breathing, I worked to clear my mind. There had to be a way out of this. We had to find a way to make it to the Oracle.

I looked toward the open field. Maybe I could get through them and out ride them. I bit down on the inside of my cheek. That wasn't going to happen. Our horses were tired from the journey.

The pock-marked man looked back at me. "For some reason, the king wants you alive, but he didn't say anything about any friends." He lifted his chin toward Celeste. "Kill the other girl."

"No!" I shouted. "Leave her alone and I'll go with you without a fight. Just let her go."

Pock-marked guard narrowed his eyes at me. "She'll come with us. If you start any trouble, I'll kill her."

I swallowed and nodded. For now, keeping him happy was the best thing I could do. "Just don't hurt her."

"If you keep up, you can ride your own horse. You try to flee," he smiled, showing his few remaining rotted teeth, "you ride with me."

I winced and turned away from him.

"Let's go." The men started to ride, keeping me surrounded. I pulled up on the reins and rode along with them. Eventually, they'd have to stop to sleep. When they did, Celeste and I could use our magic and escape. If she could get a hold of me, we could teleport. I knew we'd be traced, but if we can't fight them off, it would be our only chance. And at least it was something.

WE RODE without breaks for hours and I started to wonder if we would ever stop. Long shadows followed us along the dry road as the sun began to dip lower in the sky. Finally, the pock-marked guard, who I now knew was the captain, called for the men to stop riding.

Instead of dismounting to rest, he held up a closed fist. The men started to look around. I did the same. We were still surrounded by tall, yellow grass. No trees, nothing but the breeze.

Then a high-pitched cry broke through the silence. The guards drew their swords and half of them rode toward the direction of the noise. All at once, a large group of people came charging through the grass. My heart stopped as I remembered the undead. It took me a moment to realize that they couldn't be undead because they worked for the king, just like the guards.

In the confusion, I saw an opening and turned my horse, riding away from the attack. Glancing over my shoulder, I saw Celeste following me, along with a few guards.

"Get back here!" They shouted after us. I kept riding, as hard and fast as I could into the tall grass.

Another group of people sprung up in front of me, startling my horse. This time, I wasn't as quick and I was thrown to the ground. I rolled out of the way just in time to avoid her hooves making contact with my head.

Scrambling to my feet, I tried to grab a hold of my startled horse, but she was too fast. I ran after her, trying to catch her. Before I could reach her, somebody knocked me to the ground and pinned me down. My face was on the ground and I lifted my head to spit the dirt from my mouth. I tried to push myself up, but whoever had knocked me down was still on top of me.

"Get off of me!" I shouted. "Let me go!"

The person lowered their head next to mine and I lashed out when I recognized the smiling face. "Wiley! What are you doing? You traitor! You said you were our friend."

He put a finger across his lips. "Shhh. You're making too much noise, princess. I'm trying to help you."

I struggled and twisted on the ground, trying to break free of his weight on me. I managed to turn around so I was now on my back. He was straddling my waist and held my arms down with his. "You need to trust me. I'm not here to hurt you."

I stopped fighting him and glared at him. His long brown hair was pulled into a tail at the back of his head and looked like he hadn't shaved in several days. Despite the fact that he was holding me down, his expression looked concerned. His brown eyes seemed kind.

He leaned back. "I'm going to let you go if you promise not to run."

I didn't trust him. Not after he acted like a friend then returned with a group of bandits. But they had scared away the guards so I was willing to listen to him. "Where's Celeste, then? If you're here to help me, where's my friend?"

He let go of my arms. "We'll find her. I was told to make sure you were safe first. I'm going to get off of you now. Please, don't do anything stupid." He climbed off of me and sat next to me on the ground.

I sat up and pushed myself away from him, not entirely sure I should believe him. "What is going on?"

A horn sounded from the direction of the road. "What was that?"

He stood and extended a hand to me. I ignored it and pushed myself to standing. He dropped his hand and smirked. "You're just as tough as they said you were."

I crossed my arms over my chest. "Are you going to tell me what is going on, or do I have to use magic on you?"

"Come on, there's somebody who wants to meet you." He walked away from me, back toward the road.

I dropped my arms to my side and stomped my foot in frustration before following him. I'd spent enough time being kept in the dark by Max, I didn't want another man doing the same thing. As soon as I caught up to him, I was going to demand answers.

As we neared the road, I saw the signs of a battle that had taken place while I'd been pinned in the dirt. People were dragging the lifeless bodies of the slain guards off the road toward the tall grass. Trails of blood leaving the only record of what had happened.

Out of the corner of my eye, I caught sight of Celeste and I let out a cry of joy. She noticed me and ran over to where I was standing. "Thank the gods!" She wrapped her arms around me and I squeezed her back.

"Are you okay?" I asked, letting go of the hug.

"I'm fine, you?" She brushed her hair away from her face.

"Other than confused about what just happened, I'm fine." There were a few horses left behind, being held by people I didn't recognize. They all wore peasant clothes, none of them wore the king's crest. Other than the horses left behind and the blood stains, all remaining signs of the guards were gone. "Who are these people?"

Celeste shook her head. "I have no idea."

A woman who was several inches shorter than me walked over to us, leading my horse. "I believe this is yours, your highness." She bowed to me and held out the reins.

I took them from her. "Thank you. Are you with the White Ravens?" I knew there had been other camps, maybe there was one I didn't know about that was operating on its own.

She shook her head. "We're not the White Ravens. We're nothing. Just regular people who want to live in peace."

I looked around. These people had taken out twelve of the King's Guards. There was more to them than just people who wanted to live in peace. Rather than argue with her, I smiled. "Thank you for your help."

A boy, probably not much older than ten, walked up to Celeste with her horse in tow. "Here you are, my lady." He held out the reins.

Celeste smiled at him. "Thank you."

The people who had saved us were now gathered around us in a circle. My heartbeat quickened. They had given us our horses but didn't seem to be ready for us to leave them. I licked my lips and tried to figure out what to say or do.

Wiley stepped through the crowd and walked over to us. My unease around him was fading, but I still wanted answers.

Celeste took a few steps toward him. "You!" She didn't sound happy.

He held his arms up in front of him. "I know, I know. I didn't mean to deceive you, I promise that's not what I meant. If you'll come with us, we'll explain everything."

"We don't have time for games, Wiley," I said. "We have something we have to do. Please, let us go."

He gestured toward the setting sun. "You need to rest. At least come to our village, it's nearby. Get some food, get some rest, leave in the morning."

Why did I keep getting caught up by trusting people I shouldn't? Hadn't I learned my lesson by now? I stared at him, eyes narrowed. He was right, we did need to rest, especially after what we had been though. And we were still a full day's ride to Sir Henry's. I had a feeling anywhere we went wasn't going to be safe. But could I trust these people? They had saved us from the King's Guard. Why would they do that if they were just going to turn me in to the king?

Wiley took a few steps toward me and pulled something from his pocket. He extended his hand, showing me a scrap of fabric with the Ouroboros of my family embroidered on it. My fingers traced the familiar symbol. "Where did you get this?"

"From our leader, Sir Giles. Please, I want you to meet him." He put the fabric back in his pocket.

I glanced at Celeste and raised my eyebrows, asking her a silent question. She shrugged, then nodded.

"Alright, take us to meet this Sir Giles."

15

W e walked with the group, following Wiley into the fields we had just left. There was nothing but yellow grass as far as the eye could see. Every step we took away from the road caused more tension to rise inside me. I was starting to wonder if he was taking us to the middle of nowhere so they could attack us. "Where is this village of yours?"

He pointed ahead of us. "See that hill?"

I squinted into the dim twilight. The terrain did look like it was rising, but it was a gentle slope I hadn't noticed at first.

"We're on the other side of that rise. It keeps us out of the view of the road. We're close."

As we reached the hill, my breathing grew heavier. I was tired, my mouth was dry. All I wanted to do was get some answers and get some rest. As we neared the top, I was able to make out buildings and glowing fires below us. There was an entire village behind the little slope.

Wiley led us down the hill, right into a bustling village. Children ran to hug some of the people who were returning with us. Women and men standing outside of their homes stopped what they were doing to watch us as we walked through. The smell of cooking food floated through the air and my mouth began to water. It had been a long time since we last ate. My stomach growled and I pressed my hand to it, hoping nobody had heard it.

We stopped in front of a stable and a young brunette woman came running out toward Wiley. He caught her in his arms and lifted her up as he embraced her. She planted a kiss on his cheek. He set her down, face beaming as he turned to us. "Ashley, I want you to meet the queen of Illaria."

I tilted my head to stare at Wiley for a moment. He'd known who I was the whole time. Meeting up with us, riding with us, all of that had been a rouse. In a weird way, the fact that he had known all along made me feel a little better. When he showed up with the other people who defeated the guards, he knew exactly what he was getting into. I turned my attention to the woman he'd introduced.

Ashley dipped into a curtsy that would have made Lady Genevieve cringe. I smiled at her. "Nice to meet you, Ashley."

Learning that he had a woman waiting for him made me relax a little. The village reminded me of the one I had grown up in. There were families here, loved ones to protect. I didn't think he'd have brought us here to his home if he planned to hurt us.

"Ashley, can you take care of their horses? I'm going to take them to see Sir Giles." Wiley took the reins from my hand then reached for Celeste's. He handed them to Ashley. The woman nodded and smiled at us before leading the horses to the stables.

"This way," Wiley said with a wave of his hand.

"Is that your wife?" Celeste asked.

"Been married almost a year," Wiley said.

We walked past a few small homes. Candles glowed in the windows as twilight set in. They all had their doors open and children ran in and out of them, chasing each other. I'd never seen a place with so many children. The homes looked well lived in, comfortable. "How long has this village been here?"

"Not sure," Wiley said. "The part about traveling here from the mountains, that was all true, though I made that journey almost two years ago. I nearly died of starvation close to the place I met you. Somebody found me and brought me here. They let me stay and I made it my home."

As we walked, I started to realize the village was organized in a circle and we were headed right to the center. People were gathering, some with blankets over their arms, others with crates or stools in their hands.

A group of men carrying logs walked by. They tossed them into a huge pit in the middle of the village center. They were building a massive fire. I stopped walking.

Wiley stopped and turned to look at me.

"What are they doing?" A large fire in the middle of an unfamiliar village was too similar to the gallows I'd seen on my way to Lady Genevieve's home. Was this all some sort of plot to capture us? Were they going to hurt us after all that they'd done to save us?

"Building a fire. You came on campfire night. Once a week, the whole village gathers and we share a meal and tell stories." He smiled. "You chose the right night to come."

I lifted an eyebrow. "I didn't really choose to come."

"That's true," he said. "But Sir Giles will be here soon. I'm sure you'll get all the answers you were looking for."

He turned away and started walking again. I looked at Celeste. "You ever see anything like this before?"

She nodded. "Reminds me of feast days back home in Gallia. We used to build massive bonfires on the beach and eat and listen to the elders tell stories. Some of my best childhood memories were around those fires. We didn't get to do them at the Academy. It's more of a rural peasant thing. The nobles did more formal dinners. Not as fun."

My shoulders relaxed a little. If she'd seen something similar to this in Gallia, it was possible there was somebody from Gallia who had brought the tradition with them to Illaria. I wondered who had started the bonfires here.

People came by with more wood to add to the pit and started setting benches, stools, and stumps around the fire. A few women plopped down baskets of fresh bread and bowls of fruit on a nearby table. The atmosphere was festive and despite the fact that we were strangers, people nodded and smiled at us. I relaxed a bit more as Celeste and I found stumps to sit on. Wiley ran off to help pile more wood into the pit. This fire was going to be massive.

The sun had completely set and I was thankful that I had left my traveling cloak on. I pulled it tighter around me. Most of the activity had settled as people found seats around the fireless pit. I leaned over to Celeste. "When do you think they'll light it?"

"I'm not sure." She seemed to be just as interested as I was in the activities going on around us.

A few hoots and whistles punctuated the air and heads turned in the same direction. I followed the activity and turned to see a young woman standing on top of a stump. She had her hands up in the air, seemingly waiting for the crowd. Once the noises settled, she sent a glowing orb of fire hovering in the air in front of her.

I gasped. It never occurred to me that there were sorcerers living in a little village like this. Nobody else was surprised by her actions. This was part of life for them. Were there other sorcerers here? I stared at her, eyes darting between the ball of fire and her face.

She began to speak. "Tonight we gather, as we do each week, to give thanks to the gods and to each other for our many blessings. On this night, our thanks go to Vesi, God of Water, for what he has given us. The rain, the rivers, the sea. Tonight we honor you, Vesi."

She lifted her hands under the fireball, cradling it for a moment. Then she opened her arms wide and the fire launched through the sky into the pile of wood in the waiting pit. The fire devoured the kindling they'd thrown in and quickly grew in size, casting a warm yellow glow over the people of the village.

Everybody cheered and somebody began to play a fiddle. The somber mood shifted as people began to dance and talk and eat. Celeste and I watched for a few minutes, trying to get a feel for the event. Somebody handed me a carved, wooden goblet. I smelled the liquid, it smelled sweet, but unfamiliar.

I passed the goblet to Celeste. Her whole face lit up when she breathed it in. "It's mead. I haven't had mead since I left Gallia." She took a sip, then wiped her mouth with the back of her hand. "It's good, want some?"

I remembered back to the only time I'd had a drink. Ashton had the crazy idea that it might help me stop overthinking enough to find the element I aligned with. It had worked, but I didn't like the loss of control that came along with it. That night in the woods, with guards coming after me, had been one of the scariest moments of my life. But it was also the night when I first saw how powerful Ashton could be. He'd saved me that night and after that, everything changed. I wouldn't take that night back for anything because without it, we might not have grown to trust each other.

"Etta?" Celeste held up the goblet again.

I waved it away. "No, thank you."

She set the goblet down. "Thinking about Ashton?"

I nodded. He was never far from my thoughts. "You think he's okay?"

Celeste smiled. "I'm sure Master Flanders and Saffron are

taking very good care of him." She leaned toward me, bumping her shoulder against mine. "Besides, you know how stubborn he can be. There's no way he'll give up easily. He'll fight it and he'll wait for you. He'd never leave you if given the choice."

Her words helped. I smiled as I thought about the last night we'd spent together before he left on the scouting mission. We'd sat outside in front of a crackling fire. When he held me in his arms, I knew how much he loved me. *He will fight for me and I'll fight for him.*

Somebody pushed their way through a few people who were dancing in front of us and as the figure drew nearer, I noticed it was Wiley. Behind him was a second man, he walked hunched over and I could see that his head was covered with white hair. I stood to greet them. This must be Sir Giles.

The two men stopped in front of me and Wiley had to practically yell over the noise of the festivities. "Your highness, this is Sir Giles."

I extended a hand to the aging man. "Nice to meet you Sir Giles."

He clasped my hand between both of his. "I never thought I'd see the day." He wore a kind smile and his gray eyes sparked in the firelight.

I returned his smile. As soon as he let go of my hand, I gestured to Celeste. "This is my friend Celeste."

He reached his hand out to her. "Nice to see somebody from home."

Wiley appeared next to me with a chair in his arms. He set it next to the stump I had been sitting on. The old man shuffled over to it.

"You'll have to forgive me for not coming to your aid earlier." He fell into the chair. "I don't move like I used to. Can't ride a horse anymore."

I sat back down on the stump. "Why did you have us brought here?"

"An old friend sent a message that you would be passing by here. We've had some of our members out on the road to look out for trouble."

"What?" That didn't make any sense. Why hadn't anybody told me about this? "I'm sorry, but I don't understand any of this."

"It's a long story. Goes back to the founding of the Ravens," Sir Giles said.

I put my hand up to stop him. I knew I should be respectful, I should be patient with him, but we were on a deadline. Every minute I wasted was a minute longer that Ashton had to fight for his life. I didn't have time for subtleties. I needed answers. "Please, just explain how you knew to look for me and who you are."

Sir Giles smiled. "When I could no longer fight the king myself, I decided I'd do the next best thing. Create a refuge. A place for people who wanted to live in peace. We help who we can but we don't seek fights. We live here away from the eyes of the king. We're self-sustaining. Make all our own food and goods. Rarely travel outside our own village."

It sounded too good to be true. If they were tucked away back here, without any worry of the king or his guards, why take the risk? "So why did you come after me?"

"Because an old friend asked for a favor." Sir Giles leaned back in his chair. "Master Flanders sent a white raven with a message, asked me to keep an eye out for you."

My eyes widened in surprise. Master Flanders had been working on summoning spells with me so he could teach me how to summon a white raven, but I had yet to see one of the magical birds. The fact that he had sent one to this man meant that he must really trust him. A sorcerer who managed to call a white raven would form a bond with that bird. It was the only one you'd ever get. You had to make sure you didn't send it into harm's way.

"You know Master Flanders?" My world kept getting more complicated every time I ventured outside of the Raven camp.

"It is a very long story. And one day, I will tell you everything. But today, the short version will have to do." Sir Giles said.

I leaned back in my own chair. "Fine."

"I joined the White Ravens shortly after they were formed. I left about ten years ago, after you were discovered to be alive. I, and a few others, wanted to put you into power as the true heir. Max and those who supported him didn't want that to happen. After I convinced Saffron of your importance, I knew she'd be able to keep you safe. She was the only one who could reach Max. So I retired from the Ravens,and built a village hidden away with others who wanted to live a simple life."

A little boy ran over to us and jumped on top of Sir Giles. He was giggling and breathless. Sir Giles laughed and exaggerated being knocked backward by the boy. "Oh! You're getting so strong!"

The boy laughed again. "Is it time for stories?"

Sir Giles looked around. "I believe it is." He turned to Wiley. "Can you get the ladies some food? It's time for the main event."

He set the little boy down and then stood. The boy led him away by his hand. I watched them go, feeling a twinge of sadness for the little community we had started to build at the Raven camp. I hoped they were all safe. I hoped they all still wanted me as their leader when I returned.

"Your highness?" I looked up to see Wiley standing in front of Celeste and me with a couple of plates of food. He passed them to us.

"Thank you." I set the plate on my lap. "Does Sir Giles tell stories to the children?"

Wiley smiled and took the seat Sir Giles had previously occupied. "He tells stories to everybody. You'll see."

I took a bite of the food, some sort of fish and vegetable stew. It was different than I was used to eating.

Celeste nudged me with her elbow. "It's close to the *bouill-abaisse* I used to eat at home. There's no ocean here, but they used some kind of freshwater fish." She was beaming. It made me realize how far from home she was and how much she must miss it. As far as I knew, her parents were still alive. She had a home back in Gaillia. I wondered what it would be like to have a home that you could go back to.

I wanted that, a place that felt like home. The short time I'd spent with Ashton had started to give me the same feeling I'd had when I was safe in the little cottage with my grandmother. Her loss hadn't hurt as much after he came into my life. Now, I was faced with losing him, too. I went through the last few days in my mind, trying to keep track of how long I'd been gone from him and how long it would be until I got back. We still had quite the road ahead of us. I set the food down on the ground, unable to make myself eat any more. Just thinking about the journey we still had was making me feel tired.

Out of the corner of my eye, a blue flash caught my attention. My whole body tensed, suddenly alert. I turned away from Celeste to the fire in front of me. It was no longer orange. Instead, the flames glowed bright blue. Just like my arctic fire.

16

My eyes widened as I stared at the flames. They glowed blue and white and let of a familiar heat. *There is a water sorcerer here.* Somebody else was making arctic fire. Where was this coming from? Who was making this happen?

The flames cracked and popped and almost as quickly as they had changed, the color returned to orange. I looked at Celeste. "Did you see that?"

She swallowed the food she had in her mouth. "It looked just like your -"

Before she could finish, the flames parted, forming an empty space in the center of them, a circular frame. I noticed the woman who had started the fire was next to it, her hands out in front of her. She must be controlling the flames.

A stream of water flowed from a group of buckets that I hadn't noticed before, traveling toward the opening. It rose up like a serpent and hissed into steam when it entered the ring of fire. After it evaporated, the fire closed back around it, returning to its normal state.

My mouth dropped open. I'd never seen magic like that. I blinked a few times and closed my mouth. I realized I'd never seen magic used as entertainment. Not real magic, anyway, not sorcerer magic. Applause sounded from around me. This was expected by the crowd. The fire sorceress bowed and smiled before stepping away from the fire and sitting down on a bench next to a man who wrapped his arms around her. The little boy who had come to get Sir Giles hopped up on the seat next to her and she pulled him in for a hug.

These people were so happy. Everything in this village reminded me of how life could be. How life should be. A wave of jealousy rose inside me seeing the happy family huddled together on the bench. Would I ever feel that kind of love? Seeing a parent who was a fire sorcerer made my chest tighten. Could that be Ashton one day? Hugging his own child? Hugging *our* child. My breath caught in my chest. I never had that thought before and it scared me. I could feel the color draining from my face. What was I doing here? What was I doing with Ashton? *You won't be doing anything with him if you don't save him.*

I turned to Celeste. "We can't stay here. We have to get to Campari."

She set her plate down on the ground. "You need to take a few deep breaths. We have to sleep sometime. As soon as the sun is up, we'll leave. We won't stop until we reach Sir Henry's. Okay?"

I nodded then looked down at the plate full of food. I wasn't feeling hungry but I knew I was no use to anybody if I was weak from hunger. I forced a few mouthfuls of food while my stomach churned in protest. All I wanted to do was complete this quest. I wanted to be back at camp with Ashton by my side.

Before I could feel any worse, I heard Sir Giles begin to speak. "Tonight, we welcome an honored guest. A princess of two lands, both Illarian and Gallic."

My face felt hot as people turned to stare at me. I had never thought of myself as Gallic, but I suppose with a mother who had been Gallic royalty before marrying my Illarian father, I was. There had been so much emphasis on my claim to the Illarian throne, I hadn't stopped to think about my heritage.

"It's only fitting that on this night, when we honor Vesi, we take time to thank him for the alignment with water. It is known as the rarest of all sorcerer alignments, and like the sea itself, it is powerful and unpredictable - we have yet to understand its true depths. Tonight's tale is of a water sorceress, a true hero of our times."

The fire sunk low to the ground, no longer a raging mass of heat and flame. It glowed softly, casting a warm yellow light around the circle of people who watched with expectant looks on their faces.

Above the flames, glowing wisps of shadow or steam or something danced in the air. They twisted and writhed until they began to take on familiar shapes. A woman, a boat, a group of people. I watched in amazement.

As Sir Giles spoke, the wisps began to move, illustrating his words. "Once upon a time, there was a princess who left her home for a new land." The glowing woman climbed on to the glowing boat and the hazy form moved across the sky.

"This princess became a queen in her new land, and she was loved by all who met her." The woman was off the boat now, joined hand-in-hand with a male figure. "But the queen had a secret she didn't share with anybody. She was a very powerful sorceress and worked hard to keep that secret hidden. One day, she met the king's friend, the evil duke."

A new figure emerged. His form was tinted red and for the first time, I realized the other forms were tinted blue. A chill ran though me as I realized who the story was about. I bit down on the inside of my cheek. Where was he going with this?

"The duke, who was also a sorcerer, had a special power. He

could sense how powerful any other magic user was and he could sense the secret the queen was hiding."

I swallowed, eyes fixed on the show in front of me. The duke could sense power? What did that mean? Was he like Master Flanders who could sense alignments? My heart beat quickened. The story being played out in front of me was painting my mother as a water sorcerers. Was this possible? Could this be true? The king had told me my mother aligned with air. Was he lying to me or had he not known her true alignment?

"The duke tried to trick the queen into revealing her power, but she was smart. She showed him simple spells and convinced him of her minor power, showing that she was not a threat to him. So he ignored her." The wisp of a red duke vanished in front of my eyes.

"Now, the queen should have been happy. She was much loved by her king, but she was missing one thing. The love of a child. After many years, the gods finally blessed them with a child. The princess born to them was blessed by Vesu himself."

The woman suspended above the fire now held a bundle in her arms. The man stood behind her protectively. I felt a lump rise in my throat and had to turn away for a moment.

"There was a celebration for the birth of the princess," Sir Giles continued. "And people came from near and far to honor the child."

I looked back up to see crowds of floating people surrounding the little family. Out of the crowd, the red duke appeared. I watched as the figure walked up to the family and held the blue-tinted baby girl.

"The duke could sense the power of the gods in the girl-child and in an act of selfishness and greed, he asked for her hand in marriage."

The blue-tinted woman snatched the babe from the red-duke and the duke floated back through the crowd.

"When the duke was denied, he left the kingdom in search of a way to gain power that would make him stronger than the magic he had felt inside the child. He was worried she was the ruler from the Oracle's prophecy, the one who could stop the Darkness."

The red-duke was back, the family gone from view now. His form fluctuated from red to black.

"At this point, the duke had already started channeling Dark Magic and the Darkness had seeped into his very essence. So he left the castle in search of something to give him more power."

The duke's arms stretched into the air, a glowing yellow circle in his hands. Then, behind him four wispy-figures in all black appeared. The sight of the miniature Reapers sent ice through my veins. My fingers dug into the bark of the stump I was sitting on.

A massive group of people carrying swords and wearing helmets appeared above the fire, facing the red and black figures of the duke and his Reapers. "The king and his army rose up to fight against the duke, but he brought unnatural powers with him. With an undead army, he fought the king."

A mass of green and gray figures emerged behind the duke and my stomach knotted. I'd seen those undead up close. How would any army stand a chance against so many of them?

I stared as the yellow figures behind the blue king charged at the green figures behind the red duke. I could hear my heart beating in my ears. Then, the blue woman stepped in-between the two armies. She stretched her arms out, separating them.

My jaw started to tremble as I watched the figure of my mother standing in the middle of two armies. She stretched her arms in front of her and wisps of blue flames rose from her hands toward the oncoming foes. My heart stopped. My mother was using arctic fire.

"The queen did what she could, unleashing for the first time her true power. She saved the lives of many that day, but wasn't able to stop the duke."

The colored wisps wound together into a spiral of colored smoke, spinning around until it disappeared. I stared breathless at the empty darkness where the figures had been. My mother had tried to stop the duke. She'd been a water sorceress. She could channel arctic fire. *She died trying to save us all.*

"It is said," Sir Giles voice was soft, but strong. "That you can still feel her presence when you sail the seas between Gallia and Illaria, the two places she called home."

The people around the fire were silent. Not a word was spoken. I wiped a tear from my cheek and stared into the small fire. A hand found its way around mine. I turned to see Celeste. She had tears on her cheeks, too.

That night, in my dreams the re-enactment of the Battle of the Dead played over and over. I watched my mother die a hundred times that night, unable to wake from the repeating nightmare.

When I finally broke free of my slumber, it was still dark but I wasn't in the mood to wait around. Celeste and I were on the road before the sun rose. Our ride to Sir Henry's was nearly silent, my mind too full to speak.

17

I t was dark as we approached the farmhouse but a faint glow came from the windows. Before I had a chance to dismount, the front door opened and Sir Henry stood in the rectangle of light, a sword extended.

"I'm armed," he said. "I don't take travelers here so you better move along."

"It's me," I said as I dismounted. "Etta."

He lowered the sword and took a few steps toward us. "Etta? Your highness, what's wrong? Are you hurt?"

"I'm fine," I said. "A lot has happened and we could use a place to stay for the night."

Sir Henry began to walk. "Follow me, you can put your horses in the stable. We should get you inside before anybody sees you."

I looked around. The moonlight only gave off a little light but it was enough to see that we were surrounded by empty fields. There weren't any other homes or cities for miles. I lowered my voice as I followed Sir Henry, reins in my hand. "Do you think somebody is watching you?"

"My dear, I always think somebody's watching me. That's how I've managed to stay alive for so long."

Once the horses were cared for, Celeste and I followed Sir Henry into his home. It looked exactly the same as it had, which shouldn't surprise me. I kept forgetting how little time had passed since I left my home. So much had happened over the last few weeks that it felt like much more time had passed.

Sir Henry bolted his door closed behind us then stoked the fire. "Have a seat, I'll bring some food."

He walked away and Celeste and I found seats around the fire. Leaning back in a chair, I realized how tired and sore I was. The last few days had been a challenge.

"He seems sweet," Celeste said. "How do you know him?"

I straightened in the chair. "He helped me after the King's Guards tried to kill me. He used to work for my father."

Celeste nodded. I hadn't ever told her the story of how I joined the Ravens, but I guessed she had heard it over the last few weeks from somebody. Probably Ashton.

"Why does he live all the way out here?" Celeste asked.

Sir Henry entered the room with a tray of tea and bread. "Etta knows why."

When I didn't answer quickly enough, he continued. "I've told those Ravens that I won't join them until the true heir claims the throne." He set down the tray on a little table and took a seat. His eyebrows furrowed in concern. "Is Saffron safe?"

"Yes, she is," I answered quickly.

His posture relaxed and he began to pour the tea. "Is your escort here to keep me from talking?" He nodded toward Celeste.

I put my hands out in front to me. "No. Didn't you get Master Flanders' message?"

Sir Henry set down the teapot. "I saw a message that said you were coming here. That was it. It wasn't even signed." He frowned. "I should have known it was from him."

It was hard to tell if he was upset about the lack of information or upset by the source of the information. For now, that wasn't important. I took a deep breath, not sure where to start. "Have you heard any news since I left here?"

Sir Henry shook his head. "Nothing."

"A lot has happened, but the biggest thing was that I met with the king. He explained that Max is my half brother. When I confronted Max, he got upset and he left. I've taken over the Ravens."

A smile spread across Sir Henry's face. "That's what I've been waiting for. As soon as I found out you were alive, I began petitioning the Ravens to tell you the truth. If you even have half the strength of your mother and half the brains of your father, you'll make the best ruler Illaria has ever had."

"That's not all," I said. Closing my eyes, I called to the power within me. I felt the ice flowing through my veins. Opening my palm, I showed the blue flames dancing across my hand.

Sir Henry laughed, shaking his head. "You are your mother's daughter."

I closed my palms, extinguish the flames. "You knew?"

"I suspected. Your mother was good at hiding things, but she spent a lot of time with that guard of hers, the water sorcerer. And I've heard some stories about the Battle of the Dead." He nodded toward my hands. "Now I know they were true."

My throat felt dry, and I forced myself to swallow. How I wished I could talk to my mother. Ask her questions. I didn't even know what she was like. I wondered if she would have taught me magic herself, or if she would have kept it hidden. Would she approve of me using it so openly?

Sir Henry spoke, forcing me back to the present. "Are you training?"

"With Master Flanders," I said.

Sir Henry's eyes narrowed. "I don't trust him. Did you know

he taught the king? He was your grandfather's royal sorcerer. Retired before your father took the throne then took that job teaching the duke. It never really lined up for me."

Celeste gasped and covered her mouth with her hand. When she saw I didn't react, she glared at me. "You knew this and didn't tell me?"

"He's a good teacher," I said. He'd spent time every day since we settled in the new camp helping me learn how to perfect my magic. I have no reason to doubt him. "He hasn't caused me any harm. He's been looking out for me since he first met me."

Sir Henry sighed. "There's something not quite right about him, Etta. He seems to know things. Things he shouldn't."

I turned to Celeste. "You've been there for most of the lessons, and he's been working with you on your orb. Has he ever given you a reason to doubt him?"

Celeste pursed her lips in thought for a moment, then shook her head.

"Either way," Sir Henry said. "Please be careful. There is much you don't know about his past."

Before I could inquire about Sir Henry's comment, Celeste let out a gasp and jumped to her feet. "I've got it!"

"What?" I asked.

"It's been bothering me since the battle in Luxor," she said.

Sir Henry lifted his eyebrows. "Battle?"

I explained about the battle, giving him all the details. How I'd gone in as bait, how Celeste and I were left out and tele-ported back in. When I explained about the other sorcerers losing their magic and talking to the king on the field alone, Sir Henry nearly spit out his tea.

He leaned in, eyes narrowed. "How did you keep your powers?"

"I don't know," I said. "Master Flanders didn't even know."

Celeste was bouncing in her seat. "I think I know why. The

Black Onyx. I think it's because of your powers. You are unique. There are no other sorcerers with two water aligned parents. Your ancestry might have made you immune to the stone. That's probably why the king is searching for the other stones. He is trying to find a weakness. He can't touch you. You have bested his Reapers, survived his guards. He couldn't remove your powers. I'm guessing he thinks one of the other stones will work against you."

Sir Henry whispered. "The prophecy."

A chill ran through me. "What did you say?"

He cleared his throat. "There is an old prophecy delivered by an Oracle many generations ago."

"The one about the ruler who can end the Darkness?" Celeste asked.

"That's the one." He chuckled, and shook his head. "I never really believed it, but maybe it is true. Your magic, what you can do, it's a rare gift."

I took a deep breath. I hadn't thought about that prophecy since Master Flanders first mentioned it after the attack at the Trials. Then it had been brought up twice in the last two days. Last night around the fire, and tonight from Sir Henry. We'd had so many other things going on that I didn't want to think about the impending Darkness. Something was telling me I wasn't going to be able to ignore it for much longer. Somehow, all of this was connected.

"If I'm such a threat, why is the king letting me live?" I asked.

Sir Henry set down the cup in his hand. "Because he's arrogant and thinks he will always get what he wants. Maybe he thinks he can win you over with the other stones."

"Can he?" I didn't like the idea that the king was searching for a way to gain more power. Would the other stones work on me? With the king, death was the easy way out. I didn't want to know what he could have in mind for me with all of the power stones.

I shifted in my chair. I needed to keep my mind focused on the reason we were here. I'd have to worry about the other stones later. Right now, only one mattered.

"You're looking for the stones," Sir Henry said.

"We need to find the astral projection stone," I said.

Sir Henry steepled his fingers under his chin. "That's an unusual stone to be going after considering the power of the other ones. I assume there's a very specific reason."

Celeste and I grew quiet and it took me a moment to form the words. Explaining it was harder than I thought it would be. Even though I knew what we had to do and I knew how dire the circumstances were, saying it out loud seemed to make it more real. I realized that I was playing with my pendant and let go of it, dropping my hands to my lap. "We had an encounter with the king a few days ago. He injured a friend of ours. The stone is the only way to save him."

Sir Henry shook his head. "I'm so sorry, your highness. Whoever this friend is, they must be important if you're willing to risk a journey to find the stone."

My stomach clenched and I nodded. He was important. Of all the people I had met since that day my life changed in my grandmother's cottage, he was the most important.

"The king must know how important this person is, otherwise he would have killed them instead of sending out their essence," Sir Henry said.

I stood and started pacing the room. *It was all my fault. Everything was my fault.* My birth had caused all of this pain. I stopped moving, looking back to Sir Henry. "He asked me to marry him, when I met with him."

"He knows what you're capable of. He's afraid of you," Sir Henry said.

"We have to find that stone," I said. "We have to save Ashton. Then we have to find a way to stop the king."

"You're going to see the Oracle, aren't you?" Sir Henry asked.

"How did you know?" I said.

Sir Henry sighed. "More secrets." He shook his head. "They shouldn't be keeping so many secrets from you."

"What now?" I asked.

"The Oracle is Master Flanders' daughter. She has the gift of sight and took the post as a young girl. Master Flanders sent her there, himself. You heard the stories about princesses locked in towers? The Oracles probably inspired the stories. As far as I know, she's the only one left. In the old days, if a female child showed an affinity for seeing the future, they were taken to the Sacred City. It was supposed to be an honor to serve the gods. When the city fell, it became like a prison. I've never understood why he took his only child there and left her at the mercy of The Black Tower."

I slumped down in my chair, struggling to wrap my head around everything I had just learned. Maybe Master Flanders wasn't who I thought he was after all.

18

W e were up early the next morning to continue on our route. Campari was only two days away. The Sacred Island and the Oracle were in our reach. Flutters rose in my stomach. I was nervous about going to the Black Tower but feeling optimistic for the first time in days. I kept telling myself that we could do this. That we could find the stone in time and save Ashton. The closer we got, the more I started to believe myself.

Sir Henry was standing by the door as we prepared to say our goodbyes. "You be careful." He rested a hand on my shoulder. "Write me when you're safe."

"I will." I hugged him, feeling sad I had to leave again so quickly. He would be a great deal of help to me as I worked on a way to take down the king. I pulled away and looked at him. Why not have him help? "Will you join us when I'm back at the Raven camp?"

He smiled. "I thought you'd never ask."

"I'll send you a message when we return." Things were starting to look up.

Sir Henry waved to us as we rode from his farm. It was a

different feeling from the way I had left a few weeks ago. On that departure, I hadn't believed I was a princess and I had never wanted to rule. Now, I left as a self-proclaimed queen. I still wasn't sure that I was the right person for the job, but I was going to do whatever I could to make sure the people of Illaria were cared for.

The road to Campari was far more crowded than anything we had seen on the journey so far. Though, nobody seemed to have any interest in other travelers riding down the road. I kept my hood pulled up around my face and my eyes down as we passed other travelers. The last thing I needed was somebody recognizing me from the posters.

The poster depicted me with long, curly hair. Since seeing the poster, I had kept my hair in a tight braid around the crown of my head. It kept the curls at bay and made the length harder to guess. While at Sir Henry's Celeste and I had replaced our tattered, dirty dresses for tunics and trousers. The new clothes were a welcome change. They were more comfortable and hopefully made it harder for people to recognize us as women as they rode by.

Tomorrow we'd be riding through the largest sea port in Illaria. It would be our first real test of how the citizens of Illaria reacted to seeing me. Would they recognize me from the posters? Would they care? For the first time in my life, I was thankful for the layer of dirt and grime that travel had provided. It was like wearing a mask. When I rode in to Campari tomorrow, I was hoping I would be just as forgettable as every other traveler who passed through.

I WOKE SCREAMING, sweat beading on my forehead.

Celeste ran to me. "What's wrong?"

Looking around, I realized I was in my bedroll at the camp we had set up a few miles from Campari. The events of the last few days came flooding back. I let out a breath. "Bad dream. Ashton." A shiver ran through me. I'd dreamed that Ashton fell from a cliff and I couldn't catch him. It was too close to my current reality. I stood and grabbed my bedroll. "We should go. We've wasted too much time already."

Celeste didn't press the issue. She'd had second watch, so her bedroll was already packed up. She handed me a piece of bread and I waved it away. My stomach was in knots. Food was the last thing on my mind. "I'll eat later. Right now, I want to ride as fast as we can."

The roads were already full of people and activity. We blended right in with all the other travelers who were covered in dirt from the road. Carts full of goods to trade or ship rumbled past us. People carrying heavy bundles walked by. It was even more crowded than I remembered it from the one visit I'd made as a child.

Our campsite was closer to Campari than I'd realized. After only an hour's ride, we could see the walls that surrounded the city. The main gates were open, letting people travel freely inside and outside without restriction. I wasn't sure if they ever closed the gates, or who had control of them.

My chest tightened as we passed through. I couldn't help but feel a bit nervous about being inside a walled city. What if the king found out I was here and had the gates closed? The only way out would be on a boat and the last time I was here, the docks were heavily monitored.

My hands squeezed the reins tighter and I tried to keep my eyes from darting around too much. I wanted to blend in, to look like I belonged here. *Don't draw any attention to yourself.*

Once inside the gates, the whole world changed. Gone were the trees and grass. Our horses walked along a cobblestone road lined with shops. People swarmed around. The air was filled with the scent of food from a hundred different cultures. The city seemed to have a pulse of its own, living and breathing in time to the chaos filling its streets.

People darted out in front of us, around us, behind us. They were everywhere. I didn't remember it being this crowded last time I was here. Things had changed a lot in ten years.

We had to move into single file, Celeste dropped behind me. We rode carefully, often stopping to allow another rider or a cart to pass.

There wasn't much of a plan for our visit to Campari. Wanting to draw as little attention as possible, we figured we'd go right to the docks. The money we brought with us should be enough to secure passage.

As we rode through town, the energy shifted. Suddenly people went running past us, all in the same direction. My heartbeat quickened. Something was going on. I looked back at Celeste. She was still behind me.

We were swept up in the current of people moving toward the center of town. I fought to keep control of my horse in the chaos.

We ended up in a crowded city square. My blood went cold when I saw the cause of the activity. In the center of the square was a massive gallows. I hated that it wasn't the first time I'd seen something like this. Was this a staple of all the cities in Illaria?

Silence fell over the crowd as a group of people were marched onto the platform. They were led by two King's Guards and followed by two more. I glared at them wondering how anybody would be willing to kill innocent people so easily. My hate for the King's Guard grew more intense every time I saw them. They had to know what they were doing was wrong. They weren't undead soldiers who mindlessly followed orders. Nobody forced them to join the king. My face grew hot as I considered that maybe these men enjoyed killing and torturing.

The silence of the crowd told me that this was not a hanging they approved of. If they were executing a thief or a murderer, there would be cheers in the crowd. Instead, it was so silent that I could hear my own heart beating.

The people were spread out so there was one positioned behind each of the hanging nooses. Twelve. They were hanging twelve people. My eyes scanned the faces, looking for any connection between them. As I looked from face to face, my whole body tensed, gaze frozen on a tiny figure in the middle of the group. The girl couldn't be older than eight. Her frayed dress covered a too-thin frame and she clutched a dirty doll in her arms. Her large eyes were full of tears but she didn't cry out loud.

Heat rose inside me. Before I could stop to think about my actions, I dismounted and started walking toward the gallows.

"Etta, stop!" Celeste called after me.

I ignored her and kept walking. After pushing my way through the crowd, people began to notice me and moved aside, making a clear path. Hundreds of eyes were on me, waiting to see what I would do. Whispers followed in my wake. I heard muffled whispers as I walked through. Once or twice, the word *princess* found its way to my ears. They knew who I was, but I didn't care. Right now, I wanted to stop another senseless killing. The King's Guards were not going to kill more innocents in front of me. He'd done enough damage already. If I could prevent anybody from experiencing the losses I had, I would.

I paused in front of the gallows, eyes locked on the crying girl. A guard pulled a black hood over her head and slid a noose around her neck. My hands were clenched into fists and my breathing was shallow.

A hand touched my shoulder and I turned around to see Celeste standing behind me. "I've got your back."

Jaw set, I walked to the end of the platform and climbed the stairs. The guards didn't notice me until I was standing on the platform. A murmur rose through the crowds. I could almost feel them sending their energy to me. I felt strong.

One of the guards walked up to me. "Come to join them?"

Another guard approached. "I think this is the criminal, the one on the posters."

A third guard joined. "You're right." He pulled his sword from its sheath and smiled at me. "A hanging and reward money?" He glanced at his companions and laughed. "Who knew this would be such a great day?"

He had no idea what I was capable of. "Release all of these people and go back to where you came from."

The guard laughed and two more removed their swords. I lifted my hands, blue flames sparking in my palms. "Are you sure you want to try that?"

One of the guard's eyes widened. "It's true."

Celeste stepped next to me. She called a gust of wind that blew past us, sending our hair and cloaks swirling around us. It made her look wild. "You sure you want to do this?"

The guards hesitated for a moment, then one of them charged us, sword extended in front of him. I pushed the arctic fire from my palms. It mixed with Celeste's wind and a wall of blue swallowed up the guards.

Dropping my hands to my side, I worked to catch my breath. Celeste wasn't even winded. I definitely needed more training.

Their screams should have made me feel guilty, instead, I watched them burn and crumble to the ground. I felt detached. I didn't want to think about what I had done. I didn't want to be like them. All I wanted was to save these people. Why hadn't they just walked away like I asked? I needed to keep my mind clear before guilt clouded my judgment. I looked up from their burning bodies toward the last guard.

He yelped and dropped his sword when I locked my eyes on him. Before I could issue a command, he lifted his arms in surrender.

"Release them," I said.

He nodded. As he began to remove the hoods and nooses, the crowd erupted in cheers.

Celeste and I began to remove the hoods and ropes from the people nearest to us. A sobbing woman climbed the stairs and passed me. She pulled the hood and rope from the little girl's neck and wrapped her arms around her.

The woman carried the girl, stopping when she reached me. "Thank you."

I placed my hand on the little girl's matted hair. "It's going to be okay. I'm going to make the king pay."

The woman inclined her head to me. "You are truly a gift from the gods, your highness."

The whole crowd seemed to know who I was. I'd shown myself in front of thousands of people. Glancing behind me, I noticed the whole crowd was still standing there. They were watching me. Waiting for me to do something. Was there somebody out there right now waiting to collect on the reward? I'd put myself in terrible danger, but I didn't feel afraid.

Turning back to the task at hand, I pulled off the hood from the last remaining captive. Clear, wild, blue eyes looked back at me. Dark hair stood on end, matted and dirty. His face was covered in blood but he didn't seem to have any wounds on his face. His clothing was torn and bloody. I hesitated for a moment before I removed the noose. This man didn't look like the others. He wore the hardened look of a warrior.

There wasn't any turning back now. I'd committed to releasing these people. *Any enemy of the king must be worth saving, right?* I tried not to show my unease as I untied the rope from his hands.

The man stared at me, unblinking, as I worked to loosen the knot. As soon as his hands were free, he picked up an abandoned sword then charged the remaining guard, knocking him to the ground.

I had just killed three of the King's Guards, but this one hadn't attacked us. He'd surrendered. My anger had subsided, no longer driving my decisions. While I watched this, my conscience was torn between my overall hate of the King's Guard and my sense of what was right. Before I could object, the dark haired man shoved the sword through the man's throat.

Cheers erupted from the crowd again. Campari held no love for the king.

The man I had rescued from the noose pulled the sword from the dead guard's neck. Then he tucked the bloody sword into his belt and stared at me with blank eyes. He looked devoid of emotion. Like killing somebody had no effect on him.

I thought back to the first time I killed a man. I was sure I didn't look that calm. Yet, here I stood, after contributing to multiple deaths, wearing my own look of serenity amidst the chaos. He reminded me of myself. I could tell from his eyes, this guard was not his first kill. The thought hit me like a blow to the gut. *Is that how I looked?* How had I let things go this far? A wave of nausea rolled through me as the scent of burning flesh filled my nostrils. It was a smell that was becoming all too familiar in my world.

I glanced at the charred remains of the three guards I'd helped kill. Was I any better than them? I'd killed without hesitation. Every day, I found myself making more and more decisions that I would have to live with. I kept thinking that I didn't want people to die for me. These guards had died because of me. What was the difference? I wanted to be a good queen, a just ruler. I'd given those guards a chance to run, they chose to stay and fight. If I hadn't fought them, all of those innocents would have been hanged. How was I supposed to stop the killing when the King's Guard won't back down?

Celeste nudged me and lifted her chin toward the crowd behind me. I turned away from the bloody man standing over his kill. The people in the crowd had quieted. They stared up at me with expectant looks. They were waiting for me to say something.

The silence was deafening and goosebumps rose on my arms. Thousands of people had gathered. All of them were quiet. I'd never seen a crowd this large before and couldn't figure out how they all unified enough to wait for me to speak.

Say something, Etta. Swallowing back my fear, I stepped toward to the front of the platform. I lifted my chin and pushed my shoulders back. I needed to feel in control somehow.

"The king is hunting me. You've seen my face on the posters." I waited a moment, expecting the crowd to react. Instead, they stayed silent. "The king is afraid of me. And he should be." I waited a moment. When nobody spoke, I continued. "Because I am the true heir to the throne. Rightful queen of Illaria. And I will reclaim my throne. We will have peace again in Illaria. You have my word."

I stared out at the crowd, feeling defiant, powerful, strong. "He can come for me, but I will fight."

The crowd erupted in applause and cheers. I took a deep breath, trying to make the knots in my stomach subside. It was not easy to speak in front of people but I knew it was part of the job. And I'd accepted the position the night I sent Max away.

Movement in the back of the crowd drew my eye and I strained to see over the heads of the gathered people. A large group of King's Guards were pushing their way through.

"Etta!" Celeste was behind me, a sword in her hand. I took it from her and stood my ground, waiting for the guards to come to us.

They never drew nearer, though. The crowd was pressing in on them, pushing them away from the platform. A murmur rose and grew to a chant. "Down with the king, down with the king."

I lowered my sword and watched in awe as the people of Campari fought back against the guards. They outnumbered them and the guards were fleeing the square. Another cheer rose through the crowd and I joined in, fist in the air, crying out in unison with the crowd.

I couldn't believe my eyes. The people were turning. Down with the king.

19

Celeste and I left the platform and were swallowed up by the crowd. People reached out to touch me as I walked through, but stepped away, allowing me to pass. There were tears and cries of joy. *This is who I fight for.* My heart swelled at the sight of these people pouring their support into me. My face hurt from smiling.

Celeste led us toward our horses. She'd found somebody to watch them. When we tried to pay the man who kept them for us, he declined. My fear of being hunted for 5,000 *soldi* was lessening with every interaction I had. The people were ready for change. They seemed to know that 5,000 *soldi* wasn't worth a lifetime of rule under King Osbert.

As we readied our horses, I noticed the man who had killed the guard followed us. He approached, eyes lowered. He looked even more disheveled if that was possible. Celeste stepped between me and the man and I put my arm out, gesturing for her to step aside.

"How can we help you?" I asked.

The man looked up through the tangled mess of dark hair. "I'm here to offer my service to you, my queen."

"That's very kind of you, but I'm sure your family would like to see you."

He moved the hair from his eyes and stared at me. His gaze was clear and strong. "I have no family. The king saw to that. Those men," he gestured toward the gallows, "I've been hunting them since they killed my wife and unborn child in Greenville. They took everything from me. They would have taken my life if not for you. If you'd let me, I'd like to return the favor."

I glanced at the gallows, thinking about the killing blow this man had delivered to an unarmed guard. I wanted to say that I'd be forgiving and not take that shot, but if the king himself came to me in surrender, would I be able to restrain myself? He'd killed my parents and my grandmother. He'd tried to kill Ashton. He took everything from me. There were few people who really understood what it was like to lose it all. This man seemed to know it all too well. "The guard you killed, was he the one who killed your wife?"

He nodded. "Yes. Now he can answer for his crimes in the Astral Realm."

The punishment for murder in Illaria was death. Though the king's guards were never subject to punishment for any of their crimes. I had a hard time finding any sympathy for the dead guard. "What's your name, sir?"

He smiled. "I'm no, sir, your highness. They call me Calder."

I glanced at Celeste. She shrugged. I looked back at the defeated man. Having another hand might not be the worst idea. The warnings about trusting people rang out in my mind. I knew I should heed them, but how could I deny this man? I stared at him. He was just like me. He'd faced the same pain. If his thirst for revenge was as strong as mine had become, he'd be a powerful ally. If he betrayed me, I'd kill him.

I narrowed my eyes at him. "We're going to the Black Tower. Think you can handle that?"

"Anything it takes to get rid of the king," Calder said.

———

WE MADE our way toward the docks between the crowds that would often part just for us. The mood of the city had shifted. Smiling faces greeted us in every direction. People inclined their heads when we passed. It was as if a veil of uncertainty had been lifted. I could feel the hope spreading through the city.

I still had the sense that I hadn't yet earned the title I'd claimed. Despite knowing that I had been born royal, I didn't feel any different than the people I was surrounded by on the streets.

Lady Genevieve had said that I'd need to convince the people of my noble birth, I'd need to act like a princess. Glancing down at my dirty trousers and muddy boots, I wondered how they believed me. Smiling, I realizing it was more than appearances. These people were searching for hope, somebody who could help them find peace. They didn't care what that person looked liked as long as they delivered. *I will be that person. I won't let them down.*

Calder proved himself useful right away. Prior to leaving everything to follow his wife's killer, he'd been working at an import business in Greenville. He knew several of the captains who had vessels docked at Campari. While they all had their own routes to consider and couldn't take us to the Black Tower, they gave us names of several men who owned smaller vessels.

After three inquires, we finally found a captain willing to take us to the island. It was a short boat ride, only a few hours from shore, but the superstition surrounding the island made it a difficult sell.

We sold our horses, packed our few belongings on our

backs, and set sail within hours of securing a ship. We'd be on the island before nightfall.

I sat near the prow of the ship. It was my first time crossing the sea and the rocking motion kept me in a constant state of nausea.

"Trust me, eating something will help," Calder said.

I shook my head. Food was the last thing on my mind.

"He's right." Celeste took a bite of the dried fruit from the bag she held out to me. "Always helps me."

I turned away from the food as a new wave of nausea rolled through my stomach.

"Maybe you should try something," Celeste said again.

I glared at her.

"Or not." She laughed. "You do look sort of green."

Calder reached for the bag of fruit and threw some in his mouth. "I've never liked sailing. I'm more of a dry-land person." He tucked his feet under him, settling into a more comfortable looking position. "What are we after at the Black Tower, anyway?"

I glanced around. There were a few crew members nearby, but they seemed to be ignoring us. Still, I wasn't comfortable explaining about Ashton. While none of the men seemed to be interested in killing me for the reward at the moment, I couldn't guarantee that they wouldn't be telling the king where we went. "We're visiting a friend."

Calder nodded. He seemed to know that I wasn't sharing the truth but he accepted it without question. "Well, I'm here for whatever you need. Just let me know when we get there."

"Thank you, Calder."

Celeste and Calder shared stories about their times spent at sea over the years and I tried to listen. But as we drew nearer to the Sacred Island, my fears started to get the better of me. I wanted nothing more than to retrieve the stone and save Ashton.

I'd managed to stay optimistic until now. With the impending visit to the Oracle, my mind started to allow questions I didn't want to ask. I wasn't sure how much of the nausea was from the boat or from the fact that I was terrified that the Oracle wouldn't be able to help us.

"Etta?" Celeste was staring at me, forehead wrinkled in concern.

Startled, I shook myself back to the present. I wondered how many times she'd said my name while I was lost in thought. I adjusted my position and smiled, trying to calm my mind. The last thing I wanted to do was add to her worries. "Think I might be getting used to the rocking."

Celeste passed the bag of fruit over to me. "Eat."

I sighed. "What am I going to do with you?"

Celeste laughed. "You're stuck with me, for better or worse."

I took the bag of fruit from her and tried to let myself forget about the stakes. *I'm going to save Ashton.* The Oracle had to be willing to help us. She was Master Flanders' daughter. I took a deep breath and tried to think of something happier.

I didn't want to think about the king or his Reapers. I didn't want to think about magic rocks that had the power to control people or other damage they could cause. I wanted to enjoy the few hours of peace as we sailed over calm seas toward the Sacred City. Ignoring the nausea, I took a few bites of dried fruit.

Staring out into the white-capped waves, I tried to imagine what it might be like when we weren't fighting for our lives. Perhaps, when this was all over, we'd be able to take a ship somewhere fun, where we could just be ourselves. I let myself imagine that Ashton was sitting next to us, laughing and joking. I pictured his arm around me, keeping me warm against the wind from the sea. *Ashton, I miss you.* After this, I didn't want to let him out of my sight again.

"You alright?" Celeste asked.

I turned to her and forced a smile. "I'm fine. Just missing somebody."

She took my hand in hers and gave it a squeeze. "I know, but we'll see him soon."

Calder watched us silently. He pulled his knees to his chest and looked out at the sea. He was probably missing his family. I reminded myself that we were trying to save Ashton. He wasn't gone. I'd see him again and I would appreciate every second we spent together. The longer I stayed in this fight for my throne, the more people I lost. The king had no problem hurting those I cared about. I needed to protect them.

Instead of looking at this boat ride as another obstacle, I tried to see it as a small window of time where I knew we could be safe from the king.

Conversation was minimal as we traveled through the water. It didn't seem like much time had passed before we saw the outline of the island ahead of us.

A member of the crew walked over to us. "You sure you want to get off there?"

I looked up at him. He was a younger man with a beard and dark circles under his eyes. I wondered how long he'd been on this small boat. "We're sure."

"You've heard the stories, right?" He knelt down and whispered to me. "You aren't being taken there against your will?"

I couldn't help but smile at him. The concern was appreciated. "I'm fine, really. We're visiting an old family friend who lives on the island."

His eyes widened. "I heard the only one who lived there was the Oracle, and she's supposed to be a monster. Bred from the Astral Realm and abandoned here. Who would live there, so close to *her*?"

I ignored the fear that was bubbling up to the surface. Despite the fact that I'd grown up hearing the stories of the

Oracle, Master Flanders had assured us that we would be safe. Though, he had neglected to tell us that she was his daughter. *He must have a reason for that.* I trusted him. So I would trust the Oracle. "We'll be fine, thank you."

Heavy footsteps drew the attention of the man away from me. He jumped when he realized it was the boat's captain who had joined us. "Westley, you filling her head with your ancient superstitions?" He clapped the younger man on the back. "I think you just volunteered to row them to shore."

All of the color drained from the Westley's face. "But, but, I-I.."

"The words you are looking for are *aye, captain*." The captain lifted his chin toward the other end of the boat. "We'll be there soon. Get the row boat ready."

Westley scurried away.

The captain lifted his hat to me. "Sorry about that, my lady. Some of these country boys come to me with some strange superstitions, but I don't believe in monsters. It's just I don't much care for that island, too many rocks to get near it. Too many ships have gone down trying to reach her. Besides, what you do there is your business."

He turned to walk away, then stopped. "Do you have a way off the island? Boats won't come by there."

"We have arranged for transportation, thank you." Master Flanders had told us it would be safe to teleport from the tower to the Raven camp. With the remote location of the tower, it was unlikely there'd be a sorcerer coming along to trace our exit point. And unless anybody else had a teleportation coin attuned to the camp itself, they couldn't follow us.

My shoulders relaxed as I realized how close we were to getting back to Ashton. We just needed to get the stone from the Oracle, then we could teleport back. We could be home before nightfall if everything went according to plan. The dread I had been feeling was replaced by elation. I closed my eyes and let the warm feeling wash through me. *I'll be there soon, Ashton.*

————

WESTLEY DRUMMED his fingers on the oars while he waited for us to exit the row boat. His eyes darted from side to side, scanning the empty shore. I thanked him several times, but his responses kept coming out in stammers. He rowed away within seconds of my feet landing on the sand.

Waves washed against my ankles, soaking my boots and the bottom of my trousers. The water was warmer than the rivers and ponds I'd been in. I dipped my hand in and rubbed my thumb against my fingers, feeling the grittiness of the salt that filled the water. I wiped my fingers on my tunic and stepped onto the shore.

Ahead of me, the white sand of the beach came to an abrupt halt as it was swallowed by a mass of towering, strange looking trees. Everything was so green. The leaves on the trees were massive. Even the air here felt different. Thicker somehow. It was as if the salt from the water was suspended around us. I could almost taste it.

There were no signs of life. No buildings, no other people, no animals.

"I'm not sure what I expected, but it wasn't this," I said.

"Are we in the right place?" Celeste asked.

"Yes," Calder said. "I saw their navigation charts. We're at the island of the Sacred City." He turned to me. "Now, what are we really doing here?"

"The king tried to kill a friend of ours. We're hoping the Oracle knows how we can save him," I said.

Calder shifted the bag he was carrying. "All right."

Lifting an eyebrow, I looked at him. He hardly knew us and

he was willing to charge in through the jungle to find the Oracle. Calder was either the best ally we could have hoped for or he had lost his mind. "That's it? *All right*?"

He shrugged. "I don't really care what we do, as long as it gets rid of the king. Not even sure why I asked. I'm in, even if it's something totally crazy."

"Well that's good," Celeste walked forward, toward the jungle. "I'm pretty sure what we are about to do is totally crazy."

20

My skin was torn through my tunic from the branches and vines surrounding us. No matter how many we cut away, more sprung to life. "There has to be an easier way to find this tower."

I wiped some blood from my arm and let out a breath. "This place, it's," I searched for the words, "not right."

Calder swung at a few low hanging vines and stopped moving right next to me. "It's the sound."

We all stood silently, listening to the jungle. "There aren't any sounds." As soon as I said the words, a chill ran down my spine. The only noise was coming from us. And we were not being very quiet hacking away at vines and tripping over roots.

"That's what I mean, your highness. I've never been anywhere so quiet."

Celeste walked ahead of me. "Let's just try to find the tower before it gets dark. It's bad enough on this island. I don't want to have to camp here. We need to get to the tower, talk to the Oracle, and get out of here."

I tucked loose strands of hair back into my braid as best I

could to keep the curls off of my sweaty face. "She's right. I want to get out of here, too."

We walked for a few more minutes and I noticed that everybody was trying to be quieter with their movements. The air was wet and sticky, nothing like the air we were used to breathing. It carried a sweet scent that I couldn't place and seemed to cling to my skin.

After a long bout of silence, Calder's voice cut through the eerie silence. "Um, how exactly are we going to get out of here? We sent our boat away."

Celeste laughed. "You didn't pay much attention to what happened in Campari, did you?"

He shrugged. "I really only wanted to kill that guard. I wasn't thinking about anything else."

"You're on an island with a couple of sorcerers. We don't have to take a boat to get out of here," Celeste said.

His eyes widened. "Both of you?"

"Yes," I said.

"I had heard the stories about you." He inclined his head toward me. A smile crossed his face. "Imagine that, on an adventure with two sorcerers." He shook his head and started walking again.

We returned to as quick a pace as we could manage through the jungle. Often pausing to remove vines that managed to wrap around my ankles or catch on my clothing. It was almost as if the plants had a mind of their own. I shook away the thought. *They're just plants.*

My legs were crying out in protest as the march through the jungle continued. I ignored the pain and continued on. Finally, ahead I saw a break in the trees. The others noticed it too and our pace picked up, charging forward toward the clearing.

Emerging from the tree line was like entering nightfall without the darkness. The temperature dropped, the sticky air vanished, and I felt refreshed. We were staring across a large grassy clearing. The jungle formed a ring around it, surrounding us on all sides. It looked completely out of place after climbing through the jungle. I was so grateful to be away from the vines and roots that I didn't care if it made sense. A stone path began a few feet away from us and cut right through the clearing into the jungle on the opposite end.

"Guess we follow the path," Celeste said.

I brushed some leaves off of my shoulders and tucked in more loose hair. The others took a second to get situated then we began to walk.

"Maybe the path will be clear through the other side of the jungle," Celeste said.

My spirits were rising quickly at the prospect of being on the right path, another step closer to finding the Black Tower. The feeling didn't last long. Across the clearing from the other side of the jungle, four black shapes emerged.

A cold tingle shot through my fingers and crawled up my arms. The Reapers hadn't given me any warning. Usually, I could feel them as they approached. This time, it felt different. I could feel the tingle of magic, but it wasn't the same type of feeling. Maybe the island changed the way magic felt.

The figures in front of us began to float toward where we stood. They'd been waiting for us. My breathing picked up and my heart began to race. I scanned the tree line for the king. Was he here, too?

My friends dropped their packs on the ground. Celeste stepped forward, arms extended, prepared to raise a shield around us.

"What are those?" Calder cried.

"Reapers. Go. Hide in the woods until we call for you. We got this." I walked up to where Celeste was standing and took my sorcerer stance at her side.

"I'll use my arctic fire, Celeste, do what you can to make it stronger for me. Maybe we can send them away."

She nodded. We stood, watching the ethereal figures slide across the ground. The rotten scent of death filled the air and I wrinkled my nose. No matter how many times I smelled these creatures, I'd never get used to it. Narrowing my eyes, I focused on the two on the right. I took several sideways steps away from Celeste, never taking my eyes off of the creatures. As I hoped, they followed me, ignoring Celeste. Blue flames crackled in my hands as my whole body filled with ice. I still didn't have the best control over my power and knew I couldn't hold them off for long. I had to hope it would be enough. That we could make them go away.

While I waited for them to come into range, I did a last glance for the king. If he was here, too, we didn't stand a chance. Turning my attention back on the Reapers, I took a deep breath, preparing to launch my fire. I reached inside, feeling the ice travel through me, burning me as it moved like lighting. It was getting faster. Lifting my hands out in front of me, I screamed as I forced the magic to release.

The monsters let out a howl as they were swallowed by icy blue flames. I felt my energy draining quickly, but pushed through. Forced to squint through the bright glow of the blue flames, I tried to make out the shapes of the Reapers. I couldn't see them. Hesitantly, I called back my magic and let my arms drop to my sides. They were gone.

I was breathing heavy, that had taken a lot of energy, but it shouldn't have sent them away so quickly. "Where'd they go?"

I turned in a slow circle, expecting to see the Reapers sneak up from behind me. The jungle was silent. The smell of death was gone.

"They just disappeared," Celeste said.

The tingle of magic shot from my fingers though my arms,

down my chest and filled my whole body. It was so intense it hurt. I cried out in pain.

Then, a low rumbling noise filled the air and the ground began to shift. I struggled to keep my balance as a wall of vines and trees sprouted from nowhere in front of me.

"Etta!" Celeste ran forward, but before she could reach me, the vegetation divided us. I moved toward the vines, trying to go around them, trying to reach her. There was no way through. They were so thick I couldn't pass. "Celeste!"

I listened, but there was no response. Was she safe? I spun around to where we had entered the clearing. Where was Calder? I ran toward the tree line. "Calder?"

As I raced back to the jungle, the ground shook again, this time, knocking me down. I sat on the ground staring in disbelief as another wall of vines and trees grew from nothing, blocking my path.

I let out a choked cry as I watched the plants weave themselves together, blocking my path. My heart sunk. We'd come so close and now we were going to be stopped by this? Glancing around, I realized I was surrounded by new vegetation, trapped. I rested my forehead on my knees and took a few breaths. Was this how it was going to end? Not the king, not the Reapers, not even Max, but death by vines?

A flicker of heat rose in the pit of my stomach. I looked up and tightened my jaw. I wasn't going to go down without a fight. I was here to save Ashton. There wasn't any room for failure. I stood and brushed the dirt off my hands. There had to be a way through. All magic had a limit.

I paced around the vegetation, looking at the woven vines and tall trees. About halfway through my walk, I stopped. In front of me was an opening. The vines formed an arched doorway. It was as if they wanted me to go that way.

I hesitated, wondering if it was a trap. I did a quick walk

around then ended up back at the doorway. It was the only way out. With a sigh, I clenched my fists and stepped through.

I waited inside the arch, half expecting the vines to wrap around me and strangle me to death. Nothing happened. A few more slow steps took me into a narrow plant-lined hallway of sorts. The vines formed an arch above me, leaving only occasional spaces for the sun to shine through. It was damp and cool in the dark vine covered tunnel.

I moved through, looking for any sign of a way out. After walking for several minutes, the tunnel came to a fork. I could go left or right. I stopped, frozen in between the two choices. Which way should I go?

"Hello?" I called out to both sides of the path. No response came from either. I thought about where I had been standing and where I had last seen Celeste and Calder. From what I could guess, going left would be more likely to take me to where they were. Maybe I could find them inside this maze of vines. Then we could work together to find our way out. Celeste had a lot more magic experience than I did. Maybe she knew a spell that would get rid of the vegetation. And Calder had a sword, maybe he could cut through it.

I looked down at my hands. My most powerful spell was the arctic fire. It was possible I could create some damage with it, but I'd be risking draining too much energy. I was still feeling weak from fighting against the Reapers.

As I walked through the dark tunnels, I replayed the fight with the Reapers in my mind. It hadn't been the same as the other times I'd faced them. I'd never sent all four of them away by myself before. I'd always had Ashton with me. I bit down on the inside of my cheek and tried not to linger on the fact that I was wasting so much time. Was he still hanging on? Was he still alive? *He has to be.* I hadn't come this far to lose him.

I picked up my pace, walking faster though the tunnels. As I did, I came to more turns and I spent less time making decisions. I needed to get through this and get out of here. I couldn't keep wasting time.

After what felt like hours of walking around aimlessly, I reached a dead end. The vines blocked me in with nowhere to turn. I stomped my foot on the ground and let out a scream of frustration. "What is going on here? Where is everybody? Let me out! Do you hear me, Oracle? Let me out!"

Nobody responded to my outburst and I felt my cheeks grow hot despite the fact that I was alone. I was losing my temper at a bunch of plants. I ran my hand through my hair, tucking the fallen strands back into the knot. Despite the cooler temperature of the maze, I was still sweating.

I rolled up my tunic sleeves and turned around, headed back to where I came from. Ahead, I could make out a figure. There was somebody else in here. I ran.

21

As I neared the person in the maze, I realized it wasn't Celeste or Calder. The person turned to look at me. A chill ran through me and I froze. The young woman in front of me stared back at me with bright blue eyes. Her long dark curls were clean and shiny. She wore a white dress that was immaculate. Not a spot of dirt on it. I was looking at myself.

I looked down at my torn, dirty clothes. Streaks of blood covered my hands. I felt my hair, still braided around the crown of my head. It was falling out of the braid and had pieces of plants in it. I don't think I'd ever looked as cleaned and polished as the figure in front of me. This had to be a dream.

I turned my head from side to side and the mirror image of myself copied my movements. "What's going on here? Am I asleep?"

She took a step forward and I noticed her feet were bare. The white dress flowed behind her. "No, you're not asleep, but I'm not exactly here."

"What do you mean?" I took a step backward, away from her.

She extended a hand and turned it in front of me. As she did, I could see the shafts of light from above penetrate her skin. She was translucent. I reached my fingers out toward hers and they slid right through her. She wasn't really here. My mouth was dry. I swallowed. "What are you?"

She shrugged her shoulders. "I'm you, just a part of you that you've kept hidden away. I'm here to help you."

My hands were damp with sweat and my pulse quickened. This didn't feel right. Why was I staring at a copy of myself? "I-I don't understand. Where did you come from?"

"You created me, you called to me. There is a lot more magic inside you that you aren't aware of." She took a few steps toward me again.

This time I held my ground. "Can you help me get out of here?"

"If that's truly what you want."

"Of course it is," I said. "I need to find my way to the Black Tower. I have to find the Oracle."

"Why is that?"

I narrowed my eyes at her. "If you're part of me, you should know why."

She tilted her head back and forth again. "I don't think you really know why you're here. You keep telling yourself it's self-less, that you're here to save him, but there's something else, something darker. Something you won't admit to yourself."

I bristled, feeling suddenly defensive. How dare she tell me what I was feeling? "I don't know what you're talking about. I'm here to see the Oracle, find that stone, and save Ashton. That's the only reason I'm here. If you're not going to help me do that, you can go."

"That's fine, you can deny it all you want, but remember, you called me here. Not the other way around." She turned and started to walk away.

Panic rose inside me. What if I got stuck here? Did it matter if this spirit was saying things I didn't like? If she could help me out of here, I didn't want her to go. "Wait!"

She stopped and spun around in a whirl of flowing white fabric. "Yes?"

"Please, just help me. I have to find my friends and I have to get out of here."

She lifted an eyebrow. "What if you had to choose between finding your friends or getting out of here? What would you choose?"

My heartbeat quickened. "What do you mean?"

She walked backward through the twists and turns of the maze. I followed her, not willing to take my eyes off of her.

"Exactly as I said. If you had to choose, what would you choose? Save your friends from this maze or save yourself?"

"I'd never leave my friends behind." I was starting to feel my temper rise again. How was this spirit in front of me part of me? I wouldn't ask such a question of myself.

She placed a finger on her lips. "Even if it meant getting to Ashton in time to save him?"

I opened my mouth to speak, then closed it. The answer should be there. It should be easy to say I could never value one person's life over another, but this was Ashton. *No.* I covered my mouth with my hand. How could I even consider that he was more important? I dropped my hand and narrowed my eyes at the smiling figure in the white dress. "My friends are everything to me. Celeste, Ashton, they're like my family. I could never choose between them like that."

She smirked. "What about your new friend, then? Calder."

What about Calder? I hardly knew him. He had been willing to face death for his own revenge, and gotten what he wanted. He knew traveling with us would be a risk. Would I give up his life for my own? For the lives of my other friends? A dark thought crept into my head. A part of me was willing to sacrifice him. My breath caught in my chest. What was happening to me? How could I ever think such a thing? "Stop it!"

White-dress Etta stared at me and smiled. "I told you, there's something dark inside you. You are just like your brother."

The king had said the same thing but it couldn't be true. I could never be like Max. With a sharp intake of breath, I realized I had considered giving up Calder. That was something Max would do. *No.* Max wouldn't have felt guilty. He wouldn't have stopped those thoughts. That made us different. I might have dark thoughts, but I didn't act on them. *I am not Max.*

I glared at the smiling version of me. "I'm nothing like Max. He's only worried about power. He would do anything to claim the throne."

"What if you were asked to give up the throne. What if Max claimed it first? Would you walk away from it?"

I stared at her, walking behind her as she practically floated over the ground. Would I walk away from it? "That won't happen. Max joined the king, he switched sides."

"That doesn't' matter. He could overthrow the king. Claim the crown for himself. If that happened, would you throw in your support or would you kill him and take it for yourself?"

I didn't want to kill Max. I still didn't want to believe that he really had joined the king. There was a part of me that wanted him to come back and help me. I wanted him to support my claim on the throne. Not the other way around. "I would never kill Max. I couldn't. He's my brother."

"Which does give him a claim on the throne." The spirit version of me stopped walking and stared at me.

My heart was pounding in my ears. "No. I am the true heir. Max is my half-brother. The throne is mine."

She smiled. "You keep denying it, but you sound just like him."

I shook my head. "Take it back. You know I'm nothing like

him. He gave up everything. He betrayed everyone he loved. I wouldn't do that."

"Yet, we are here. You have left the Ravens to fend for themselves while you selfishly try to save a single man." Her words seemed to echo through the maze, sounding over and over in my head.

"No," I said. "He had to be saved."

She took a step closer to me and spoke softly. "Would you have done this for any other member of the Ravens? Did you even feel sad when you heard the king killed Nathan?"

I bit down on the inside of my cheek. She was right. If it had been somebody else, I probably wouldn't have gone. The realization nearly knocked me over and I struggled to find my breath. I felt like I was suffocating. I wanted to be a good queen. I wanted to serve my people well but I had left them all to save one man. And I'd do it again. "It's Ashton."

White-dress Etta's eyes narrowed. "But you are supposed to be the queen."

The word spiraled through my mind. *Queen.* Nobody told me what I was supposed to be doing. There were no rules, no teacher, no-one to model it for me. Remembering back to when I first joined the Ravens and the power that Max had demanded by his mere presence sent a shiver through me. *I'm not Max.*

I stared at her. "Maybe I wouldn't go after the stone myself if it weren't Ashton, but I'd make sure I did whatever needed to be done to save an innocent life. I'm not Max and I'm proud of that. I am going to be a great queen."

Mirror-image-me smoothed her dress. "What if it comes down to the two of you? Would you kill him for it?"

"No!" I was shouting now. "I can't kill Max. I don't want to kill anybody!"

"Not that that's stopped you in the past." She turned around and walked forward. I followed her. The hot prickle of tears were rising in the back of my eyes. She was right. I never wanted to kill anybody but had left a trail of bodies in my wake. The guard in Redding, the sorcerer at the trials, the guards in Campari.

She glanced over her shoulder at me. "Though, I suppose you don't always have to be the one to do the deed yourself. How many have died under your orders? Or to protect you?" She turned away from me and kept walking.

It was getting harder to breathe. I couldn't even count all of the bodies that had fallen in my wake as a result of others trying to defend me. *Is this the kind of queen I'm going to be?* I looked down at my hands and started screaming. They were covered in wet, red blood. It dripped from my hands into a puddle on the ground in front of me.

The next thing I knew, somebody was shaking me awake. "Etta? Etta, can you hear me?"

I shot up from the ground and pushed myself away from the person leaning over me. My heart pounded in my chest and as my vision cleared, I recognized Calder. I covered my face with my hands. It had all been a dream. Dropping my hands, I looked up. My heart dropped into my stomach. I was still inside the maze, looking up at a ceiling formed by twisted vines.

I covered my ears with my hands and squeezed my eyes shut. Was this ever going to end? I took a deep breath and opened my eyes. Calder was staring at me, eyebrows knitted together in concern.

He reached out and placed his hands on top of mine, lowering them from my ears. "Are you okay?"

I shook my head. "No. I'm not okay."

"I know," he said. "Me neither."

22

I was suddenly overwhelmed with gratitude toward Calder for volunteering to come on this trip. Without him, I'd be alone right now, trapped in a maze with a version of myself that reminded me of all of the terrible things I'd done. "Thanks, Calder."

"For what? I hid in the woods until I saw the vines growing. I tried to reach you two, but they grew around me." He ran a hand through his dark hair. "Do you know some kind of spell or something that can get us out of here?"

I shook my head. "I wish I did. I only started using magic a few weeks ago."

"Really? I thought all noble kids were tested and trained young. My family are merchants. I mean, we were well-to-do, but not nobles. Yet, even I was tested." He looked away and shoved his hands in his pockets.

"You were?" I realized how little I knew about Calder. While I had agreed to trust him quickly, he came with a lot of secrets. I considered my own past. I supposed we all had secrets. "It doesn't matter right now. We need to find Celeste and get out of here."

I noticed that the sword Calder had carried through the jungle was sitting on the ground next to us.

"Did you try that on the vines?" I inclined my head toward the sword.

"That was the first thing I tried. They seem to be made of something stronger than any plant I've ever seen." He picked up the sword he had tossed to the ground and tucked it under his belt.

We started walking through the narrow tunnels, doing our best to navigate at the intersections. Calder and I walked silently side-by-side, hoping we'd hear something that would give us a clue to where Celeste was.

"You still want to go to the Oracle after all of this?" Calder asked.

His question took me off guard. I had never thought about quitting. "I have to. If we don't, my friend will die."

"Is this friend worth your life?"

It was a question I should put more thought into, but my answer came quickly. "Yes."

"Wow." A hint of a smile crossed Calder's face. "What's his name?"

Calder had held the woman he loved in his arms while she died. He'd chased after her killers to exact revenge and was now on a potentially deadly quest to inflict more harm on the person who was responsible for her death. If anyone understood the lengths I was willing to go to, it was him. "Ashton. He's a fire sorcerer, one of the best."

Calder raised his eyebrows. "I have a feeling we'd be searching for this Oracle even if he was a shoeless peasant."

I smiled, knowing I'd give up all the riches in the world to be with Ashton. "Yes we would."

We were quiet for a while as we kept walking through the maze. It was hard to tell with the vines above us, but it seemed to be getting darker. I didn't want to be stuck in here overnight and started to walk faster.

The feel of being trapped in here was starting to wear on me and I balled my hands into fists, then released them over and over again. There was no place for me to expel the nervous energy coursing though me. Every second we wasted in here felt like I was letting Ashton down.

Calder set his hand on mine. He must have noticed me fidgeting. I looked over at him.

He pulled away his hand. "Tell me about your Ashton. What's he like? How'd you meet?"

Warmth spread through me at those words. *Your Ashton.* He was mine, if I could get him back. I thought back to the morning I'd found him waiting outside my tent and couldn't help but smile. "I suppose it's your typical girl-meets-boy story. You know, fighting against Reapers, being attacked by the king's sorcerers, that whole thing."

Calder laughed. "Ah, I see. The ol' life-or-death experience bonding. Yes, very common. Happens all the time."

I laughed at his playful sarcasm. At the time we had gone through those events, there was nothing funny about them. I wondered if I'd be able to look back on this maze and our trip to the Oracle and laugh one day.

Calder kept talking with me, asking questions and sharing stories about his wife and their life in Greenville. After a while, my fingers relaxed and I was feeling less overwhelmed by my surroundings.

"Etta!"

I froze. Turning to Calder, I whispered, "did you hear that?"

He nodded.

My heart started racing. *Celeste?* "I'm here! Celeste, is that you?"

"Etta! I can hear you. Don't move. I'm coming to you." The

voice sounded like Celeste but after what I had experienced earlier, I wasn't ready to trust this maze until I could see her for myself.

A few seconds later, a breathless Celeste came running toward me. She launched herself at me, pulling me into an embrace. "Is it really you?" Her face was tear-streaked and dirty. Whatever she'd been though in the maze hadn't been easy.

"Are you okay?" I asked.

She nodded. "I'm fine. I just want to get out of here."

"Me too. Any ideas?" I still hoped that she might know a spell that would help us.

Celeste extended a hand toward Calder. "Your sword, please."

He pulled it from his belt and handed it to her.

Celeste held the blade across her open palms and stared at it for a while. I leaned in closer, trying to hear her whispered words. While she worked, I looked up at the vines. Between the gaps, I could see that the sky was no longer blue, it had been replaced by the gray of twilight. We'd lose all of our light soon.

I looked back at Celeste. She held the sword for a few seconds longer then handed it back to Calder. He took it without comment.

"Try it now," she said.

He shrugged then took a deep breath before swinging the sword at the vines in front of him. The blade sang as it cut through the foliage. The severed greens shriveled and lost their color. I touched one of the gray vines and it crumbled to dust. Hope filled me. "Do it again."

Calder swung again, cutting down more vines. He kept going until he'd cleared a hole in the wall that we could pass through. After cutting down the vines for four more walls, he looked tired, though he wouldn't admit it and refused to let one of us take over. He stood in front of the next wall, catching his breath.

He lifted the sword in Celeste's direction. "What did you do to it?"

I looked over at her, she looked almost as tired as Calder. Dark circles rested under her eyes that I hadn't noticed before.

"Two spells," she said. "One, strengthened the sword itself. The other allows it to draw magic from me to help break the enchantment."

"Celeste, why did you do that?" I was worried for her. I now realized that the look she had was probably how I looked before I passed out from using too much magic. She was being drained of her magic with every swing.

"It was the only way," she said. "It'll be fine. We have to get to the Oracle."

"I'm really not sure what's going on here," Calder said. "Should I keep going?"

"Yes," Celeste said.

Calder looked at me for reassurance. I hesitated. How much magic could she afford to give? I didn't like it, but if there were another way she knew to get out of the maze, Celeste would have done it. This was the only way. With a sigh, I nodded. Getting out of this maze and getting to the Oracle were too important. Ashton's life hung in the balance.

Calder pushed his sleeves back up and turned to face the wall of vines ahead of us. He used the sword to cut and hack at the vines and they fell away as dead, gray strands.

A thump next to me took my attention away from Calder's progress. Celeste was on the ground, unconscious. I dropped to my knees and checked her for breathing. She seemed to be alive, just drained of her energy.

"Your highness!" Calder shouted.

I looked up at him. He was breathing heavily and his forehead was covered in sweat. He wore a huge smile that faded as soon as he saw us on the ground. He dropped the sword and ran over to me. "Is she alright?"

"I think so, just too much magic." I glanced up and noticed that the vines he had cut away didn't lead to another wall. I could see trees and jungle through them.

"Calder! Is that it? Are we out?" Flutters filled my stomach. Then I noticed that the vines were growing back.

"Help me!" I grabbed Celeste's arms and started pulling her. "The wall is closing up!"

Calder glanced back at the wall. Then, in one movement, he picked Celeste up and threw her over his shoulder. We ran for the opening, making it through just as the vines swallowed up the hole he'd cut away.

I took a deep breath as relief flooded through me. We'd found a way out of the maze and we were alive. Ahead of us, in the moonlight, was the jungle.

In the distance, I could just make out a stone pathway that began at the tree line. A breeze blew past us and the jungle moved with the wind. I shuddered, imagining the thick foliage swallowing us whole. There would be no turning back. We needed the stone to save Ashton and we needed to get help for Celeste. I glanced at Calder. "Follow the path?"

He shifted Celeste's weight on his shoulders. "Follow the path."

23

The trek through the jungle moved more quickly this time. The path was surprisingly free of growth or obstacles. It was as if the jungle now welcomed us. My eyes rarely left Celeste's prone form, draped over Calder's shoulder. I could not figure out how he was able to carry her, I was just thankful he was able to.

My breathing was heavy and every muscle in my body was tense. No matter how hard I tried to protect those I cared about, I never seemed to succeed. Celeste's unconscious form seemed to merge with Ashton's in my mind and the voice of the white-dress-Etta from the maze echoed through my head. Was I risking too much for one man?

My cheeks flushed with heat. I knew the answer to that question. I knew I would do anything to save Ashton. I wondered if I had a right to drag my friends, new and old, along with me on such a dangerous quest. I was thankful this was almost over. As long as the Oracle helped us, we'd be home before sunrise. After this was over, I'd have to seriously consider my actions before rushing into things that could get me, or other people killed.

As we walked along the road, signs of former civilization

began to appear. Crumbled stone foundations, piles of rocks, the occasional fire pit or other ruin. Most of the remains were being reclaimed by the jungle. Vines and trees grew through them, around them, embracing them. I wondered how long the city had been deserted for the jungle to be so lush. Had this all been here when it was a thriving city?

The deeper we went into the trees, the darker the shadows became. The foliage around us created a canopy that often blotted out the sky. The unnatural quiet we had experienced since arriving on the island seemed to follow us. Our footfalls and the sounds of our labored breathing were all that could be heard in the damp, heavy air.

The ruins became more frequent, closer together. Some of them even started to look almost livable, though they'd need roofs. "We have to be getting closer." I wasn't sure if I was talking to myself, Calder, or the unconscious Celeste in front of me.

We followed a bend on the path and stopped, frozen in our tracks. In front of us, was a tower made of dark stone. It looked as aged and crumbling as the other structures we had passed, yet somehow, it still stood. A shiver ran through me. The tower did not look at all inviting. Or safe.

I took a deep breath. This had to be the Black Tower. All that was standing between us and saving Ashton was the Oracle inside the tower. "Let's go."

The tower was even taller than I originally thought once we reached its base. I had to tilt my head back as far as it would go to see the top. It broke through the canopy of trees, soaring toward the sky. I reached out and touched the stone, brushing my fingers on the surface. They came back covered in soot. The black color of the tower was not from the stone itself, but from a layer of grime and soot that had collected over the years. I wiped my fingers on my trousers and circled the base of the tower, searching for a door.

Calder gently eased Celeste on to the ground. "How do we get in?"

I looked up at the tower again. It had some rectangular slats cut into the stone near the top. Other than that, there were no openings. "I'm not sure."

Calder walked up to the tower. "Maybe we just need to knock."

I put my hands on my hips. "I'm sure that's it, Calder. Go for it."

He shrugged, missing the sarcasm in my voice, and knocked three times on the side of the tower.

I turned toward the jungle. "Maybe we can make a rope with some of the vines."

"Um, your highness." Calder grabbed me by my shoulders and spun me around.

My mouth dropped open. A door had appeared out of nowhere on the side of the tower. "Knocking." I shook my head.

Calder picked up Celeste. "After you."

The door opened directly to a dark stairway. A lump rose in my throat. There was nothing inviting about this dark stairway. I closed my eyes for a moment and focused on the reason I was here. We were going to save Ashton. I clenched my fists and headed up the dark stairs. *I am not going to lose him.*

Calder let out a few grunts as he climbed the stairs with Celeste in his arms.

I stopped walking and looked behind me. "Do you need some help?"

He shook his head. "Just keep moving. Stopping and starting is the hardest part."

Quickly, I resumed the climb. The stairs wound their way around the inside of the tower, hugging the walls. Glancing above me, my heart sunk. The stairs went all the way to the top. *Of course.*

Finally, out of breath, thighs burning, I reached the top. A single door met the end of the staircase. Afraid to throw off Calder, I pushed the door open without pausing to knock.

I stepped inside a circular room. It took up the entire space of the tower. A few sconces with glowing, tall white candles dotted the walls. A small fire flickered on one side of the circular wall. The other side was lined with bookshelves that spanned two or three stories. A large ladder was propped against one of the shelves.

Looking around again, I noticed that the ceiling was lower on the half of the room where the fireplace was. A ladder was propped against the ceiling. It was a loft.

Walking to the ladder, I paused in front of it. "Hello? Oracle? I'm sorry to disturb you, but we have an emergency." No response. "We could really use some help."

A shuffling noise sounded above me. Somebody was up there. Panic rose inside me. Had the king left a trap for me? What if it wasn't the Oracle up there?

I let out a long breath when I saw a woman in a white dress climb down the ladder. She was a small, frail looking being. Long, blonde hair plaited into a braid, hung down below her waist. She didn't look much older than me.

Hopping from the ladder to the floor, she spun on her bare feet and faced me. "He finally sent you, did he?"

Glancing at my friends first, I turned my gaze to her icy blue eyes. She cocked her head from side to side, as if she was studying me.

"Yes, Master Flanders sent us."

"I know. I've been waiting for you. I really thought I'd see you sooner, but that's the funny thing about the future. It can change so quickly."

I wasn't sure how to respond to her, so I just started talking. "We had an incident, out in a giant vine-maze."

I wanted to yell at her for having a vine-maze on her island in the first place. It was no wonder people didn't visit the Sacred Island unless they were already dying. It now occurred to me that most of those people probably never made it this far. How long had it been since she'd had a visitor? Right now, that wasn't important. What mattered was helping Celeste and finding that stone for Ashton.

I walked over to Calder, who still held Celeste in his arms, and pulled him toward her. Calder stepped forward and the Oracle walked to meet him. She placed her hand on Celeste's forehead. "She just needs to rest. She'll be fine by morning."

I let out a breath, releasing some of the tension I had been holding. At least she was safe.

The Oracle pointed to the side of the room near the bookshelves. "You can rest over there for the night. I'll get you all set up with some blankets." She turned and walked away.

"Wait!" I ran after her and set my hand on her shoulder. "Please, we came here because we need your help."

She looked at me, silently willing me to continue.

"Our friend. He's in trouble. The king sent his essence from his body. We were told there is a stone we can use to help him get it back."

The Oracle blinked a few times, staring at me with her icy blue eyes. "There is such a stone. You are looking for the Astral Stone. It has long been kept by the Oracles."

I straightened, practically bouncing up onto my toes. "Yes, that's the one."

"I'm afraid the stone isn't here."

My shoulders dropped. How could this be? We'd come all this way. We had to have that stone so we could save Ashton. "What do you mean? Where is it?"

"When the king made me move to this tower, the stone

stayed behind with an older Oracle. She is no longer with us in this realm, but the stone remained behind."

"There's another tower?" I asked. I had heard tales of the Black Tower on the Sacred Island, but never of a second one.

"It's an older tower, in Delios, mostly used for training new Oracles. If you travel there, you should find the stone. The city is abandoned." The Oracle looked up, her expression suddenly vacant. She stood quietly for a moment, not doing anything.

I took a tentative step toward her. "Oracle?"

She blinked a few times, then looked at me. "I'm sorry, sometimes visions come when I don't ask for them. It's been happening more often since you came out of hiding. The future is less certain than it used to be. Too many variables."

I had no idea there was so much different magic existing around me. The Oracle's ability to see the future was so different from my own magic. I wanted to ask about my own future. Would Ashton be okay? Would I defeat the king?

The Oracle touched a finger to my cheek. "I know what you're thinking. And no, I cannot tell you that. All I can share is that the king is sending a company of guards to Luxor. They will kill everybody there. If you go, you will defeat them and save the people who live there. If you do not go, you will find the stone that can save your friend. My vision does not tell me if you can do both. You'll have to make a choice."

24

—————

I stared at her, hoping I had heard her incorrectly. I let the words sink in for a moment, trying to find a way to make them sound different in my head. "Could you be wrong? Could it change?"

Her gaze softened. "I'm afraid that part of the vision was very clear. The king's guards will attack Luxor. They are already on their way there."

I turned away from her, trying to wrap my mind around what she was telling me. *If I go get the stone, I can save Ashton, but at what cost?*

"Your highness." Calder tapped me on the shoulder.

I jumped at his voice. I'd almost forgotten he was here. Rubbing my eyes, I turned to face him. The exhaustion I'd been living with for the last few weeks was catching up to me today. "Yes?"

"You have saved so many people already. Save Ashton. The way you talk about him, you don't get love like that more than once in your life." He swallowed. "Let me tell you, as somebody who lost the most important person in the world, the pain I feel daily will never cease. I'd sacrifice the whole world to have her back in my arms."

"What's going on?" Celeste's voice came from behind me.

"You're awake!" I ran over to her and sat down next to her. *Finally, something good happened.*

"Where are we?" She looked around the room, her eyes stopping on the Oracle. "Are we?"

I nodded. "We're in the Oracle's Tower. Your magic got us out."

She let out a long breath. "Thank the gods. I thought we'd be trapped in there all night. Now, what is this about Ashton?"

"The Oracle says we will find the stone that will save Ashton but there's a problem in Luxor. The king's guards are going to attack. If we go there, we can stop them, but we might not be able to do both."

"We have to get the stone." Calder looked at me. "You don't even know those people."

"Actually, I do." My mind replayed the battle with the king a few weeks ago. I remembered Celeste and I at the Tiger Lily Inn, walking through the empty streets. The people knew what was coming. They'd hidden away and tried to support us as best they could. Calder hadn't known us then. He didn't know what we had been through.

"Your highness, this is a war. Sometimes, people die. You have to save Ashton." Calder's hands were in fists. He was still covered in blood and had that wild look in his eyes I'd seen when we first met. I wondered if he was living through the death of his wife all over again in his mind.

"How could you say such a thing?" Celeste said. She gripped my hands in hers. "You know what Ashton would want. If you let all those people die, and he wakes up to find out what you did, you're going to lose him. You know that."

I pulled away from her and pressed my palms into my eyes.

How could I make a decision like this? The man I love or a whole town full of people I'd never met.

"Only you can make the choice," the Oracle said. "They are both noble quests."

Calder and Celeste were silent. I knew what they were each thinking. The Oracle was right, this was my decision. If I go on to truly become Queen of Illaria, I will be faced with decisions like this all the time. What was more important, my people or my heart?

I closed my eyes and thought of Ashton. I remembered our first kiss by the archery range. I could still feel the heat of his mouth on mine. I touched my lips, trying to hold on to that memory. Then, my vision changed and I saw Ashton on the ground in front of the king. He looked so helpless. That stone was the only thing that could save him. Was Celeste right? If I let the King's Guards kill the people of Luxor, would Ashton ever forgive me?

I thought of how he'd selflessly thrown himself in front of me when the Reapers first came for me. How he'd volunteered to help the people at the Trials escape without a second thought to his own safety. He was willing to give his life for the cause but I didn't want to lose him.

What would I want him to do if it were me who needed rescued? Would I want him to sacrifice the town to save my life? I swallowed. *No. You'd want him to go to Luxor.*

Opening my eyes, I looked at the Oracle. "You said you don't know if it's possible to do both but if I go to Luxor first, I will save the town."

She nodded.

My heart felt like it was breaking. "Can you tell me the fastest way to get to the stone after we leave Luxor? We were told teleporting wasn't safe."

"Wait here." The Oracle turned away and climbed up the

ladder to the loft. After a short wait, she returned, clutching something in her hand.

She handed me a small leather bag tied with a ribbon. "Black Onyx Dust. A little of this on the place you teleport from will mask any trace."

I stared at the bag, amazed by how much I was still learning about magic every day. "I never knew there was such a thing."

I held the bag in my hand, my heart swelling with hope. Celeste and I had been to Luxor before so she could teleport us directly there. With this, we might actually be able to accomplish both tasks. "Thank you."

The Oracle smiled. "There's one more thing." She stretched out an open hand. "You'll need this." She held a brass key that stretched the length of her palm.

"What is it?" I asked.

"It's similar to the teleportation coins you've used. It's an Oracle key. You can't teleport to this tower or from this tower without it." She lifted her hand closer to me.

I picked up the key. "I don't know how to thank you."

She inclined her head in a slight bow. "No thanks needed." She looked up at me. "If you find the stone, come back to my tower and I'll show you how to use it before you return."

I closed my fingers around the key. There were no words for how grateful I felt in that moment.

"Are you sure about this, your highness?" Calder said. "You don't owe these people anything."

"Yes I do, Calder. I've made a vow to protect the people of Illaria from the king. I have said over and over that I am done with having people die for me." I swallowed back a lump that had risen in my throat. "Besides, Celeste is right. Ashton would never forgive me if I saved him at the cost of all those innocents. He's been fighting against the king since he was a child. If the situation were reversed, I'd expect him to think of the Illarians first, me second."

"That will never happen, your highness," Calder said. "I don't know Ashton, and I'm sure if you both say he'd want you to sacrifice him, it must be true. But they couldn't sacrifice you. When you're queen, you life matters more than others. Without you, there's nobody to step in and protect the people."

I held my breath for a moment. Was I more important than the rest of the people in the kingdom? *I'm no different, I just have different parents.* "No, that's not true, I'm not any better than anyone else."

"Yes you are," Celeste said.

I stared at her. How could she say that?

"If something happens to you, who else is going to rise up against the king? Max joined him. There's nobody else," she said. "We help everyone in Illaria by keeping you alive. "

The Oracle raised her hands in front of us. "My children, what you say is true. While I am forbidden from directly telling somebody their future, I can tell you that I often see several different versions of the future. There is a version where you become queen. There are many where you do not. The decisions you make in the next three months will determine the path for all of Illaira. Even if you do not become queen, what you do will have consequences for the entire kingdom for generations to come."

"What does that mean?" I asked. How could she say something like that and not elaborate? "In *one* version I become queen? Does that mean the odds are against me?"

The Oracle shook her head. "I have already said too much. The future is constantly changing. Every decision made by every person impacts it. Some people have a stronger connection to the world and their decisions hold more weight. You are one of those people. That is all I can tell you."

I stiffened. What did that mean? How did my decisions hold more weight in the grand scheme of the world? I rubbed my temples, trying to ease the throbbing that had seeped into my head.

The Oracle walked over to the fireplace. It had been reduced to embers while we talked.

"You should sleep here tonight. You'll be safe. If you intend to save the people of Luxor, you'll need to be there by midday tomorrow." She added wood to the fire then turned away from us and climbed up her ladder.

We were left standing in the dim room alone. Celeste covered a yawn. "I am tired. Maybe we should sleep."

A pile of blankets and pillows sailed over the edge of the loft onto the ground. "Thank you!" Celeste called up as she collected them. She made quick work of laying them out into beds of sorts for the three of us.

Not long after the others settled in, I heard steady, deep breathing. They fell asleep quickly. In the quiet of the room, I whispered to Ashton, even though I knew he couldn't hear me. "I have to go to Luxor first but then I'm going to get the astral projection stone. I need you to stay strong for me. Keep fighting. I promise, I will come back for you. I will return your essence to your body. We will be together again in this world. You can't leave me. Promise me you'll stay strong." I wiped a tear off my cheek. "I love you, Ashton."

When I woke the next morning, it took me a second to remember where I was. Part of me had hoped I'd wake to find it had all been a nightmare. Today was the day we should be finding that stone. Instead, we were off on another mission. How long was Ashton going to hang on? I kept trying to tell myself I was doing the right thing, but it was hard to quiet my selfish desires.

When I looked over at my friends, I saw Celeste was already awake.

"He's going to be fine," she said. "We're going to get the stone and we're going to save him."

I bit the inside of my cheek. I wanted to believe her. I had to believe her or I wouldn't be able to fight in Luxor. Pushing the blankets away, I sat and surveyed the room. The fire had died down and the gray early dawn light filtered in through the high windows.

Calder was still asleep, snoring softly under the covers. I was glad we all got a good night's sleep for a change. We'd be on the move again this morning and I didn't know when we'd get another chance to rest. I knew that sleep would be hard for me to find until Ashton was safe.

Light footsteps drew my attention away from my friends. The Oracle was padding toward us on her bare feet. She wore the same white dress from the day before but now her long hair hung loose around her face. It went well past her hips without the braid to hold it in place.

"Anybody hungry?" she asked.

I didn't feel hungry at the moment but I couldn't remember our last meal. "I should probably eat something."

"I'll make porridge." She walked toward the fireplace and busied herself with a large pot.

"Thank you," Celeste and I said in unison.

I smiled at Celeste. "Thank you, too. For being here with me."

She reached her hand out to mine and squeezed. "There's nowhere I'd rather be."

"Think we should wake Calder?" I asked.

She extended her foot and pushed her toes into his side. "Calder, wake up."

Calder turned away from us and started snoring again. We both started laughing. It felt strange, having such a normal moment with a friend amidst such turmoil. We were heading, once again, into battle. The laughter faded away and I pressed my lips into a tight line.

Knowing that we'd win didn't seem to help alleviate any of the nerves I was feeling. My stomach had the same pre-fight knots I'd come to know in my last few encounters with people who were trying to kill me.

"What is it?" Celeste asked.

A dark thought crossed my mind. "The Oracle said we'd save the people of Luxor, but she never said if we'd be able to save ourselves."

25

W e stood in the center of the tower, Celeste between Calder and me, grasping each of our hands. Sandwiched between our hands was the key the Oracle had given me. It was the only way we'd be able to teleport in or out of this tower.

Celeste was going to have to teleport two people since I still hadn't learned the skill on my own. She looked pale with worry. It had been less than two weeks since she first teleported somebody besides herself. Interestingly, I had been the cause of that experimentation. "You're going to do great."

She glanced at me. "First thing we're doing when we get back to the Raven camp is teach you how to teleport like this."

"Agreed," I said. Then I looked at the Oracle. "Thank you for your help."

She smiled and lifted her hand in a silent goodbye.

I squeezed Celeste's hand. "Alright, Celeste. It's now or never."

She squeezed my hand tighter. "Calder, hold on. Don't let go, no matter what."

"Got it. I'm not letting go for anything," he replied nervously.

Remembering back to my first time teleporting, I couldn't help but smile. It still was far from my favorite thing to do, but it did get easier. "First time's the worst. Just hang on."

The Oracle touched her three middle fingers to her forehead and lowered her hand toward us. It was the blessing of the three gods: Sky, Water, and Underworld. My whole body tensed, caught off guard by the gesture. I'd gone most of my life only seeing this sign used in the most dire of circumstances. It was something I associated with death.

Goosebumps rose along my arms. I wondered if I was expected to return the blessing. Before I could respond in any way, gray smoke rose up from the ground, clouding my vision. The Oracle seemed to be smiling as the darkness of teleportation swallowed us.

Calder let go of my hand as soon as we were on solid ground and he tumbled forward. Resting a moment on all fours, he stared at the ground. He looked like he was going to be sick.

My first time teleporting hadn't been that long ago but it felt like a different life. I squeezed my hands into fists, thinking of the power I could call from them. How had so much changed so quickly?

I stared at the town of Luxor in front of us. It didn't hold fond memories for me and a chill ran through me. Last time we'd been here, we'd failed to defeat the king. This time, we were again facing a battle but our goal was different. Luring the king in to try to kill him was much different than defending a town of people who just wanted to live their lives. Somehow, this fight felt more noble.

Celeste dropped to Calder's side and helped pull him to standing. "It'll be easier next time."

"Next time?" Calder shook his head. "It might be easier to deal with the King's Guards."

We'd been going non-stop since he joined us and he still

wore the blood of the guards he had killed on his clothes. As we walked, I started to wonder about the rest of his story. "Calder, you said you hunted down the guard that killed your wife, but you were already covered in blood before you killed him." I regretted asking as soon as the words left my mouth.

The color drained from his face and he stopped walking. Celeste gave me a scolding look. I understood her silent message. The man had lost everything. Asking him to relive something so gruesome was not kind.

Calder looked up at me. "It's my wife's blood. We were in the market district in Greenville. A group of guards came through. They were drunk. Somebody said something insulting about the king. Didn't matter who said it. The guards didn't care. They started killing anybody who was in the way. I pushed her behind me, away from the fight, and a guard stabbed her from behind. Like a coward." His eyes narrowed and his upper lip curled. It was as if he was watching the whole scene replay in his mind. "I didn't attack him because I was too busy trying to keep her alive. They were gone before I realized she never had a chance."

"Calder," I reached for his hand. "I'm so sorry. I shouldn't have asked you about that."

Dropping my hand, he pulled on the edge of his tunic. "She made this for me." He laughed. "She was a terrible seamstress. It's the only one she made that was suitable to wear. Fitting that I wore it the day she died."

He took a deep breath. "If we can keep somebody else from losing their loved one, maybe I can start to forgive myself."

"It wasn't your fault, you know," I said.

"Do you believe that?" he asked. "About any of the people you loved who died? Do you think it wasn't your fault? Do you blame the king for Ashton?"

I knew exactly what he meant. He wasn't blaming me. We shared a unique bond. Deep down, we knew that we hadn't caused the deaths of our loved ones, but there was no way to avoid the guilt and the pain their deaths caused. No way to wonder if it wasn't somehow our fault or if there had been something we could have done differently to prevent it.

My fingers traveled to the pendant tucked under my tunic. I closed my hand around it. My parents, my grandmother, Master Edward, so many people had died for me. The list was getting longer the further down this road I traveled. Part of me wondered who would be next. Ashton's near-lifeless body haunted my vision. We had to take care of the people of Luxor fast. I couldn't lose Ashton.

I stared ahead at the town. Last time we'd been here had been to set a trap for the king. Celeste and I had stood in this very spot with Master Flanders. Last time, we were told people were watching out for us. This time, we were on our own.

"Now, how exactly are we supposed to stop the King's Guards from taking out this entire town?" Calder's color returned and he was standing tall, focused ahead of us.

"I don't know." The same thing had been nagging at me since the Oracle told us about the task. "We don't even know what we're walking into. We don't know how many guards, or what they are going to do." I looked at Celeste and Calder. They both looked worn and tired and the sun had only just begun its climb into the sky.

"I guess we need to think like king's guards," Celeste said.

"How would the King's Guard take out an entire town? And how would three people stop it?" I stared down at the main street. It didn't have a huge population, but I knew that the streets got busy once the day started. People would be out trading and visiting friends. "The Oracle said something about midday. I guess we need to start exploring, see if we can find anything suspicious. I'm not even sure where the guards would be."

"Sounds good to me." Calder started walking and Celeste and I followed behind him. I reached up to my neck and made sure that my pendant was tucked under my tunic. Unlike my last visit, I didn't need people knowing who I was. There were still the posters to worry about. I couldn't count on every place we visited being as supportive as Campari.

"Do we have a cover story?" Celeste asked.

"Bandits stole our horses?" I suggested.

She nodded and we continued silently toward the main road. As we approached, I saw the Tiger Lily Inn and considered stopping inside. The innkeeper had seemed supportive, but I couldn't guarantee she would be working. The last thing we needed was to alert somebody to my presence who could contact the king. I was still considering going inside until I saw the poster hanging from the front door. I elbowed Celeste and lifted my chin in the direction of the poster.

She shook her head, and smiled. "Good thing you don't look anything like that right now."

I smiled back. There was a definite benefit to the unintentional disguise the dirt gave me.

A tingle rose in my fingers and my whole body tensed. "Celeste?"

She froze for a second, then kept walking. "I feel it."

"Feel what?" Calder asked.

"Magic," I said. My stomach knotted. I wasn't expecting to feel magic when we arrived. "We aren't the only sorcerers here."

"She did say *guards,* didn't she?" Celeste asked.

I tried to remember the Oracle's exact words. I spent most of the time there being so worried about Ashton that I didn't pay as much attention as I should have. "I think so."

"She also said the future can change," Calder said. "If the people who are attacking changed, does that mean the outcome will change? Maybe we should go."

I pressed my palms against my temples. *Why isn't anything ever easy?* If the future has changed, has something changed with Ashton? *Maybe we should go find the stone right now.*

Nearby, the squeak of shutters being pushed open echoed through the abandoned street. I turned to see a shopkeeper getting ready for the day ahead. He poked his head out of the window and looked at us, eyes narrowed.

I lowered my voice. "Maybe we should get moving. We're starting to draw attention."

The man was walking toward us now. The three of us started to walk away when he called out to us. "You three, wait a minute."

I took a deep breath and turned to face him. The last thing we needed was to cause a scene. We'd politely explain that we were looking for an inn, and be on our way.

The man caught up to us and stood in front of me. He was an older, though not yet fully gray. Flecks of white stood out in his dark hair and beard. He had warm, brown eyes and a round full face. "You all look like you could use some kindness. Come on in, my wife was just making breakfast."

"That's very kind, but we're fine, just passing through," I said.

"Please, in these troubled times, if we don't help each other, who will?" he said.

My stomach clenched. *I will.* At least, that's what I was trying to do. A moment ago, I was considering leaving these people defenseless. Now I knew I couldn't do that. I was here for a reason.

I wanted to save the people here, but I found my thoughts wandering to Ashton. *Please let us do both.* As we followed the man into his shop, I found myself praying to the gods. If there was any chance they'd listen, I needed them to know that I was willing to do anything to save Ashton.

We sat around a table in the back of the shop. The tingle of magic crept through my limbs and filled me with unease. I couldn't tell what was causing the response inside me. It had to be something inside this house. My fingers gripped the edge of the chair tightly as my eyes darted around the room. I wondered if this was some sort of trap. Was there even such a thing as truly kind people in this world anymore?

The man who had led us in walked around the corner after showing us to the table. He returned a moment later with a blonde woman, belly swollen with child. She smiled at us and set down a tray she carried in her hands. "Welcome to our home."

She seemed nice but it still took everything I had to force a smile in return. "Thank you for having us."

She sat down at the table, shifting a few times to find a position that would accommodate her stomach. "I'm Kaylin."

The man set down another tray and settled into a chair next to his wife. "I'm Dax, sorry I didn't introduce myself sooner. We don't have company often. Sometimes I forget myself."

Kaylin nodded to the tray in front of her. I glanced down at the sliced bread and bowl of jam.

"Help yourself," she said.

The three of us hesitated.

"I'm sure you know a detect poison spell," Dax said.

My mouth dropped open. *Does he know who I am?*

He laughed. "I could sense your magic from a mile away. I'm sure you can feel mine, too."

I blinked a few times and focused on the tingling. I needed to learn how to read it better. "I could feel something, but it seemed too strong to be just one person."

He nodded. "Just me and a few magical items. They can cause a pretty strong pull to those who are sensitive to magic."

"You're a sorcerer?" Calder said.

Dax nodded. "Took my trials a long time ago. Haven't used it much since then but started practicing a bit when Kaylin here fell pregnant. Just in case the little one shows any signs of channeling magic."

Calder leaned back in his chair and put his hands over his face. "My life is never going to be normal again, is it?"

"Take it you're not a sorcerer?" Dax said. "Don't worry, Kaylin's not, either. You're not alone."

"Wait." I hadn't spent a lot of time thinking about what a sorcerer would do after the trials. They couldn't all work as masters teaching the next generation. Were there jobs for sorcerers? "What are you doing here? Couldn't you be working for a noble or something?"

Dax smiled. "I am a noble. But I'm the third son, so I didn't have much. But this beautiful woman agreed to be my wife and we wanted to have a fresh start. So we moved here. We thought we'd be free of all of the politics of the court." He shook his head. "Seems that follows you anywhere you go. The king's sorcerers can be pretty hard to shake."

Warning bells were ringing in my head. This man had been part of the court? Had he worked for the king? Was he still working for the king? My heart was pounding. I tightened my grip even more on the edge of the seat and tried not to betray my fear. Despite the warmth of the room, a chill ran through me. "Why are you inviting people you don't know inside your home if you're worried about the king's sorcerers?"

At this point, I was ready to run. Was he talking about himself? Trying to catch me off guard?

"I'm sure you learned that every sorcerer has a unique power, right?" he said.

I nodded, curiosity winning over my desire to flee.

"I can sense if a sorcerer has ever used Dark Magic. When I felt your group approach, I could tell that none of you ever have."

I relaxed a little. "And you are against Dark Magic?"

He smiled. "Please, use a truth spell against me or something so you can trust me. I'm one of the good ones. And I can tell you are, too. I wouldn't have invited you into my home if I thought you'd be a threat to my family."

Calder reached across the table and picked up a slice of bread. Before I could react, he started eating. "He's right, your - um, lady. Man's wife, man's baby, most important things in the whole world. Not worth risking."

My cheeks flushed at Calder's near use of my title. *Why hadn't I told him to call me Etta like everybody else?*

Dax lifted an eyebrow. "So it's true. The heir is a sorceress." A smile spread across his face and he patted his wife's hand with his. "We may just get to raise our baby in a peaceful kingdom, after all."

He turned to me. "I take it there's something that brought you here to Luxor."

I looked at my friends. Calder's mouth was full of food. Celeste gave me a slight nod. She seemed to approve of sharing with these people. He'd said the right things, seemed like he was a good person. I'd taken a chance trusting Calder and he turned out to be a helpful ally.

"We have word that there's a group of guards coming here to punish Luxor for helping me." I bit the inside of my cheek, trying to cover the nauseous guilty feeling that was rising inside me. This whole thing was my fault and I had considered walking away from all of these people.

"Where'd you hear this?" Dax asked.

"The Oracle."

Dax stood and walked away from the table, disappearing from view. He returned with a large, wooden staff. "Didn't think I'd have use for this again."

"A staff?" I wasn't sure how that was going to help us.

He nodded. "It's been attuned to my power. One of the magical objects I keep here. Helps me to channel the energy around us. It's a skill that can help those of us who align with earth. Gives us another point of contact with the ground."

"You don't have to help us," I said. The last thing I wanted was to be the cause of losing another good person. Too many people had offered to help me and had paid with their lives. I didn't want anyone else to join the ever-growing list. "It's going to be dangerous."

"Are you sure you want to do this?" Kaylin said. "If you go out there, word could get back to the king. He could find you."

Dax smiled at his wife. "I can't run from him forever. We both know that. I've turned him down one too many times."

"Turned him down?" Celeste looked as uncomfortable as I felt. "What do you mean? Did you fight for him?"

Dax sat back down, propping the staff against the table. "You may have noticed that the king only has a small group of sorcerers who work with him. Have you ever wondered why it's such a small group?"

I had wondered about that, but I thought it was just due to people not wanting to work with him.

When none of us spoke, Dax continued. "He collects sorcerers, but only the best. You've heard of his power? He knows who the strong sorcerers are."

I nodded.

"I have a feeling it's why you are still alive. If he wanted you dead, you would be. In fact, if he allows any sorcerer he meets to live, there's a good chance he is hoping to add that person to his collection."

The king has let me live several times citing that he wants me to join him rather than kill me. He'd also met Ashton on several occasions and never lifted a finger against him until he took away his essence. Was it possible Ashton was one of those rare sorcerers he was after? "Does he usually kill random sorcerers he meets without reason?"

"Sometimes. If he doesn't see a use for them, he knows that they could be a threat if they team up with other sorcerers."

"Why not just force people to join him? Or take the less powerful sorcerers?"

Dax shrugged. "From what I've heard, he has his sorcerers train in Dark Magic. You have to have a certain level of skill to perform spells like that. The weaker sorcerers wouldn't be able to channel the Darkness. He also knows that if they don't come to him based on free-will, they could turn against him. In fact, if the small group of followers decided they were done with him, their power would be enough to take him down."

"You don't have to do this, Dax." How could I ask this man to put himself and his family at risk? "The Oracle said we'd defeat the guards."

Dax smiled. "How do you know the Oracle didn't see me joining you?" He squeezed his wife's hand. "I'll be fighting with you."

"We can move somewhere else," Kaylin said. "We've started over before. We could do it again."

"You're welcome to join the White Ravens." I looked around the comfortable room I was sitting in. If they did that, they'd be giving up a lot. "We don't have much, but we can keep each other safe. Only if you need to. I'm sure you don't want to raise a baby in a tent."

"Thank you, your highness." Kaylin inclined her head. "We can live anywhere as long as we're giving our baby the best chance for survival and a happy life."

I smiled. When we left on this journey, I thought I was going to have to protect myself against my own people. Instead, they were rising up with me. They were ready to fight the king and take back Illaria.

26

W e didn't know when the guards would arrive or where they would come from. Dax took us to the town temple where we were able to climb to the top of the tall building and sit on the roof. Watching and waiting for an attack we knew was going to happen was harder in some ways than walking into an ambush. The waiting made me think of every worst case scenario possible. I imagined the Reapers floating into town. I pictured the king and hundreds of undead soldiers following behind them. I shuddered, recalling the vacant, white eyes and gray skin of the undead. Tucking my feet under me, I closed my eyes for a moment and tried to think of something happier. This time, my mind wandered to Ashton's nearly lifeless form. My whole body tensed and I clenched my teeth together to keep from reacting to the vision.

Celeste leaned into me, breaking my trance. "You okay?"

I nodded.

"You're lying." She took my hand in hers. "We're going to make it. We're going to save him. But right now, I need you to stay with me. Focus on what is happening now."

She was right. If I was distracted, it could cost us. Even

though it was a battle we were told we would win, there was still a possibility that fate could change. "You're right."

I cleared my throat, drawing all eyes to me. "We need a plan. We can't just attack a company of king's guards without one."

Three faces stared at me, waiting for what I'd say next. What should we do? How do four people take on an entire company? "Calder, I'm going to have you stay at the edge of town. Warn people to stay indoors and avoid the fight. Do whatever you need to do to keep them safe and away from the battle."

He frowned. "I can help, you've seen me fight."

I pursed my lips. "I know you can but this is a sorcerer fight."

He didn't look happy, but he nodded. "Alright."

"Dax, Celeste, I'm open to suggestions. What do you think?" I wasn't sure what Dax's strengths were or how the three of us could work together.

The rest of the wait went quickly as we discussed strategy and options for taking on the guards. Dax knew a lot about what we could expect from the guards as they entered the town. They were coming to send a message. His best guess was that they'd be focused on burning buildings and killing anybody who got in their way.

We had to stop them from reaching town.

As the sun neared the midpoint of the sky, we spotted the guards coming from the south. It was time.

WE MADE our way back down to the ground floor and headed right through the heart of town. The four of us walking through the busy main street drew quite a few head-turns but we were too focused to worry about the scene we caused.

Calder held back at the edge of town as Celeste, Dax, and I walked to meet the guards. The guards rode on horseback, easily a hundred in all, perhaps more. We stood our ground just outside of the town limits, waiting for them to approach. I let my hair hang loose around my face so I better matched the posters. Dax and Celeste stood on either side of me. They both wore an expression of calm. Three seemingly unarmed people standing outside of a town wouldn't do much to dissuade the guards. We were counting on them recognizing me.

As they approached, they began to slow down. They were apparently curious enough about us. One rider sped up, ahead of the others. He rode toward us as the others halted their progress. Stopping in front of me, he looked down from his horse, eyes narrowed. "You're the princess from the posters, aren't you?"

I lifted an eyebrow. "Am I?"

He seemed annoyed by my lack of information. "I'm afraid you'll have to come with me."

I laughed. "Come with you? I don't think so." Clasping my hands in front of me, I tilted my head from side to side, examining him. He wore the black leather armor of the King's Guards, the fiery red phoenix with its wings around a skull was emblazoned on his chest. He was likely muscular under his armor. Possibly a good fighter. Maybe that's why he was the leader. His angular jaw was tense as he stared back at me.

"I think you misunderstand what we are doing here," I said. "You see, I've come to give you a chance to leave safely. You and your men can turn around and leave now and no harm will come to you."

It was his turn to laugh. He laughed so hard, his whole body shook.

I could feel my cheeks burning.

"You are amusing, miss," he said. "I can see why the king would rather keep you alive. Come on, I'll even let you ride with one of the guards so you don't have to walk the whole way."

A smile crept back onto my face. "You have no idea what you just walked into."

Next to me, Celeste raised her arms in the air, building a shield around us. We were bathed in the shimmery cover before the guard realized what was going on.

His eyes widened and he turned his horse back toward his company. "They're sorcerers! Take them down. Try to keep the princess alive if you can. Archers, ready your bows!"

Arrows launched from the oncoming guards hit the shield and fell to the ground in front of us. Celeste didn't even look tired from the effort of holding the shield.

On my other side, Dax lifted and dropped his staff, then lowered himself into his sorcerers stance.

I focused my attention back on the horses racing toward us as I lowered myself into my own stance. They weren't shooting arrows anymore and I knew it was going to be my turn to strike soon.

The ground in front of us moved, rising and falling like waves in the ocean. Horses fell, trampling riders. Some ran off in the opposite direction, other continued to run forward, riderless. The ground continued to shift, dismounting nearly all of the guards. A few guards turned and rode away, apparently afraid of engaging us further.

"Drop the shield," I called. "Give me wind."

The shimmer faded from view and I focused on the sky. Using every ounce of energy I had, I called to the clouds. Celeste brought wind, making the clouds easier to manipulate. The sky darkened as gray clouds filled the previously blue sky.

The sounds of chaos from the guards intensified. I glanced from the sky to the men in front of me. There weren't any horses with riders coming for us anymore. They looked disconnected and confused.

My hands began to crackle with energy as I called to the

storm. I could feel it building. Rain started to fall in heavy drops, soaking us in seconds. I lifted my hands toward the sky, feeling for the power of the lightning I knew was there. Directing everything toward the guards, I called to the lightning, dropping my arms to my side in a single rapid movement.

As the lighting touched down, I turned away, momentarily blinded by the brightness. The hair on my arms stood on end. Turning back to the guards, I worked to catch my breath. *That better be enough.* I didn't have anything left, and I knew it. As the smoke cleared, I saw that any remaining guards were headed in the opposite direction.

A rush of relief rolled through me as I watched them leave. We'd done it. We'd won.

"We did it!" Celeste pulled me into a hug.

Dax looked tired, but he wore a smile. "The king won't be happy about this but it should keep them away for a while."

I pulled my hair into a quick knot at the base of my neck and turned toward town. I froze in my step, stomach full of knots. Standing at the edge of town, surrounding Calder were several hundred people. They were armed with whatever they could find. Axes, swords, daggers, rocks.

A cheer rose up from the people and they ran out to greet us. "Long live the queen!"

They were here to fight with me. They were going to fight back against the king's guards. The people were starting to stand up for themselves. Just like in Campari, they were willing to risk upsetting the king to join me.

Amidst the cheers and celebrations, we were swept into the city as people continued to chant. As the crowd made its way through the streets, people tore down the posters with my face on them. Like in Campari, they tore them up. The people of Luxor were no longer hiding their hate of the king.

THE CELEBRATION in Luxor continued as we ducked inside Dax's home. While we had been encouraged by many of the towns-people to stay and join in their revelry, my mind was focused on only one thing: saving Ashton.

Dax closed the door behind me. "Thank you for your help, Dax. We couldn't have done that without you."

"I'm happy I was here to help. Are you sure you have to leave again so quickly?" He set his staff against the wall.

"We have somebody counting on us," I said.

Kaylin walked into the room, hand resting on her belly. "Won't you at least take a day to clean up and get some rest before you run off again?"

"We don't have time." I looked at my companions. Calder was still wearing the blood of his dead wife. Celeste looked like she hadn't slept in weeks. Neither of them were complaining. I had asked so much from them on this journey but it was finally time to save Ashton. I didn't want to wait.

"It's only a few hours until sundown, surely you have time to rest," Dax said.

I looked at my friends. Neither of them said a word. I knew they'd support whatever decision I made. "We're already late."

Dax's forehead wrinkled and his brows pressed together. "You just used a lot of magic. If you're attacked on the road, you won't be able to defend yourself. You need at least a little time to rest."

I hesitated. I didn't want to put off getting to Delios any longer than we already had, but he did have a point. I turned to Celeste. "An hour?"

She nodded. "I am just as eager as you to get going, but he's right, we aren't in any shape to defend ourselves." She glanced toward Calder. "And at least one of us has to have a bath."

Calder looked at his hands and down at his clothes. "I suppose since I'm not dead yet, it wouldn't hurt."

Kaylin walked over to Calder. "I think Dax's clothes will fit you. I don't think you'll be able to get the blood out of these."

Calder's whole body tensed.

"Kaylin," I said. "Do you think maybe just the tunic could be saved? It's okay if not all the blood comes out."

Kaylin looked at me and a silent understanding passed between us. I'm sure she didn't know why it was important, but she knew that tunic meant a great deal to Calder. "Of course, I'll wash it with some salt, should clean up better that way."

"Thank you," Calder said.

Kaylin led him out of the room, presumably to somewhere he could find water.

Dax had been leaning against the wall and pushed himself to standing. "That magic took a lot from me. Don't ever quit practicing." He shook his head and walked toward the front door. "Come on, I'll take you to the inn. You can get cleaned up there while you wait for your friend."

Dax led us to a small inn a few doors down from his shop. The innkeeper was more than happy to fill some tubs for us. Celeste and I ended up in different rooms with a tub of water for each of us.

I didn't want to waste time with something so frivolous, but went ahead and washed up in the cool water, anyway. When I stepped out of the bath, the water was a murky brown.

Frowning, I put my dirty clothes back on and left the room. I tried to think of how much time we'd spent in town already. How was Ashton? Was he still waiting for us or had his essence given in and left our realm?

I waited in the hallway outside of Celeste's room. While I stood there, I tried to send my thoughts to Ashton. *Hang on, Ashton. We'll be there soon.*

Celeste's door opened and she stepped out, hair soaking wet, just like mine. As we silently walked down the stairs to the lobby of the inn, she worked it into a braid. My wet hair was piled on top of my head and tied in place with a ribbon I found in a pocket. The back of my neck was wet from the dripping hair.

"What's the plan?" Celeste walked next to me back to Dax's.

I wished Celeste had been to Delios so we could teleport directly there. We'd have to go to the nearest city that she had visited instead. I pictured the map of Illaria I had spent hours pouring over it with Sir Henry. The closest city to Delios was Greenville. "We should teleport to Greenville. We can find horses there and ride the rest of the way."

"Sounds good to me," she said.

I couldn't believe that after everything, I was going to end up in Greenville. What was it about that city?

Calder was waiting for us when we arrived. I was grateful that my friends had not taken their time getting cleaned and ready to go. We had probably been here less than an hour and we were ready to leave.

I didn't even greet Calder before I started in on our plans. "We have to teleport again. Should be easier this time."

Calder's face looked a little green at my news.

"Is there anything we can do for you before you leave?" Kaylin had been sitting at the table and stood.

"Kaylin, Dax, you two have done so much already. Thank you for your kindness." I smiled at each of our hosts. "And truly, if you need a place to go, you are welcome with the White Ravens."

"Thank you, your highness. If we need to leave Luxor, we'll look for you." Dax inclined his head.

"We should get going. Thank you, both." Celeste poured some of the black onyx powder on the floor, then moved on top of it. She reached her hands out to us. "Are you two ready?"

I clasped her hand in mine and gave her a squeeze so she knew I was ready.

"Thank you, again," I said to our hosts. "I'm sure we'll meet again. Take care of that future sorcerer."

Dax and Kaylin raised their hands to wave goodbye as the gray smoke spiraled around us, engulfing us in darkness as our feet left the ground.

27

G reenville was everything I expected it to be. In the chaos of the crowds, they didn't even notice three people tele-porting right inside the main gates.

The flow of traffic into and out of the city was like a current, pulling us deeper into the heart of the city. We passed street vendors with rows of fabric and children running in large groups.

The smell of unwashed people, horses, and unfamiliar food assaulted my senses. I thought Campari was large, but it had nothing on Greenville. How would we even find anything here? Our mission was to find horses so we could ride the rest of the way to Delios but I didn't even know where to begin our search.

Celeste bumped into me as she ducked away from an oncoming carriage. "It seems busier than the last time I was here." She had to almost yell for me to be able to hear her over the chatter of people, cries of shopkeepers, and rattle of carts.

"It's my first visit." I pulled the hood over my face as we passed a poster with my picture staring back at me. It was too warm for a hood, but I quickly noticed I wasn't the only one wearing something to cover my face. I had the feeling that there were a lot of people in Greenville who didn't want to be found.

"This way, I know where we can find some horses." Calder led us down a narrow alley way that took us away from the crowded and busy streets. It was quieter here and I felt my heart slow to a more normal rhythm.

"Have you been to Delios before?" I didn't know if an Oracle Tower was a place people would go see if they lived close enough.

"No." He turned, leading us down another alley way. "It's not a place people like to go. Delios is an ancient city. Nobody lives over there anymore. With the Oracle gone, there isn't much reason to go."

"How long will it take us to get there?" It took all my willpower to not look at the sun every few minutes to see how much time had passed since we left the Black Tower. How long had we been gone already? The days were starting to blend together. Despite the adrenaline pushing me onward, I was feeling tired. We'd have to rest eventually.

"It's probably a two-day ride." Calder stopped in front of a gray door and knocked.

My heart sank. *Two more days.* If only Celeste had been to Delios before, then we could teleport there. For a moment, I considered asking her to make a blind jump, then stopped myself. Master Flanders had warned of how dangerous it was to teleport to a new place.

We waited in silence for a moment before Calder knocked louder on the door. A rustling noise came from the other side, following by a loud crash. I took a few steps back and exchanged a nervous glance with Celeste.

The door opened to reveal a portly man with a red face. A stack of crates came pouring through the door. He jumped away, rubbing a spot on his elbow.

"I told you not to store things in front of this door." Calder smiled at the man.

"Cal?" The other man's face filled with a grin as he ushered us inside. He kicked the crates out of the way and shut the door behind us. "What are you doing here? You're a wanted man. They've had guards here looking for you." He narrowed his eyes at me. "She's wanted, too. Since when do you travel with royalty?"

"It's a long story, Holden. Right now, I just need to call in a favor," Calder said.

"You got it. What can I do?" Holden asked.

Calder lowered his voice. "We need horses and enough provisions for a two-day journey."

Holden stroked his chin with large fingers. "For a one-way trip?"

Calder nodded.

A half-smile rose on Holden's face. "You still have something against your father-in-law?"

Calder's expression darkened. "You have to ask?"

Holden looked at all of us standing there. "You three wait here. Give me an hour, two at most. I'll have your horses."

Holden walked through the dark curtain that separated the room we were standing in from whatever else was in the building. Calder sat on one of the overturned crates. Celeste and I sat across from him on crates of our own.

"How do you know Holden? Can we trust him?" I asked. The thought of waiting in a back room with no windows was making my insides squirm. If Holden went off to get the guards, we wouldn't have a chance.

"We can trust him. He wants nothing to do with the guards, trust me. He's got more secrets than all three of us combined." Calder rolled up the sleeves of his tunic. "We've known each other since we were kids. His parents died when he was a teenager. He had to find a way to take care of himself. If there's crime in Greenville, Holden is the center of it. He runs this city."

"And you think we can trust him?" I wasn't feeling as confident as Calder looked.

"I'd trust him with my life. His methods might not be legal, but he'll get the job done and he's loyal. Besides, he owes me."

I wanted to object again, when I realized that all of us in this little room were criminals. We were all on the run from the crown. There were wanted posters plastered in cities across Illaria with my face on them. Calder had killed members of the King's Guard, and so had I. How many members of the Ravens were on the wrong side of the law even before they joined our resistance group? If anything, the fact that he was a criminal should make me trust him even more. I was a criminal and all of my friends were, too. So much had changed in my life. I stifled a laugh.

"What's so funny?" Celeste asked.

"Just thinking about what my grandmother would have thought if I brought all of my new friends over for dinner." I imagined opening the door to let in Saffron, Ashton, Calder, and all of the other people I'd met over the last several weeks. "Grandmother, I'd like you to meet my friends, they're all hiding from the law, but they're really great people."

Celeste smiled and spoke in her best old-lady voice. "Nice to meet you. Can I hang up your weapons for you?"

I laughed louder, and covered my mouth with my hand to keep it in.

Calder shook his head. He was smiling. "You're going to draw too much attention to us back here."

"Sorry," I said, my face hurting from smiling.

"Where are we, exactly?" Celeste asked.

I looked around the dark room. It was piled with crates and smelled faintly of something old that I couldn't place.

"Holden runs a wool shop out front." Calder nodded toward the curtain.

"What did he mean about your father-in-law?" I asked.

Calder fidgeted on his crate. "Let's just say, we never got along. If it hadn't been for my family's money, he'd have shipped his daughter somewhere far away just to keep us apart."

"Does your family still live here?" I was curious about his life before the gallows. He'd looked so wild and dangerous when we met. It was hard to believe that he'd come from a wealthy upbringing.

"Some of them," Calder said. "I'll tell you about it one day, just not today."

"Sorry to pry," I said.

"It's fine." Calder smiled. "I know you mean well. I'm just not ready to dig into all of that yet."

As we waited, we tried to find things to talk about that wouldn't remind us of all the things we were sad about. We all had lost loved ones or were in danger of losing them. In the silences that filled the gaps of our conversations, my mind always wandered back to Ashton. Was he scared? Was he in pain? Was he still waiting for us?

It was during one of those silences that the curtain moved. Holden stepped into the room, a look of triumph on his face. "You three ready to get on the road? Three horses waiting in the back, compliments of Sir Magritte."

Calder stood and embraced his friend. "Thanks, Holden."

"Any time, my friend," Holden patted Calder on the back. "When you're done gallivanting around, I could use your help on something that would benefit from your delicate touch."

Calder glanced at me and cleared his throat before looking back at Holden. "I'll be back soon." Calder moved away from his friend.

Standing, I reached my hand toward him. "Thank you."

Holden shook my hand. "Good luck, your highness."

The three of us left through the door we had come in to find three horses complete with supplies, ready for us. Without waiting, we climbed on and rode out of the alley way back to the streets. After several minutes of winding through the crowds, the streets emptied. We were away from the marketplace and the cobblestone road turned to dirt.

"Come on," I called to my companions. "Let's get away from town." I picked up the pace, eager to be away from people who could recognize us and turn us in to the king.

The horses were well rested and traveled quickly down the dirt road. The further we got from town, the less frequent other buildings and people became. As the sun dipped lower in the sky, I felt exhaustion pulling at me. I couldn't keep fighting it. We had a long day and needed rest.

As we led the horses to a stream, I wished there was a way we could have teleported to Delios so we could get the stone and get back to Ashton faster. I didn't even want to think about what would have happened if we couldn't get as close as we had. Riding all the way here without teleporting would have taken weeks.

Celeste dug through the saddle bags and found three bedrolls and some food. We found a semi-flat area under some trees to take a break and eat before getting some sleep. "I'll take first watch."

"You two should sleep first," Calder said. "I've heard how using magic can make you tired. You both used magic today. I didn't."

Did I trust him enough to take watch while both Celeste and I slept? "What if something happens? It would be better to have one of us to fight."

Calder laughed. "No question about that. If something happens, I'm waking both of you up so you can defend me."

I looked at Celeste. She gave a nearly imperceptible shrug. She wasn't objecting. If I didn't trust Calder, I sure gave him lots of opportunities to hurt us over the last few days. He hadn't taken any of them. "Okay, but don't let us sleep too long."

"I'll wake you in a few hours," he said.

I scooted down into the bedroll and closed my eyes.

It was still dark when Calder shook me awake. I blinked a few times, wishing in my daze that I had asked for more than a few hours of sleep. Before I could say anything to him, he left.

I sat up and saw him waking Celeste. He wasn't supposed to wake us both. That meant something was wrong. I moved to my knees, suddenly alert. "What is it, Calder?"

"Not sure. Listen." He grew quiet.

I sat and listened in the dark, eyes scanning the trees around me. The moon was a sliver in the sky, not giving us much light. The leaves rustled in the wind. It was quiet, not even the sound of any nocturnal animals. Then I heard it, a dragging sound. The hair on my arms stood on end. That was not a normal nighttime sound.

28

MAX

Max walked into the still sleeping town. The streets were empty, the sky black. Footsteps behind him reminded him that he wasn't alone. He stopped walking. Nora caught up to him and stood next to him.

"You don't have to be here for this," he said.

"I want to."

"Are you here because your father asked you to be here?" Max wondered if King Osbert had sent her to make sure the job got done. It was clear from the moment the king had issued the order that Max was being tested yet again.

"I'm here because of you and me, we're in this together." She smiled at him.

Max stared at her. He was conflicted about Nora. Some days he couldn't stand her, other days he was looking forward to having her as his queen by his side. Today wasn't one of those days. For some reason, the thought of having her watch him murder everybody in an entire village all at once made him queasy. He'd become a monster and he hardly recognized himself anymore. Sometimes, he blamed her for it, other times he wanted to shelter her from it.

"You know what I have to do while I'm here." He took her hand in his and gave it a gentle squeeze.

"I know. I'm here to help you."

He shook his head. "No, I don't want this blood on your hands."

"It's a war, Max. There's going to be a lot more blood before we're done with this."

Max could feel the Darkness rising inside him, it twisted and turned, slithery tentacles of hate and anger filling his insides. Every time he did something like this for the king, the Darkness took a stronger hold on him. He was worried he'd lose control. Nora was already unpredictable. He didn't want to see what would happen to her if she added all of these deaths to her already long list of destructive deeds.

Max brushed her red hair away from her face and tried a softer approach. "Look, I can't do this if I'm worried about your safety. Why don't you go ahead to Delios. Start looking for the Astral Stone. I'll meet you there when I'm done here."

Agreeing, she placed her hand on the back of his head and pulled him in for a kiss. "I'll see you soon."

In a cloud of smoke, Nora left Max standing alone.

He took a deep breath, trying to prepare himself for what he had to do. As Max knew all too well, desperation made you do things you wouldn't normally do. The king wanted to scare Etta by sending the undead. He wanted to make her feel desperate. To do that, he needed bodies.

Max removed the pouch from his robes and untied it with trembling fingers. *You want this. You want to be king.* He worked to steady himself. Weren't sacrifices part of getting what you wanted? Wasn't this a war? Even if he wasn't in a battle, he was still fighting against the king. The king just didn't know it yet. *You won't have to be his errand boy for much longer.*

Max dumped the contents of the pouch into his open palm. Careful not to breathe in the dust, he called to wind, blowing the crushed substance into the sleeping town. A lump rose to his throat and he tried to push away the thoughts of the innocents who were about to take their last breaths.

29

J umping to my feet, I moved over by Celeste and whispered to her. "What do you think?"

"Not sure," she whispered. "Definitely something or someone out there."

Where had I heard a sound like that before? My heart was pounding. I was forgetting something. I should know this. My blood froze. It reminded me of the undead the king had summoned. They'd dragged their feet when they moved toward me. I'd seen her fight the undead and I'd seen how difficult it was to get them to stay down. "Celeste. What's the best way to kill the undead?"

"You don't kill them. They're already dead." Calder said.

"Yes and no," Celeste said. "You have to destroy their heart. Then they can't keep going. Fire is the most effective."

The horses started to whinny and stomp. They could sense the monsters heading our way.

"Is it me or does anybody else think that maybe we should just run?" Calder said.

"Calder's right." I bent down and grabbed my bedroll. "They don't move fast, we should go."

I shoved my bedroll into a saddle bag and mounted my horse. "Ready?"

"Yes," Celeste called.

"Me too," Calder said.

"Let's go." I pulled on the reins and led my horse back to the road in the dark. We rode as quickly as we could by the light of the moon. After a few minutes, I looked behind me. My shoulders relaxed when I saw the empty road. I was getting tired of always looking over my shoulder. Getting back to camp would be a welcome reward at the end of all of this. At least the wards over the camp kept us from being attacked without some warning.

We slowed down. Calder and Celeste rode on either side of me. I felt bad that Calder hadn't slept at all. The few hours I had snatched helped me feel like I could ride for another whole day.

"Do you think that really was the undead back there?" Calder asked. "Or was I being paranoid?"

"Doesn't matter," I said. "It wasn't worth staying to find out." If it really had been undead, how had the king found us? Did he have a trap waiting the whole time or was he following us?

As if reading my mind, Celeste spoke. "Do you think it was coincidence? Or a trap set in case we went that way?"

"I wish I knew," I said. "All I know is that I want to get this stone and get back to Ashton as quickly as we can."

"Agreed," Celeste said. "Calder? Are you going to be alright to ride? Do we need to stop?"

"I couldn't sleep if I wanted to," he said. "The idea of undead soldiers after us will keep me awake for months."

"I think there's a town ahead," Celeste said. "We should try to get past it before dawn so we don't draw attention to ourselves."

We picked up the pace again and rode in silence as the black sky began to lighten. Dawn was indeed approaching. Calder had let us sleep longer than he should have. I glanced at him from time to time, worried he'd fall asleep on his horse, but he didn't look even the slightest bit tired.

Buildings and homes grew in frequency as we neared the town. We slowed down and moved to single file as the road narrowed. The entire town would only take minutes to ride through. It wasn't much larger than the village I'd grown up in.

The sky was streaked with pink and orange as the sun began its ascent. People would be moving about the town soon. I looked at the buildings as we rode through. There were no signs of life. My stomach twisted as I remembered riding through Redding, the town empty of all people. I hoped this town was full of sleeping people and that it hadn't been emptied by the king. Part of me wanted to knock on a door, just to see if anybody was home, but we didn't have time for that right now.

We rode past the edge of town and the knots in my stomach began to loosen. Maybe it was all in my head. It was still early and there was no reason for people to be out and about before the shops even opened for the day.

My companions moved up next to me as the road widened. We rode until the sun was fully risen, then stopped to take a break and rest the horses. Calder's eyes were bloodshot and he looked paler than usual. He needed a break.

"Would it be safer to rest during the day and ride at night?" I asked.

Celeste looked from me to Calder. "I think that's a good idea, perhaps just a few hours?"

"Please, don't do this for me. I'm fine," Calder said.

I shook my head. "You're not fine. You need to sleep."

Calder didn't look convinced, but he unpacked his bedroll and settled down on the ground. Celeste and I tended to the horses and he was asleep before we finished.

Celeste settled on the ground next to Calder. I watched as

she traced designs into the dirt with a stick. I sat down next to her and closed my eyes, feeling the gentle breeze on my face.

Crack.

The snap of a twig brought me to my feet. Celeste stood next to me. We both spun toward the direction of the sound.

The trees around us were suddenly filled with noise. This was not the same slow, dragging noises we had heard yesterday. Whatever this was, it was moving much faster. The horses started stomping their hooves on the ground and tried to pull away from their secured positions.

"What's going on?" Calder stood next to us, apparently woken by the horses.

I spread my fingers at my sides, feeling the tingle of magic growing inside. "Get behind us, Calder."

Next to me, Celeste struck her sorcerer's stance and I followed her example. I took a deep breath in as I felt the blue sparks of my arctic fire begin to surface on my palms.

With a roar, a mass of people broke through the trees. Young, old, men, women. They all had the same pale gray flesh of the undead I saw outside the king's castle. Fire was our best defense. *What I wouldn't give to have Ashton with us right now.*

A rush of wind blew past me, knocking back some of the charging figures. Celeste was calling the wind. I concentrated as best I could as more undead approached us. Reaching inside, I called to fire. Maybe this time, I could make it happen, and perhaps Celeste could help me make it stronger.

The blue sparks in my palms gave way to orange flames. I jumped in surprise and my heart leapt. They were nothing compared to what I'd seen from fire sorcerers, but it was all we had and I had made it. "Celeste, help me."

She nodded and placed her hands behind mine, giving me wind to grow the flames. It wasn't enough. The flames stayed contained to my hands. "We need more fire! I can't do it! I'm not strong enough."

Wind blew past me. Celeste was doing everything she could to keep the creatures from reaching us. Her wind knocked them off track, but they regrouped quickly.

"Here!" Calder was standing next to me. He had several large branches in his hand. He'd wrapped cloth around the tops. "I dipped them in oil. Light them."

I raised my hands, using my small flames to light the cloth on fire. They reacted quickly to the oil and Calder held two flaming torches in his hands. He handed one to me and we started to wave them at the monsters approaching us. They stepped back from the fire.

"Light the ground," Celeste said. "It's covered in dry leaves. It'll go up in minutes."

"Set the whole forest on fire? Are you crazy?" I shouted.

"Do you want them coming after us? You know fire is the only way." She stood there with small flames of her own in each palm. "Do it, Etta."

Calder stood frozen with the torch extended in front of him. He was waiting for my decision. One of the undead rushed at me, wrapping ice cold arms around my throat and dragging me to the ground. I dropped the torch in my hand.

I shoved my elbow into the monster's stomach and it gripped me even tighter. Calder wrapped his arm around the creature's head and pulled backward. I heard a sickening crack as the head broke away from the body, dangling limp from the neck like a flower that had been almost completely broken from its stem.

Despite the fact that the head was no longer attached to the body, the undead woman kept squeezing around my neck. Calder locked his arm around her waist and pulled her away, dragging me with her. I lurched forward and fell on top of the creature. The fall was enough to finally break her grip on my neck.

I pushed myself off of her and called to the fire again, managing a small flame. Not taking any chances, I placed my hand directly on the dead woman's chest. She caught on fire, not even uttering a cry of pain as the flames consumed her.

My fallen torch had already started a fire nearby. These creatures were not going to stop. "Burn the whole thing."

Calder threw his torch at the oncoming creatures and Celeste lit a few patches of dry leaves with the flames in her palms. Black smoke rose quickly from the damp areas under the dry leaves and the flames devoured the forest floor.

Our horses were in a panic at this point. It took every ounce of my strength to hold on to my mare as she tried to throw me. Once I untied the restraints, she couldn't run fast enough.

We rode for hours, afraid to stop, afraid to look back. All I wanted to do was find the stone and get back to Ashton. I was done with adventures. The king wasn't coming after me himself, he hadn't sent Reapers, but I would almost rather face off with him than the undead. He kept saying he wanted me alive. Why had the king sent the undead after me? *He's trying to scare you.* A chill ran through me. All those people had been killed to send me a message. He wasn't going to stop hurting people until I gave him what he wanted, but I would never join him. The only way this would stop was if I made him stop. When I returned to the Raven camp, I would find a way to earn their trust. We had to work together to save Illaria.

I risked a glance behind me. The smoke from the fire was like a signal to the whole world of where we had been. I didn't think I'd ever get the smell out of my nose. Had we done more harm than good? I thought of those people who had been turned into undead soldiers. The king would have continued to control them until somebody could destroy their heart. They might have served him in their death for years.

"Celeste, Calder, promise me something."

My friends turned to look at me.

"If the king ever turns me into an undead soldier, kill me." I don't want to live like that, or rather, die like that. I never want to be controlled by anyone.

"Same here," Celeste said. "We did those people a favor, Etta."

"I say we make a pact," Calder said. "If any of us goes down, we make sure the king can't bring us back."

There was a reason that the dead were burned in Illaria. What used to be a funeral reserved for warriors had become the norm. Nobody wanted to be brought back after their death. "I'm in. If any of us fall, we give that person a warrior's funeral." I was going to say more, but the sight in front of me caused me to pull up on the reins and stop to stare.

A cloud of black smoke that looked like the one behind us rose from the earth. It was coming from Delios.

30

The three of us exchanged worried glances. I was the first to regain the ability to speak. "How fast can we ride?"

"Only one way to find out," Celeste said.

I pulled back on the reins and headed toward the smoke, toward Delios. What would I do if the stone was already gone? Were we riding into a trap?

My shoulders tensed at the thought. I slowed my horse down and let my friends catch up to me. They rode on either side of me. My breathing was fast, heart pounding. After taking a moment to catch my breath, I looked at each of them. "This could be a trap, neither of you have to come with me. You can stay behind or go back."

Celeste looked determined. "You know my answer, Etta."

"I'm with you, your highness," Calder said.

I glanced behind. The sun was dipping low in the horizon. "It will be dark when we arrive."

"So we lose the horses and sneak in under the cover of night. Sounds perfect," Celeste said.

"This one's smart," Calder said. "We're teleporting back, right?"

"Yes. Okay, so that's the plan. We get into Delios, as soon as possible, we send the horses away and we get to that tower." I took a deep breath. "We get that stone, and we save Ashton."

"Let's do it," Celeste said.

This is going to work. I set my jaw and squeezed my legs around my horse. We were so close to saving Ashton. *As long as the stone is still there, we'll find it.*

The smoke grew stronger as we neared Delios. My chest burned from breathing in the fumes. I rubbed watery eyes and focused on maintaining my pace to get there as quickly as possible.

As evening set in, the stars were shrouded by smoke and we rode under an inky black sky. The extra light would have been helpful but the road was pretty clear so we were able to continue, though slower than we would have liked.

Delios was abandoned so homes or shops sat vacant. No candles in windows, no fireplaces in hearths. Again, I missed Ashton's fire. He could have created one of his floating fire orbs for us. I wondered if Celeste could create one that would be strong enough to follow us, then thought better of it. Calling more attention to ourselves wasn't a good idea if we were riding into a trap.

We rode by some broken cabins and crumbling fences. This must be the outskirts of town. In the darkness, I couldn't see the Black Tower that was supposed to dominate the city, but we had to be close.

"It might be time to walk," I said, pulling back on the reins. I coughed. Though we couldn't see the smoke in the dark, I could tell it was getting stronger.

After checking the bags for anything we could use on the last part of our trip, we said goodbye to our horses. They rode away from us pretty quickly. I don't think they wanted to continue.

Our footsteps were silent on the soft dirt road as we walked.

Buildings grew closer together and larger as we approached. It was eerie to walk though yet another abandoned town. Was Illaria full of cities that were inhabited by ghosts?

There were no side roads. Everything was on this one road. I wondered what it used to look like and what happened to the people who had called this place home.

"The Oracle said the tower was at the center of town, right?" Calder said.

"I think so." I looked away from a temple with a large dome to Calder. He had stopped moving. "Why?"

He pointed ahead. "I think we found it."

In front of us was a smoking pile of bricks. Panic surged through me. I ran ahead without thinking.

"Etta, wait!" Celeste cried.

I ignored her. My heartbeat pounded in my ears, my stomach was twisted in knots. *This can't be the tower.* If the tower was gone, how would we find the stone? Was it still here, buried in the rubble or was it gone?

When I reached the brick, I fell to my knees. In the dark it was harder to see details, but it looked just like the brick from the other tower. Hoping for more success, I called fire. It came easier this time, and I was able to make a small orb of flames in my palm, lighting the scene. It was the tower. At least it used to be.

I forced myself to stand and walked in a circle around the destroyed building. There were places where the brick was still smoking from the fire that had been used on it. Whoever had brought this building down had done it today. We were so close. If we hadn't gone to Luxor, we'd have made it in time. I clenched my teeth. We'd wasted too much time. Ashton's life was on the line and I'd chosen strangers over him.

Celeste put her hand on my shoulder. "We could still find it here, Etta. The king might not have taken the stone."

I shook my head. "How do we find such a small thing in this big pile of mess?"

Celeste dropped her hand. "There are ways. Master Flanders had you working on summoning spells for weeks."

A flicker of hope rose up inside me. A summoning spell. We could bring the stone to us. "Calder."

He ran over to us. "What can I do to help?"

"Think you can be on watch?" I asked. "We won't be able to pay attention to what's going on around us while we work. If you hear or see anything suspicious, let us know."

"I can do that." He turned and took a few steps away from us and stood, looking out into the dark.

"How do we summon something when we don't know exactly what it looks like?" I asked.

Celeste had already taken her sorcerer stance. "Well, it was white when Master Flanders told us about it, but I think it's more important to focus on the meaning of the object. Think of the essence of the stone. Think of the purpose of it, what it can do. Reach out to anything magical. It's probably the only magical item here."

My throat was dry and sore from the smoke. I licked my lips and swallowed. If that stone was still here, we had to find it. This was not going to be easy for me. I had just recently learned summoning spells and while I had success with them, it had been for specific items that were nearby. Taking a deep breath, I closed my eyes and thought about the stone. It was a stone that allowed a person to leave their body. It had magical properties from a sorcerer who had been trapped inside. I wrinkled my nose. The thought of using a stone that contained the essence of another sorcerer made me uncomfortable. But I'd do it. I needed to save Ashton. I'd do whatever it took.

Reaching out with my magic, I tried to feel for anything that felt like it contained power, anything that spoke to me. After several minutes, I opened my eyes and shook out my hands. I wasn't having any luck.

Celeste was standing with her eyes closed, unmoving. She was in her own world. I watched her for a minute before returning to my own stance. Closing my eyes again, I thought about what I would do with that stone. I would use it to save Ashton. Could anything else be done with it? Maybe that wasn't a strong enough idea. I pictured me holding a white stone and guiding Ashton's essence back to his body. I imagined him waking up. Something pulled inside me and my heart began to race. My eyes snapped open and the feeling vanished. I cursed. *So close.* There is something magical out there, waiting for us to find.

Taking a deep breath through my nose, I dropped into my stance again, and repeated the process. Again, I felt the pulling sensation, but couldn't quite get hold of it. I opened my eyes and stepped closer to Celeste. She was still focused. Her hands were loose at her sides. I clasped her hand in mine and closed my eyes. Instead of focusing on finding the stone myself, I poured all of my energy into Celeste. I imagined all of my magic traveling through my body and into my fingers. My fingers tingled and I pushed that sensation into Celeste's hand. She needed the extra magic. If we worked together, maybe she could latch on to the source and summon the stone.

Celeste gripped my fingers, squeezing so hard I was losing feeling. I fought against the pain and continued to send my magic into her. She stumbled backward, letting go of my hand. I opened my eyes to see her on the ground, breathing heavily.

I dropped to my knees next to her. "Are you okay?"

She looked up, a smile on her face. She raised her hand and sitting in her palm was a smooth, shiny stone on a gold chain. In the dim light of the fire, the stone looked almost silver. This had to be the Astral Stone. I could feel the magic radiating from it. I pulled her into a hug. "We found it!"

Calder ran over to us, joining us in a group hug on the ground.

I wiped tears of joy away from my eyes. We were going to save Ashton.

CELESTE GRASPED the key the Oracle gave us and reached out a hand to me and Calder. "Ready?"

I pulled the gold chain of the newfound stone over my neck and clasped her hand. "I'm ready. Calder?"

"I've never been more ready to leave a place."

I knew what he was feeling. The crumbled tower and the abandoned town were something from a nightmare. Even without Ashton's life on the line, I'd be eager to leave.

"Hang on, you two." Celeste squeezed my hand as a cloud of gray smoke began to rise around our feet. I held my breath and squeezed my eyes closed. Ashton's smiling face filled my thoughts. He'd be safe soon. I smiled as I felt my feet leave the ground.

We landed hard on the stone floor of the Oracle's tower. As the smoke cleared, I looked around the circular room. It was the same as we had left it. "Hello? Oracle?"

A soft rustling sound behind me drew my attention toward the ladder that went to her loft. She descended, bare feet padding across the stone. "Welcome back."

A thump next to me caused me to jump and I turned. Calder was on the ground, all color drained from his face. "Calder!" I dropped down next to him. "What's wrong?"

"I'm fine," he said through gritted teeth. "Just hurt my leg when we were fighting the undead. I just need some rest."

I looked down at his legs and noticed a large tear across his trousers. The dark fabric and the night sky had masked the fact that they were soaked in blood.

Celeste was next to him now and she rolled up the fabric to reveal a large gash across his leg. His thigh and calf were smeared with blood. "Calder, how have you been riding with this? Why didn't you tell us?"

"I'm sure it looks worse than it really is. I hardly felt it," he said.

Celeste shook her head. She tore the trouser from his leg and wrapped it around the wound. "We need to do better than this, but I need to stop the bleeding first."

"Don't worry about me. We did this to get that stone to save Ashton. I'm going to live. Do what you need to do." Calder tried to stand up.

In the short time he'd been with us, he'd earned his place in my little circle of friends and it hurt me to see him in pain. I put my hand on his shoulder. "Stay here. Celeste will take care of you."

Celeste nodded. "Talk to the Oracle, find out how to use the stone."

I kissed Calder on the top of his head, then stood up and walked over to the Oracle. "We found it." I pulled the stone from around my neck and held it out to her.

She reached for the stone and took it from me. Her expression hardened and she pressed her lips into a tight line. "Where did you find this?"

"At the Black Tower in Delios, at least what was left of it. It was destroyed when we arrived. We had to summon the stone to find it."

Her brow furrowed. "Destroyed?"

I nodded. "It was smoking ruins when we arrived."

"I didn't see that coming." She sighed. "It's already happening."

"What? What's happening?" Her worried expression made me nervous.

"The Darkness is clouding my visions. Oracles have always struggled to see what happens when Dark Magic is used, but when a sorcerer channels the Darkness, it's impossible to see." She passed the stone back to me.

I held it in my hand and looked down at the shiny metallic surface. I knew the Darkness was something I should be worried about, but right now all I wanted was to take care of Ashton. "I'm sorry about the tower."

"It's not the tower I'm concerned about," she said. "It's the fact that you have the wrong stone."

31

I felt like I had been punched in the stomach. A buzzing sound filled my ears, and for a moment, I lost touch of what was happening around me. *This can't be.* I opened my mouth to speak, then closed it again. My body began to tremble, it was as if everything good in the world had been ripped away from me.

"No." I shook my head and held the stone up to her. "This has to be it. It's magic. It was at the tower. How can it be the wrong stone?"

"I'm sorry," the Oracle said. "Whoever destroyed the tower must have taken the stone you needed. I didn't realize this one was being stored there, too."

"What am I supposed to do with a useless silver rock?" My voice got louder with each word. She'd sent me to get the stone. She'd told me it was there. But she had warned me that if I stopped to save Luxor, I was risking not getting there in time. I didn't think she meant I wouldn't find the stone. In the back of my mind, I kept thinking I could do both. I wasn't ready to accept that I was actually going to lose him.

I struggled to breathe. It was as if the world stopped, frozen in that moment. Numbness filled my body and my mind raced. I couldn't pin down any single feeling or expression. I could barely keep myself from collapsing to the ground in a heap.

If I couldn't save Ashton, what was the point? A wave of anger rose inside me and I welcomed the sensation. It felt better to be angry.

"I sacrificed Ashton for nothing." My hand made a fist around the useless stone.

The Oracle took a step toward me. I stepped back, nearly running into Calder. My whole body felt like it was vibrating. I had never felt anger like this before.

"You misunderstand." The Oracle stopped moving. "That stone in your hand, it's the one the Oracles never knew the location of. It's been lost for a long time." She placed her hand on top of my closed fist, easing open my fingers. "Etta, you found the Dragon Stone."

I blinked at her, trying to process what she had said. "The Dragon Stone?"

She nodded. "It is possibly the most powerful of all the stones if you can learn to wield it. This changes everything."

My hands fell to my side, the stone falling to the ground. I didn't care about power right now. I wanted Ashton. If this stone couldn't save him, it didn't have any use to me. "You keep it. I don't care." I walked toward the fireplace, running my hands through my hair. *What am I supposed to do now? Do I sit here and wait for Ashton's essence to go to the Astral Realm? Do I start planning a funeral for him?* A lump rose in my throat. More than anything, I hated feeling helpless. What was the point of having magic, of having power, if you couldn't use it to save the person you loved?

Celeste was standing next to me now. She bent down and picked up the stone. "Etta, I'm so sorry."

I turned away from her, not wanting to look at her right now. She was the one who had told me to go to Luxor. She was the one who convinced me to save the people over Ashton. She set a hand on my shoulder and I shrugged it away. I didn't want comfort right now.

"There has to be another way," Celeste said. I could hear the pain in her voice. The anger eased a bit as I remembered that she'd known Ashton longer than me. They'd been friends a long time. She was probably feeling just as heartbroken as I was right now.

I looked over at her and saw that her eyes were filled with tears. A lump rose in my throat at the sight.

"There may be a way," the Oracle said.

Calder cried out in pain behind us. I glanced at him and saw that he was trying to clean his wound himself.

Celeste put her hand on my shoulder again. This time, I let her. Her jaw was set in a determined look. "I'm going to take care of Calder, you figure out how to fix Ashton."

I nodded and stepped over to the Oracle. She spoke quietly, words meant just for my ears. "There may be another way, but it's a risk. It could fail and leave you both stranded apart from your bodies."

I turned away from the fire, face to face with the Oracle. "Show me." If there was a way to save him, I'd do it. The risk didn't matter. How could I go the rest of my life knowing I might have been able to save him but I'd put my own life before his? I'd already put the lives of strangers before his.

"If you do this, there's no going back." Her face was grim. It looked like the words pained her.

I stared at her, unblinking. "You know something about what's going to happen, don't you?"

She frowned. "I know many things, Etta. The path you take right now, the choice you make, could have dire consequences in Illaria. Not just for you, but for the whole kingdom."

"What does that mean?" I covered my face with my hands

and rested them over my mouth. Her words were confusing and frustrating. My vision blurred as tears formed. I wasn't sure I wanted to hear any more. I didn't want to sacrifice Ashton. I wanted to be selfish. I wanted him back with me.

"Please." My words came out choked. "Can I save him and save Illaria? I don't know what I'd do without him."

She looked down at her bare feet, then back up to me. "If you go this route, it will make things harder for you. But in the end, Illaria will be stronger for it."

I blinked back the tears. For the first time, her words sounded hopeful. I could work hard if it meant saving my home and the man I loved. "That doesn't sound so bad."

"Are you sure?" she asked. Her face had returned to its impassive expression. She wasn't going to give me any more information.

There was no choice. I wasn't going to give up on Ashton. "I have to try. You don't know how much he means to me, please. Tell me what I have to do."

She sighed. "I was in love once, too. I took the easy way out. I've regretted that every day of my immortal life. It haunts me."

My shoulders dropped as a wave of sympathy rolled though me. What would it be like to live beyond all of your loved ones? The Oracle lived here alone for far too long. She had probably seen more than any other person in the whole world.

"Come with me." She walked toward the ladder and I followed.

I didn't say a word to my friends as I climbed to the loft but I felt their worried stares on my back. I didn't want them to talk me out of doing something that put my life at risk.

The loft was bathed in a warm glow from candles hovering around the room. They floated at varying heights, casting unusual shadows against the walls. The Oracle held an interesting mix of magic to be able to enchant objects like that. My eyes traveled the room, looking at the large space. It was cluttered with shelves full of objects, bottles, and jars. It reminded me of an apothecary.

The Oracle stopped in front of one of the shelves. "Are you sure you're up for this?"

"I don't care what it is. I'll do anything."

She took a deep breath. "What I'm about to show you is considered Dark Magic. It's against guild law. If anybody finds out you did this, you'll never be granted permission to practice magic within the guild. If you do, you'll be an outlaw."

"If anybody finds out?"

She nodded. "This is not something you enter in lightly. Using Dark Magic always comes with risks. It leaves its mark on your essence. It will follow you until you die. You will be changed in a way we can't predict. If you survive."

"What do you mean, changed?" I asked.

The Oracle shook her head. "There's no way to know for sure. It takes different forms on every sorcerer."

If I did this, there was no turning back. Nobody could ever know. I bit down on the inside of my cheek. I knew using Dark Magic was forbidden. I knew the guild took rule breakers very seriously. Technically, I wasn't even able to practice magic on my own unless it was life or death since I had yet to pass my trial. Then there was the change to consider. I didn't linger on the decision long. If a dark mark on my essence was the cost of Ashton's life, I would pay it.

"And Ashton? What will happen to him?" I wanted him back with me, but I wanted the Ashton I loved. I didn't want an undead version like the king controlled. It was only worth it if I could bring back *my* Ashton.

"It's possible there will be a side effect on him, but he won't be touched by the Dark Magic the way you will. He won't have to know." She stood. "Do you want to do this?"

"It'll bring his essence back?" I said.

She nodded.

I thought back to when I had last seen Ashton. He was so pale. It didn't look like there was much life left in him. If he was still alive, it was now or never. I wasn't an expert on magic, but I had a feeling he didn't have much time left. If there was a way to bring him back, I had to do it. "I'm ready."

The Oracle turned to the shelf and pushed around some vials and bottles. She opened a small box and removed something. When she turned around, she held an ornate silver vial with a purple jewel on it. Inside the vial was a dark liquid. I wrinkled my nose at the cloudy substance. "What is this?"

"It's Belladonna root."

"Nightshade?" I had learned to avoid the deadly berries from this plant as a child, but also knew that the apothecary sometimes used them in recipes for certain medicines. You had to be careful when working with it. I wasn't sure about the roots.

The Oracle handed me the bottle. "It's the most poisonous part of the plant."

My stomach twisted. I had a feeling I knew what she wanted me to do with this. I tilted it slightly, watching the mud colored liquid move around the vial.

"You'll need to bring yourself to the brink of death so you can reach the astral state without the stone. As I said, it's risky."

Purposefully ingesting poison was a risk but it didn't seem on par with raising the dead. I wasn't doing anything to hurt anybody else. "How is this considered Dark Magic?"

She handed me a black ribbon I hadn't noticed her holding before. "It's not the poison part that is using dark magic, it's the part where you bring yourself back. To ensure that you won't die, you have to cast a spell on yourself to grant a second life. You're going to be cheating death."

"I thought Dark Magic was only the magic where you were

removing somebody's free will?" I wasn't sure how preventing my own death applied.

"This is more than that," she said. "You're going against the will of the gods. It's the darkest kind of magic there is. Second only to bringing back the dead."

I swallowed. Doing this would put me close to the same category as the king. I stared at the vial in my hands and thought of Ashton. There was no going back now. I was going to do whatever it took. "What do I do?"

She wrapped the black ribbon around my right hand. "You'll need to channel the astral realm. You have to reach out to the depths of yourself. Find the darkest area of your mind. When you reach that place, you have to hold on to it while you drink the Belladonna. If you don't hold on to it, you'll die. If you are successful, your essence will leave your body and you'll have a few minutes to find Ashton before your body calls your essence back. You have to get him back to his body before your essence goes back to your body." She paused. "Etta, if you don't get back to your body in time, you will remain in the Astral Realm forever."

There were so many ways this could go wrong. Her directions weren't very specific. I could die before I even left my body. And if I was successful, I could still fail to find Ashton's essence and return it in time. I took a deep breath. The only option was to not fail.

32

I closed my fingers around the ornate bottle and looked up at the Oracle. "Come back with us. You don't have to stay here alone."

She shook her head. "I can't leave."

"Why not?"

"I'm bound to this place by the king. Only the ruler of Illaria can give me permission to leave." She folded her hands in front of her, an unreadable expression on her face.

"Do you want to leave? You must miss your father."

For a split second, darkness crossed her expression, before it returned to normal. I couldn't tell if I had really seen the subtle change.

"I don't even know my father. He had me sent to the tower when I was four years old. Until another from my family line comes to replace me or the king grants me leave, I'm to remain here, bound to the tower."

I felt guilty coming here to get help and then leaving her alone. "Is there anything I can do to repay your kindness? Can I release you when I re-claim the throne?"

She smiled. "You have done enough. We'll meet again. But

now, the time has come for you to return to your friend. Send your injured friend away for help and ask Celeste to keep guard for you while you perform the spell. You don't want anybody there while you are working."

I swallowed hard. The bottle in my closed fingers was feeling heavier by the second. "Is Ashton going to be okay?"

Her gaze softened. "I can't tell you that. Even if I wanted to, the results are too muddled when Dark Magic is used."

I took a deep breath. It was time to go. Finally time to save Ashton. Everything we'd been thorough had been leading up to this. I just wished they had gone according to plan. I smiled at the Oracle. "Thank you, for everything."

I climbed down the ladder where Calder and Celeste were waiting for me. He'd gotten worse while I had been upstairs. I walked over to them.

Celeste pulled me aside. "He lost quite a bit of blood, but I got it stopped. I think it's going to be alright." She lowered her voice to a whisper. "Did you figure out a way to save him?"

I nodded, unable to fake a smile to reassure her. She seemed to understand that whatever I was going to do was not something I wanted to talk about.

The Oracle came down the steps with a jar in her hand. She passed it to Celeste. "For your friend, this will help prevent infection."

Celeste took the jar. "Thank you."

The Oracle stepped back. "You three better go, time is running out."

My stomach twisted into knots at her words. "Celeste, you still have the coin from Master Flanders?"

She dug into her pocket and pulled out a red coin. Without one of those, we couldn't teleport directly inside the ward of the Raven camp. My anxiety eased a little at the sight of the coin. It would make getting back almost effortless.

Calder winced as he tried to stand on both legs and limped over to where we were standing.

"We'll get you help as soon as we're back at our camp," I said.

"Remind me not to volunteer next time." He was pale but at least his spirits were good.

Celeste grabbed hold of each of our hands. "Ready?"

"Ready." I nodded to the Oracle as gray smoke rose from the ground, swallowing us. We were going back home.

The portal coin took us right outside of Master Flanders tent. I shouldn't have been surprised. It was nearing sunrise, the camp wouldn't stay quiet for long. For now, I was grateful that we had a reprieve from prying eyes. We'd have enough questions to answer as soon as everybody woke.

Celeste and I helped Calder to the entrance of the tent. I peeked inside. "Master Flanders?" The tent was empty.

"Come on," I said. "Let's get Calder in here and then we can find Master Flanders."

My mind was racing. Every so often I felt for the vial that I had tucked into my pocket to make sure it was still there. As we went through the motions of getting Calder situated on a chair, I barely registered what was happening. All I could think about was getting to Ashton and what I would have to do when I did.

"Calder, we're going to find Master Flanders and send him to you. He'll take good care of you," I said.

"I'm fine. Go, already. Save your love," he said.

I smiled. "I will."

Celeste and I ran from Master Flanders' tent to the barn as quickly as we could. We didn't pass anybody as we darted between tents and through the common area. As we reached the barn, I saw light glowing through the holes in the walls.

We slid open the large, rotting door and saw Master Flanders sitting on a chair near the front. His eyes were closed and he was breathing slowly. Gently, I shook him awake.

He rubbed his eyes and smiled when he saw us. "You're back."

I nodded. "Yes, and we made a new friend who needs your help."

"Here." Celeste handed him the jar of salve the Oracle had given her. "The Oracle said to use this. Can you fix him? He's in your tent."

Master Flanders stood, taking the jar from Celeste. "Did Delphina explain how to return his essence?"

I nodded.

"Find me when it's done." Master Flanders left without another word.

As soon as he was out the door, Celeste turned to me. "What do you need from me?"

"Stand guard. Nobody comes in here," I said.

She nodded then walked through the door, sliding it shut behind her.

My eyes traveled the room, looking for the only thing I cared about. I found him lying on a bed behind the large table in the center of the room. He looked just as pale as he had when I left him.

Tears threatened as I ran to Ashton. Dropping to my knees, I rested my hand on his chest, feeling for breath. The rise and fall was subtle, but it was there. He was still breathing. I pushed the hair from his forehead and kissed him. His lips were cold. "I'm here, Ashton. Don't worry, I'm going to save you. We're going to be together again."

Thinking back to the Oracle's directions, I dug the black ribbon from my pocket. When I reached for the bottle in my other pocket, I took a quick glance at it. If I stopped to think about what I was going to do, I might lose my nerve. I had to do this. I leaned over Ashton's still body and kissed his forehead. Then, I sat back and closed my eyes. I cleared my mind, emptying it of all thoughts, ignoring my fears, quieting that little voice that questioned everything. I had to find the darkest place, the place where I could go to cheat death itself. Memories popped up in my head that I didn't recognize. Fire, screams, flashes of faces from people I didn't know. I pushed them away, searching for the darkness inside me. How was I supposed to get there?

A face came into view, lifeless eyes staring up at me from a puddle of blood. It was the guard I'd killed accidentally. My heart beat faster as I fought against the memory. I didn't like the way it made me feel. Then, I felt the cold steel of a blade against my throat as the memory of Patrick threatening me came crashing into view. The incident seemed to play through my mind at lightning speed and suddenly, I was looking at his dead body. And I was happy. I wanted him dead. The feeling caught me off guard, but I held on to it. It was pure anger. Hatred. Everything dark about me coming out at once. I pushed through the discomfort, until I reached a place where all I could see was darkness. I'd found it.

I allowed myself to take a deep breath before I pulled the stopper from the vial. *Here goes nothing.* I tossed the contents back, grimacing as I swallowed the surprisingly sweet liquid. For a moment, nothing happened. Opening my eyes, I realized I'd never even questioned the Oracle's directions. I was so desperate to save Ashton, I'd believed her without doubt.

In front of me, Ashton's breaths turned raspy. He was struggling to hang on. I tried to speak, I wanted to yell out to him, but it was as if I couldn't remember how to form words. My head felt heavy. Ashton's form blurred, giving him the impression of having three heads. I tried to focus on him, but couldn't concentrate. My eyes felt heavy and he blinked in and out of my view. Toppling forward, I landed with my head on his bed.

The world around me was colored in shades of brown. All

other colors were missing. My dark curls were a tangled mess on the back of my head. My breath caught in my chest. I wasn't in my own body anymore. I was looking down at myself, passed out on Ashton's bed. I turned in a slow circle, taking in the room. The dingy wood turned a murky brown. The ground under me seemed uneven. Everything was different. I stretched my hands out in front of me. My fingers were transparent. I could see right through them. I couldn't feel my heart beating or the rise of my chest. I wasn't breathing. My essence was functioning outside of my body.

Knowing I didn't have long, I began to feel panic rise. I never asked how I would find Ashton's essence. "Ashton?" My voice sounded distant, different than I was used to, but it was still there. I leaned over his body, hoping I could get a clue from his prone form. Nothing.

I walked around the barn, calling out Ashton's name. How was I supposed to find him? Moving around the room, I realized that I didn't need to walk. I could float. Out of the corner of my eye, I caught a glimpse of something. I spun around to see a ghostly form near the ladder to the old hayloft. "Ashton!"

He turned, his movements were slow, his body sagging. His eyes looked unfocused, like he was looking past me. When I reached him, I tried to wrap my arm around him, but they swept through him as if he were made of air. "Ashton?"

He raised his head, and reached a hand toward me. He looked so broken. How much time did he have left? If I had waited any longer, he probably wouldn't have been here for me to find.

Focusing on his form, I placed my hand on the small of his back. I managed to give him a little push. "Come with me. I have to get you back to your body."

I pushed again and he started to move. It was slow going, but eventually, we made progress. As we neared his body, my vision started to blur. I shook it off, and kept pushing him toward his physical form.

He stopped in front of the pair of us, unconscious on the bed. His eyes widened into a look of panic as he looked from us to me.

"It's okay," I said. "I'll go back into my body as soon as you're in yours."

He shook his head and pointed to my body.

"No, you've been here longer. You need to go first." I staggered backward for a moment, and then caught my balance.

Ashton pointed to my body again.

"Ashton, we don't have time to fight. We are both going to die if you don't go."

His shoulders slumped lower than they already were. With a backward glance at me, he stepped onto his sleeping form and laid down. If I could breathe in this form, I'd have been holding my breath as I watched him. The seconds ticked by, feeling like hours. Then, his eyes blinked open.

A wave of relief washed though me. I had done it. I'd saved him.

Just then, the whole world went black. I couldn't see my body. Stumbling blindly, I reached forward, hoping I was in the right place to find myself. Diving to the ground, I aimed for the place I thought my physical form should be.

Surrounded by silence, in complete darkness, I floated. Feeling like I was neither alive nor dead. Had I made it back to my body? Was I in the Astral Realm? Was Ashton safe?

Something grabbed at my waist and pulled. A voice sounded in my head. *Give in.* It took me a second to realize that the voice and the pulling were taking me toward the darkness. I fought against it, using everything I had to get away from the pulling but it felt like it was coming from inside me. It was as if I was battling against myself.

A shock of pain shot through my body like a bolt of lightning. I screamed as light came flashing back into view. I had never felt pain like this. As if every part of me was on fire from the inside out. "Just let me die!" If I had to feel this, I didn't want to live.

"Etta!" A voice called to me from the distance. It was Ashton. That was what I was fighting for. I did this for him. How could I give up when he was waiting for me? Using the concentration I put behind channeling my magic, I called to the power inside me. I wasn't going to give up. I was going to beat this thing.

A different type of pain shot through my head as it hit the hard ground of the barn. It knocked the other pain away. I was staring up at the thatched roof, my body sprawled across the floor, covered in sweat.

A warm hand brushed damp hair off of my forehead. "Etta?"

"Ashton?" I let out a breath. Was this real? We were both alive?

He leaned down and kissed my forehead. I reached a hand up and touched his cheek, I had to make sure he was real. "You're alive."

"Thanks to you," he said. "Whatever you did, please don't ever do it again. I was so scared."

My brow furrowed. I knew I had screamed, but it had all happened so quickly—it was worth it for both of us to be here together.

"You were screaming for ten minutes," he said. "I wasn't sure you'd be able to make it back. It was as if somebody was trying to take you away from me."

Slowly, I sat up, giving myself a moment to adjust as the room spun. I cheated death. In the pit of my stomach, a gentle pull hung on to me. It was as if it were reminding me I wasn't supposed to be here. Like part of me didn't make it back. Forcing a smile on my face, I looked at Ashton. "I'm okay. It's over. You're safe. That's all that matters."

He shook his head. "Etta, when are you going to realize how important it is for you to be safe? Everything we're doing, it's pointless if we don't have you. You can't keep charging in to danger every time one of your friends is in trouble."

How could he say that? Didn't he know how important he was to me? If I didn't have him, I wasn't sure I would be able to breathe. He kept me on track. He gave me strength when I wanted to quit.

"Etta?" I turned to see Celeste peeking through the door. Her eyes welled with tears when she saw Ashton. She ran into the barn. "Etta, how?"

I didn't have an answer for her. What was I supposed to say? Nobody could know that I used dark magic to bring him back but I'd have to come up with an excuse. Before I could speak, she was running toward him and pulled him into a hug. "It doesn't matter," she said. "Thank the gods you're both alive."

She let go of Ashton and hugged me. "I don't care what you did. You did the right thing."

Hugging her back, I fought back tears. She and Ashton were my family. I knew I'd do anything for either of them, no matter what Ashton said. I'd been so lonely most of my life and I wasn't going back to that. I would hang on to them with everything I had.

M ax rubbed his thumb over the smooth surface of the white stone in his hand. It was smaller than he expected, more like a jewel than a stone. He wondered if the Oracle would convince Etta to go through with drinking the deadly nightshade. If she'd be willing to cheat death to save Ashton.

For a moment, Max's thoughts shifted to Saffron. She'd occupied a lot of his thoughts lately as he heard reports of what Etta was going through to save Ashton. He closed his fingers around the stone and began pacing the room. He didn't like thinking of her so often, but given their past, it was hard not to.

He should have heard something by now, some sort of news from the king. If Etta was successful in saving him, the rift she'd open from coming back from the Astral Realm would cause a permanent channel for the Darkness. Max wasn't strong enough yet to read that himself. The king would send word, though. He just had to wait.

The fire roared in the sitting room. He walked over to it and watched the flames dance. The Dragon's Keep was quiet tonight. Nora was at her father's castle. Most of the members of the

Order had gone out for the night. He used to enjoy the silence. Now it gave him too much time to think.

Without warning, a booming noise sounded through the keep, and the whole room shook. Max dropped the stone into his pocket and called his flames. He didn't know who would be stupid enough to attack the keep, but a wave of relief washed through him. A battle was just what he needed. No time to think when you're fighting. He left the sitting room, headed for the cave entrance.

A loud screeching noise rang through the hallway. Max picked up the pace, moving toward the noise. Heart beating, adrenaline coursing though his veins, he felt more alive than he had in weeks.

As the marble under his feet gave way to stone, the temperature dropped. It was a welcome contrast to the heat rising from the fire in his palms. Without waiting to see if the intruder was friend or foe, he launched a fire ball into the depths of the cave, illuminating the darkness.

To his surprise, a larger fireball came back at him. He dodged it, and threw more fire in the direction of the assailant. This time, when the flames passed through the cave, he saw the silhouette of his attacker.

Max sent his fire in the direction of the sconces that lined the cave. One by one, they sprung to life, swallowing the darkness.

He dropped his hands to his side, extinguishing the flames and stared face to face with a dragon.

"Etta!"

I pulled myself away from my friends to see Saffron rushing through the open barn door. She covered her mouth with her hand as her eyes found Ashton. After letting out a sound somewhere between a cry and a laugh, she ran toward us and managed to wrap her arms around all three of us.

"You did it," Saffron said through sobs.

I'd never seen her cry before and her response brought tears to my eyes. The four of us laughed and cried together for several minutes before we had to stop to catch our breath.

Saffron stepped back and wiped the tears from her cheeks. She was wearing the first genuine smile I'd seen on her since Max left. Or maybe it was the first genuine smile I'd ever seen. She ruffled Ashton's hair as if he were a kid. "I don't think I could've handled you leaving, too."

Ashton hugged her and warmth spread through me. I'd saved him for me, but Ashton meant so much to so many people. Saffron released him and turned to me. "You found the stone?"

I swallowed as a lump rose to my throat. I hadn't figured out what I was going to tell people about how I brought Ashton's essence back. "Not exactly."

"What do you mean?" she asked. "How did you?"

Before the conversation could continue, Master Flanders walked into the barn, Calder limping behind him. Master Flanders' wasn't wearing his usual smile. I wondered what Calder had told him about our time with the Oracle.

My fingers found the pendant around my neck and I slid it up and down the chain, trying to cover the anxious flutters that had risen inside me. Would Master Flanders punish me for using Dark magic? Would he turn me over to the Guild? I knew what I had done was wrong, but if I had to do it again, I would. Ashton was worth it every time.

Master Flanders stopped a few paces inside the barn. "Etta, we need to talk."

Ashton set his hand on top of mine and furrowed his brow. "Everything okay?"

"It's fine." I kissed his cheek. "I'll be right back."

I turned and walked toward the barn door where Master Flanders was waiting for me. Calder moved next to me and leaned in to whisper. "I'm sorry, Etta. I told him that we never found the stone."

I rested my hand on Calder's shoulder. "It's alright. You didn't do anything wrong."

"Calder!" Celeste called out from behind me. "Come meet everybody. I was just about to tell them about Greenville."

Calder walked over to the group while I continued toward the door. Master Flanders had stepped outside and I joined him.

We stood outside the barn in the gray pre-dawn light. Master Flanders looked older than he had before I left. I shook the thought away. *Must be the light.* I clasped my hands in front of me, waiting for the lecture that was sure to come.

His expression softened as we stood there in silence. He

seemed to be studying me, as if looking for any physical signs of injury. "How do you feel?"

The question took me off guard. I expected him to ask me about the stone, or the Oracle, or lecture me for using Dark magic. I shifted my feet. "I'm fine."

He narrowed his eyes and seemed to study me again. The silence was making me nervous. Did I look different to him? Had something physically changed? The Oracle had said that using Dark magic would leave a mark. My palms were sweaty and I felt guilty for letting him down. "I'm sorry. I had to do it. I had to save Ashton."

He let out a long sigh. "You should never have to resort to Dark magic. I'm afraid this is all my fault."

"What's your fault?" I wasn't in the mood for Master Flanders' cryptic messages. A flicker of recognition made my insides jump. He spoke like the Oracle. *His daughter.* It made so much more sense to me now. Sir Henry had even said that Master Flanders knew things he shouldn't. "The Oracle, your daughter."

He nodded. "I thought I could trust her. She seemed like she'd put that part of her past behind her."

"What part of her past?" I asked.

"Osbert." He shook his head. "It's complicated. Needless to say, I made a mistake. I'm sorry."

At this point, I was completely confused. The Oracle had helped me. She'd given us the Black Onyx powder and the way to find the Astral Projection Stone. When that didn't work, she helped me save Ashton. "What are you sorry for? She helped me. I made a choice."

"This is bigger than saving Ashton, Etta." His mouth turned down and he looked like he was struggling with what to say. "You're one of the strongest sorcerers in the land, but there's darkness in you. The king could feel that."

My chest tightened and I shook my head. I didn't like where

this was going. How could the Oracle be working with the king? And if she was, why did they want me to bring Ashton back with Dark magic?

"They used your love for Ashton as a way to make you travel to the realm of the dead, then back again."

"That doesn't make any sense," I said. "Why have me go to the Underworld? What purpose did it serve? And how do you know?"

Master Flanders hesitated a moment. "I can see the mark it left on you because I've been there myself."

"You?" I stared at Master Flanders, eyes wide. "What happened?"

"That's not important right now. What matters is that your return has caused a great change in the balance."

Something had changed in me, but I didn't yet know what that was. I knew I'd have a price to pay, but I thought only I would have to pay the price. I didn't think my actions could hurt anybody else. If the king wanted me to do this, what was he gaining? "What does all of this mean?"

"You opened a bridge, Etta." Master Flanders' shoulders slumped. He looked defeated. "There's a tear in the Underworld from where you left it, leaving a permanent channel to the Darkness. Anybody using Dark magic can tap into it, and strengthen their magic. It also means that the Darkness inside of you is going to be harder to fight."

My knees gave out from under me and I collapsed to the ground. All I wanted to do was save Ashton. How could something so noble be twisted into something so terrible? "I didn't mean for any of this to happen. What's going to happen now?"

"You're going to learn to control the Darkness. You'll fight against it." He sounded confident but I wasn't sure I could do what he asked. I never realized I had Darkness inside me. Was that what I had been feeling the last few weeks? That pull toward the anger. The extra power. A shudder ran though me. Was I already channeling it on my own? "I don't want to use Darkness. I didn't want to help the king."

Master Flanders' joints cracked as he knelt down next to me. "I know. They found your biggest weakness and used it against you. They planned it perfectly. They knew I'd send you to the Oracle to save him. Then they distracted you, made you feel desperate, and offered a solution. It was a game. One we all lost."

I ran my hands over my hair and rested them on the back of my neck. This was too much. I'd set out to save the man I loved on a selfish quest that may have cost the entire kingdom. I had to be the worst queen in the history of the world. Who else would hurt their own kingdom so badly?

"Etta," Master Flanders said. "There has always been Darkness in you, but you've kept it hidden. Some of us are drawn to it."

I looked at him, surprised at his words. *Some of us.* "You?"

He nodded. "There's a reason I agreed to teach the young duke how to channel his magic. I wanted to help him find his strength and power without the need to reach into the Darkness he carried with him. I'd overcome it myself, but at great cost. I didn't want to see another young person go through the same thing."

"But he used his Darkness," I said. This was not making me feel better. I didn't want to turn out like him.

"Yes, he did," Master Flanders said. "I failed. But that doesn't mean I can't help you."

"How can you help me? I keep doing everything wrong." I reached for my necklace again, squeezing it in my hand.

"No. You don't." He pointed to my hand clasped around the pendant. "If you were the king, you would never have saved those people in Luxor. You probably wouldn't have even gone after Ashton. You have been controlling it on your own without any training. With help, you'll learn how to shut it out completely."

"You think I can do that" I asked.

He smiled. "I know you can, Etta."

The sun was beginning its ascent. The sky streaked with pink, reminding me that I wasn't dead yet, which meant, I could still fight. I may have been the one who caused more harm, but that seemed to motivate me more. If anything, I owed it to the people of Illaria to try.

"What do we do now? How do we stop him now?" I asked.

Master Flanders stood, and offered his hand to me. "We write your uncle in Gallia. We ask for an army. We fight."

Shouts sounded behind me and I turned to see a group of Ravens running toward the barn. I was swept up into the crowd and somebody lifted me onto their shoulders and carried me inside the barn. The chants and cries were happy, but I had no idea what was happening.

The man who had been carrying me set me down then picked me up and spun me around. I couldn't help but smile. "What's going on?"

He set me down again and I recognized him. It was Josiah, one of the scouts we'd sent to Greenville. My heartbeat quickened as I searched the group for Greg. He was here, too. They'd both made it back from Greenville alive, and apparently brought good news that most of the camp had already heard.

"Annalise?" I asked. We'd sent them to search for the girl from Master Edward's message, if they were in this good of spirits, they must have found her.

Josiah shook his head. "No, Annalise. It's bigger."

My heart sunk. I'd been so hopeful that they'd found her and could have used some good news.

Greg put his hands up in the air. "Quiet down, quiet down."

The crowd had grown to nearly a hundred people, all

wearing smiles on their faces. It was contagious. Despite being disappointed about Annalise, I found myself smiling again.

Ashton found me and stood next to me, clasping my hand in his. We'd never shared our relationship with the rest of the camp, but I wasn't going to hide it anymore. I'd worked too hard to have him back and I wasn't about to let him go.

A few people in the crowd whispered his name and somebody shouted. "The queen saved Ashton!" Cheers erupted and my smile grew.

Josiah's forehead creased. "What happened to Ashton?"

"Long story," I said. "What is this big news?"

He climbed up on the table in the middle of the barn and bowed to me. "Your highness, I'm sorry you weren't the first to hear, but I couldn't keep it to myself."

My spirits lifted. I could get used to hearing good news. "Yes?"

Josiah's smile widened. "The people of Greenville heard about what you did in Luxor and Campari. They tore down all the king's colors and hung blue flags wherever they could. You should have seen it, there was blue fabric hanging outside every window."

My heart raced and a surge of pride ran through me. My family's color replacing the king's red.

Greg took a step forward. "Tell her the best part."

Josiah's eyes lit up as he continued. "The people rose up against the King's Guard. They expelled them all from the city then closed the gates. They declared war on King Osbert, called him a false king. They cheer in the streets for the Queen of Illaria."

"What exactly did you do in Luxor and Campari?" Ashton asked. "You must have been busy while I was stuck here."

"You have no idea," I said.

Saffron joined Josiah on the table. "We need music! We need to celebrate!"

The crowd cheered as more people flooded into the barn. Somewhere behind me, somebody began playing a fiddle and several others joined in.

I looked at Ashton. "Have you ever seen Saffron like this before?"

He shook his head. "No, but it's a nice change from how sad she was after Max left." Aston froze for a moment, all the color draining from his face.

Panic welled up inside me. Was something wrong? I pulled him over to the back of the barn, away from the music and dancing that was taking place near the doors. "Ashton are you okay?"

He swallowed and looked me in the eyes. "Etta, do you know what happened to me?"

The smile was gone from my face now. "Your essence was removed by the king. I had to bring it back."

He shook his head. "No, that's not what I meant. I mean, I know my essence was removed, but it wasn't the king who did it."

He looked down and let out a sigh then looked back up at me. "Etta, it was Max. He really is working for the king."

My heart dropped to the pit of my stomach and I felt like something inside me shattered. As much as I wanted to deny that Max was working with the king, I had secretly clung to the small hope it was a ruse, that Max was on our side. This ripped that hope completely away. How could Max ever harm Ashton? How could he use such Dark Magic to do it? He could have killed Ashton.

That tendril of anger I'd felt before slithered up through the empty place inside me. The place that never returned from the Astral Realm. It called to me, encouraging me to pour all of my anger and hatred onto Max. How could he have done this to Ashton? To Illaria? He abandoned us all by siding with the king.

Sparks rose in my palms, the feeling caught me off guard. Startled, I squeezed my hands into fists and swallowed back a lump that had risen in my throat. *What is happening to me?* It had to be the Darkness. Master Flanders was right. *I need to learn to control it.*

My eyes found Ashton's. His eyebrows were pressed together in concern. He reached a hand out and covered one of my hands. "I'm sorry, Etta."

His touch was soothing and as I stared into his eyes, I felt my control resurface. If anyone had a right to be angry at Max, it was Ashton. He'd been like a brother to Ashton and yet, Max had nearly killed him. I relaxed my hands. "I'm just glad you're safe. Let's not talk about Max tonight."

Ashton leaned in to me so his face was inches from me. "Let's not talk at all tonight." He flashed a mischievous smile then wrapped an arm around my waist. In one fluid movement, he pulled me in to him and our lips met. The hair on the back of my neck stood on end and goosebumps traveled across my skin. Every part of me tingled.

I slid my fingers through his hair and pulled him in tighter. Our bodies were pressed together. For that moment, everything was right with the world. Every sacrifice I made was worth it.

Somehow, we managed to break away from each other. Cheeks flushed and breathless, I stared into those green eyes, feeling completely happy.

Whoops and cheers and laughter filled the air and my cheeks flushed scarlet. "Kiss her again!" somebody yelled from the crowd.

Ashton pulled me in to him and pressed his lips against mine. Cheers surrounded us. As we ended the kiss, I laughed. I'd been so worried about what people would think of the two of us, but nobody cared. They wanted to find reasons to celebrate. Love was one of the best reasons of all.

Ashton and I were swept up into the party. Somebody lifted us onto their shoulders and people cheered as we were carried around the room.

The energy was pure joy and even if I wanted to, there was no way I could worry about anything right now. The Ravens had gone so long without a reason to be happy. Ashton's return from death and the events in Greenville were more than we could have hoped for.

I was lowered to the ground and found myself surrounded by people who wanted to talk to me and ask me questions. Ashton and I were separated as people pulled us in all directions.

After several long minutes talking to most of the members of the Raven camp, a hand clasped mine and pulled me away. I turned to see Ashton smiling back at me.

He led me toward the music where people were dancing. Twirling me around, we joined in the fun and I laughed as we danced until I couldn't catch my breath anymore.

The sun rose higher in the sky and I fought against the exhaustion of the last few weeks but I didn't want the day to end. I hadn't had anything to celebrate since finding out the truth of who I really was. The last few weeks had been marked by death and loss and fear. I was worried that once this party ended, it may be a long time before we could find time to celebrate again.

A few hours ago, I had thought all hope was lost. Now, I had Ashton by my side and the people of Illaria were fighting back. Everything was coming together. *I can do this.* For the first time, I felt like I could be the queen my people expect. We could do this. We could defeat the king and take back Illaira.

ABOUT THE AUTHOR

Thank you for spending your time in Illaria with me! I hope you enjoyed the book. Book Three of the Illaria series will be available soon. I look forward to sharing more of Etta, Ashton, and Celeste's journey with you!

This book was published independently. One of the best ways to help support independent publishing is to leave an honest review. Please take a few minutes to share what you thought about this book by reviewing it on Amazon or Goodreads.

Sign up for my mailing list for the most up to date information on new releases.

Keep in touch by finding me on social media

www.dyanchick.com

ACKNOWLEDGMENTS

Thank you to all the people who support my writing journey. Putting your work out there in the world for others to see is difficult and I wouldn't be able to do it without my family and friends. Thank you to my husband for putting up with me spending so much time writing and for smiling while I talk about writing or my imaginary worlds nonstop. Thank you to Lori, the best critique partner anyone could ask for. Seriously, you keep me going when I feel like giving up. I can't wait to see where this journey takes us both. Becky, thank you for being one of the first to read this book - your kind words gave me the confidence I needed to move forward. Thank you to my editor, Laura, and my cover artist, Clarissa. You ladies are awesome. Anne, thank you for the additional editing and proofreading, it really helped make my job easier. I also want to give a shout out to my ARC team. Thank you all for being excited about Illaria and taking the time to read my work. Finally, an extra special thank you to my mom who taught me how strong we can be when faced with adversity.

49961382R00156

Made in the USA
San Bernardino, CA
09 June 2017